*the*

# LOVERS

T

# Eden Bradley

## *the*

# LOVERS

THE LOVERS

ISBN-13: 978-0-373-60551-4

Copyright © 2010 by Eden Bradley

Recycling programs for this product may not exist in your area.

For questions and comments about the quality of this book please contact us at Customer_eCare@Harlequin.ca.

www.Spice-Books.com

**Printed in U.S.A.**

This book is for all the writers' groups that are so crucial to any writer, but which have played an especially important role in my life. A huge thank-you to Romance Divas—my Divas are the best! Thank you also to the members of Los Angeles Romance Authors.

But, most of all, this book is dedicated to my fellow Smutketeers: R.G. Alexander, Crystal Jordan and Lilli Feisty, who have stuck by me through the brainstorming and the inevitable meltdowns, the exhilaration and the moments of self-doubt.

I also must thank my agent, Roberta Brown, for daring to shop this book, my editor, Susan Swinwood, for allowing me to write this book in the way it needed to be written, and to them both for championing this story.

Last, but never least, to S, for bringing love into my life.

# CHAPTER ONE

It's dark, and there are hands on my naked flesh. The scents of incense and sex in the air, the earthy fragrance of fresh sweat. Stroking, stroking, fingers and tongues, on my belly, my breasts. I turn to offer my hardened nipples to those seeking mouths.

Ah, yes, hot and sucking and the pressure building between my legs. Silky hair fluttering like sensual wings over my parted thighs.

*Yes, kiss me there…*

Soft fingers spreading the lips of my sex wide, then slipping inside my body. Pleasure like an electric current, humming in my veins, making me hot and shivery all over.

*I'm going to come soon.*

My eyelids flutter open. It's still half-dark, but there is a silvery cast to everything now, and I can see them. Bodies writhing beside me: men, women. Beautiful naked flesh against my own. And that lovely mouth at my breast, sucking, sucking. Fingers plunging into my wet pussy, my hips arching, heat racing over my skin. And then that mouth between my thighs—*oh, yes!*—pulling my hard little clit in, sucking, hot, wet mouth and silken tongue, sliding, sucking, harder…

*Oh, yes, going to come!*

My body gives a hard lurch and I am awake. I blink.

*Oh, yes…on the train.*

My body still buzzing with near climax, and I have to force a deep, calming breath into my lungs. Had I made any noise? Moaned as I slept? My clit pulses still with unshed need. I squeeze my thighs together. It doesn't help.

*Calm down.*

I pick up my bottle of water and take a long, slow sip, looking out the window as the train grinds to a stop in front of the tiny, old station house. Goleta, California. I could have been in any small town in the country, and suddenly wish I were. Why had I decided to come here?

A few other passengers are rising to their feet, gathering their belongings, but I can't seem to make myself do the same.

*Stupid. You never should have done this.*

But no, this trip is about forcing myself outside my comfort zone, the solitary existence that had begun to drive me crazy. When I'd agreed to come here, to the Santa Barbara coast, it had seemed the perfect opportunity, the perfect way for me to get out of my own head for once. To learn to interact with the human race, as my therapist, Terry, had been encouraging me to do for months. Who better to spend time with than other writers? A limited group on this yearly retreat, people I've spoken to online for some time. Safe.

Maybe.

But my pulse is thready, humming unevenly in my veins, a sharp, staccato beat. I push my long, unruly blond curls from my face, my hair suddenly too heavy, too hot, against my neck. I'm always threatening to cut it, but I never will.

Maybe I should have just stayed home. Everything is simple at home. Just write my books. Do my online promotions from behind the safety of my glowing computer screen. I don't have to interact with anyone but the girl at the Starbucks down the street from my apartment in Seattle, and the handful of friends I've known forever. They all thought this trip was a great idea, too. I'm not so sure.

*Time for a change, Bettina.*

Yes, that's why I came.

*Just do it. Get up. Don't be such a chicken.*

Grabbing the slouchy canvas-and-leather bag that holds my laptop, several books and my wallet, I stuff my sweater into the bag and move down the narrow aisle lined with blue vinyl seats, past the small squares of grimy windows. I step out of the stale air, my back and legs stiff from more than thirty hours of travel, and pull in a deep breath of cool and lovely sea air.

Nice.

I see a row of eucalyptus trees to one side of the station and inhale once more, pulling their tangy, fresh scent into my lungs. See the silhouette of hills in the distance against a stark blue sky, the uncut grass scattered with tiny wildflowers in yellow and purple. Feel the *space* around me.

Maybe this is why I've come. Maybe things are going to be okay.

I smile, pleased with the concept.

"Bettina, is that you?"

Viviane Shaw waves at me from the other end of the platform, impossible to miss with her deep, husky voice, her willowy height, and even more, her black-and-purple hair. My closest friend in the online writers' group where we met, Viviane had been the singer in a well-known punk band in the early eighties, and even now, at forty-six, she dresses in jeans and T-shirts and too much silver jewelry that looks exactly right on her. Her smile is warm, and as I approach her, she pulls me into a tight, lilac-scented hug.

"I'm sorry my train was so late." I step back, out of her arms, a little unsettled by Viviane's embrace, even though I liked it.

"You don't need to be sorry, doll. Not your fault. Anyway, it gave me a reason to hang out in town and do some shopping." Viviane stands back and looks at me. "You're even prettier than your pictures, Tina. Wow, can you believe we've been talking online for two years? I feel like I *know* you. It's always so weird, isn't it, meeting people for the first time you've only known online. No matter how many years I've been hosting these writers' retreats, I never get over it."

"I don't really know. This is the first time I've met anyone from our online group. Or from online at all."

"Well, it's about time then, isn't it?" Viviane smiles at me, and I feel a little less uncertain. She's gorgeous, with high, curving cheekbones and enormous light brown eyes that tilt up a bit at the corners. She seems like an exotic creature to me, colorful and vibrant and more youthful than I am myself, somehow, even though I'm eighteen years younger. "You must be tired. Are you hungry? We can stop on the way to the house, if you like."

"No, thanks, I'm fine. I ate on the train."

"How was your trip?"

"It was long. Beautiful, when there was enough light to see by. And I loved the motion of the train. It was soothing. Mesmerizing. It felt like an adventure."

She smiles at me. "I think you've needed some adventures. Small ones, anyway."

"You're right, I do. Maybe I'll have some here. Small ones." I smile, the last of my nerves vanishing during this simple conversation. "Ah, I think I see my luggage."

We retrieve my two small black bags, and Viviane leads me through the parking lot to a silver SUV coated in a layer of dust. A large, black nose is pressed to the back window.

"I brought Sid with me," Viviane says. "I hope you don't mind."

"I like dogs. I've always wanted to get one, but living in an apartment in the city isn't the best scenario for a dog." Sid has an enormous, blocky head and one of those toothy grins with loose, floppy jowls that make him look perpetually happy. He snorts and rumbles as Viviane opens the tailgate. "Is he friendly?"

"Oh, yeah, he loves everyone. He just looks vicious. Sid Vicious, get it? Stay there, Sid, good boy."

Viviane holds the barrel-chested bulldog back by his wide, studded collar while I pile my bags into the back of the car. I stroke Sid's head, making his stumpy tail wag at a hundred miles an hour, before I go around to get in on the passenger side. Viviane starts the car and music blasts from the stereo, some cacophonous metal song, as she pulls onto the street.

She turns the knob to lower the volume on the stereo. "My place is only about fifteen minutes away, so it won't take long. It really is good to have you here, Tina."

"Thank you so much for having me."

"No need to be formal, doll, it's just me, same as I am online." Viviane pats my knee. "Don't look so worried. This is a casual group. We're spending almost the entire summer together, they'll all feel like family before you know it. And you've been talking to all of us for so long. None of us are that different in person. Although you're even more shy, I think."

"I suppose I am. It's sort of the bane of my existence," I admit, feeling a real sense of ease with Viviane. It's almost impossible not to.

"So you said when we talked on the phone. But I really think this will be good for you."

"I hope so. I've been feeling so…stuck. And not just with my writing."

Uneven rows of quaint old houses stream by outside the windows, separated by fields of grass, eucalyptus trees and a few ancient oaks among the stands of rock on the low hillsides where cows wander, staring at the road. It's as though they're watching us. Watching the world go by. Maybe that's what I've been doing all this time.

"I honestly don't know how you write that angsty women's-fiction stuff," Viviane tells me. "I could never come up with enough high drama. Especially if there's no payoff at the end."

"And I don't know how you write romance, even your darker work. I'm not sure I even believe enough in love. I could never write about it."

Viviane's features go soft for a moment; I can see it even in profile, the scenery flashing by in a blur of green and blue behind her head. "Oh, I believe in love. I always have. I always will."

"You miss him still," I say quietly, then immediately wish I'd kept my mouth shut.

"Malcolm? Yeah, I do. It's been thirteen years since I lost him, but once you love someone, it never really goes away."

"Yes, well, once you love them, I suppose…"

Viviane turns to me, one dark brow quirked. "You've really never been in love, Bettina?"

"No. Never. I've had a few boyfriends, but none ever inspired any real passion in me. They were all…okay." I shrug. "No more, no less."

"Well, when it does happen, that's when you'll believe in

it. Because you won't be able to do otherwise. It's a powerful force, love."

I smile at her. "So you say in all your books."

"Have you read all my books?"

"I try to read at least a few from everyone in the group. Patrice's historical mysteries, Kenneth's war epics, and I love Audrey's urban-fantasy stuff. I've even read some of Leo's horror comics."

"And Jack's thrillers?"

"I think they're brilliant. I think he's brilliant. But his work is too disturbing for me. I know we all write dark—that's what brought us together—but I'm a wimp at heart, I guess."

"No, I can hardly take it, either. His work is so psychological, it messes with my head. His stuff will give me nightmares even more than Leo's gore comics. Ah, this is my street."

The "street" is really a long unpaved road lined with more of the towering eucalyptus trees. Green fields give way to rockier terrain as we near the beach, and I roll down the window so I can breathe in the salt of the ocean.

"This is beautiful. Peaceful."

"Isn't it? I fell in love with this place the moment I saw it. I don't think I could write anywhere else. I think you'll like it."

"I think I will, too."

We bump over the end of the road and pull up behind a sprawling, two-story, Spanish-style bungalow with a tiled roof and high, arched windows. Bougainvillea climbs the white stucco walls, and more eucalyptus and a few cypress twisted by the wind shade the rambling house. We get out of the SUV, Viviane letting the tailgate down so Sid can jump out, hefting his brown-and-white bulk to the ground at a startling speed for such a heavy creature. I can hear the thundering of waves in the distance, and the air here is even sharper, cleaner, than it had been at the train station.

"We'll get your bags later," Viviane says. "Come on and meet everyone. Well, everyone who's arrived so far, anyway."

She leads me around the side of the house and in through what turns out to be the kitchen door. Inside, the kitchen is a large, open space with terra-cotta-tiled floors, and thick, cobalt tiles on the counters. The ceilings are heavily beamed, and there's a fireplace at one end of the room, surrounded by chairs made of woven brown leather, a low table of heavy, raw beams in a dark wood. The place is like something out of a magazine, except homier. I love it instantly.

In the center of the kitchen is an island, and a thin, birdlike woman in her early fifties with short, mouse-brown hair stands there, chopping vegetables on a large cutting board.

"Bettina, this is Patrice Michaels, our historical-mystery author."

Patrice smiles, a small crooked lift of her thin lips. She has a narrow face, sharp, dark eyes, and I feel even more intimidated by her than I have talking with her online. Patrice is known for her blatant and sometimes brutal honesty, but she's a talented writer, and has been in the business longer than any of us. She's generous and an enormous source of information on writing craft and the publishing industry. Still, I don't know that I'll ever feel entirely comfortable with this woman and her dry, shrewd appraisal of me.

"Hello, Bettina. I see you've arrived safely."

"Yes, thank you."

"Dinner will be ready in an hour."

"Patrice is an amazing cook," Viviane interjects, making the dour, older woman really smile.

Viviane can make anyone smile. I'm glad she'll be here to help me ease into this, that I won't be on my own with the rest of the group. Viviane is the one I've talked with the most, the one I trust. I would never have made this trip otherwise.

"Bettina!"

I turn to find a heavyset man with a thick head of silver hair and watery blue eyes coming in the kitchen door, a happy smile on his face. Kenneth Bergen.

"Kenneth. It's so good to meet you."

He comes to me and takes my hand in both of his, a warm, comfortable embrace. "Oh, you're lovely. Isn't she, Audrey?" he asks over his shoulder.

She's standing in the doorway, a waif of a girl, although I know Audrey LeClaire is in her early thirties. She's all long, dark hair and huge, smoky-blue eyes fringed in the longest dark lashes I've ever seen. With her olive skin and tiny frame, she seems like some woodland sprite come to life. Except that her breasts, barely contained beneath her bikini top, are almost too large for her body.

Why am I even noticing?

"Yes, beautiful. Come say hello, Bettina. Don't worry, I won't bite." Audrey smiles, her lush mouth parting, a dimple appearing in one cheek, and she comes to wrap her arms around me.

She smells of lemons. And sex.

My body heats.

*What is wrong with me? Must be that dream…*

I pull back and Audrey is still smiling. "Yes, you really are a beauty, Bettina." She reaches out and gives my cheek a small pinch, and I find myself blushing as she moves away and loops an easy arm around Kenneth's shoulders. "You behave yourself, now, Kenneth. What would your wife think of you surrounded by all these gorgeous girls?"

Kenneth goes a bit pink, but looks pleased. "She knows I

love only her. But I have enough of the artist's eye to appreciate you lovely ladies."

"You're a shameful old flirt," Viviane teases. "Come on,
Bettina, let me show you where you'll be sleeping. I've put
you in one of the cottages."

My body is still buzzing with my unexpected response to
Audrey's touch as I follow Viviane through the bright, airy
house. It's all open space, the living and dining areas separated
only by a graceful arch. The furnishings are heavy imported
pieces, overstuffed sofas with piles of richly colored throw
pillows, everything gorgeous yet livable, comfortable. A bank
of tall windows framed by a pair of twisted cypress trees look
out over the sandy dunes leading down to the beach.

The heavy front doors stand open. Every detail about this
place is welcoming, and I tell myself again that everything
will be fine, that coming here was a good decision.

We move through the doors and outside, where we cross
a large patio tiled in terra-cotta. More bougainvillea climbs
the walls, delicate, coral-colored blossoms littering the tiles.
Enormous pots of rosemary and lavender are scattered around
the edges of the patio, lending their fragrance to the salt air.
Black wrought-iron chairs sit around a long wooden table,
and there is an outdoor kitchen built into the far wall of the
house. Sid is there, sitting on a dog bed by the door, but gets
up to greet us. Viviane bends to scratch his big, grinning head.
More tail thumping. I give him a pat, his fur short and coarse
under my palm.

Standing, I look out to where the dark blue and green
waves curl and crash on the beach. "This place is incredible,
Viviane."

"It is. It's my dream home. I came here looking for refuge
after Malcolm died, and just…stayed. It soothes me, even
now."

"This isn't the kind of place anyone would want to leave."

"I'm glad you think so. I've been hoping you'd be comfortable here. Okay so far?"

"Yes, thanks."

"Even after meeting Patrice?"

I laugh. "Yes, although I have to admit she scares me a little."

"Oh, her bark is worse than her bite. She's a nice woman. She just has a flinty exterior. But she'll loosen up after she's been here a few days and I get a few bottles of Pinot Noir into her. Good wine is her Achilles' heel."

"Thank God she has one."

Viviane grins at me. "Come on, the cottages are this way."

We follow as Sid trots down a path of loose gravel hidden between two cypress trees. On the edge of the sand two small wood cabins with corrugated-tin roofs sit close together. They each have a small porch hung with ferns and flowers in baskets. Grass grows in tall clumps here and there. It's all a little wild and primitive, but cozy. Adorable. Like something out of a storybook. Or maybe that's just the writer in me.

Viviane leads me to the one on the right and swings open the wood door, which is painted a bright blue. Inside, a queen-size bed covered in a handmade blue-and-white quilt dominates the small, homey space, flanked by matching bedside tables. Beneath a pair of paned windows, a double-wide chair done in white canvas and piled with pillows sits next to a round wooden table large enough to hold my laptop and a few books.

"It's perfect." I move over the wide-planked wood floor to look out the window. The place smells of old wood and the salt of the sea. "Who's in the other cottage?"

"No one yet. We'll see where everyone wants to stay. I thought I'd give you one of the cottages, rather than a room in the house, so you'd have more quiet time. I had a feeling you might need some space away from the others now and then. But if you'd rather be in the main house I can switch people around easily enough."

"No, I love it here, it's perfect. Thank you, Viviane."

Viviane smiles, gives my hand a squeeze, and I'm so grateful to her. But I feel unable to tell her how much this means to me, to be invited here. To be safe with her while I'm trying to stretch my wings a little.

"You're welcome. And you look exhausted. Why don't you rest for a bit. I'll send someone down with your luggage before dinner."

"I am sleepy, even though I napped on the train."

My long, dreamy nap. My dream...

*Don't think about that now.*

"I'll see you at dinner, then. Come on, Sid."

Alone, I pull in a deep breath, then another, trying to calm down from the excitement of meeting everyone as I drop my tote bag on the end of the bed, then sit next to it. I turn to look through the sheer curtains at the glorious view outside. The sky is beginning to go a little hazy with the late-afternoon fog, but through the small stand of cypress trees is a clear view of the dunes and lower down, the beach. Waves crash on the shore in shifting tones of blue and gray and green, bits of seaweed caught in the foam, golden-brown against the white. The sun is cutting through the deepening fog, touching the crests of the water in dazzling light. The beach is deserted, peaceful.

I let out my breath, feel my shoulders drop. I'm so tired after my long night on the train. Maybe a short nap, or even just lying still for a few minutes, wouldn't hurt.

Pushing my bag aside, I lean into the pillows, letting myself truly relax for the first time since I left my apartment in Seattle. The bed is soft, the hypnotic rhythm of the ocean lulling. I close my eyes. And remember my dream on the train. The same one I've been having off and on for months. Always that sort of orgy, where I can't tell one person from another. Just hands and mouths on my flesh, desire rising in my body like pure heat. And always, I wake at the very last moment, needy, dazed. At home I would reach into my nightstand drawer for my vibrator, bringing myself to orgasm alone in my bed.

Too much alone. That's what Terry says, and I know she's right. But those empty relationships have worn me down and I don't feel ready for another one anytime soon.

Still, my body is pulsing with need now, just thinking about the dream, my breasts aching subtly.

It's been too long since anyone has touched me. Months. And I don't miss it so much in my day-to-day life. But I've been having the dream more often. It's becoming more and more real to me. And even when I use my vibrator, as I do almost every night and sometimes during the day, even after I make myself come, I am left needy.

Why did I leave it buried in my suitcase?

*Just calm down.*

But knowing I am without release makes it even worse.

My own hands have never done anything for me; I need the vibrator. It was an epiphany when I bought my first one, furtively ordered over the internet at twenty. I spent an entire weekend with that purple, buzzing phallus between my thighs, coming and coming. The next one was pink and textured. The next shining chrome. Oh, yes, I quickly became a connoisseur of sex toys. Anything that moved, vibrated, pumped. So much easier than dealing with a man I wasn't really interested in. No boring dates, where I had to stretch to find something to talk about. Just my plastic friend, a little lube, maybe a sexy book. And now these dreams, where I wake on the verge of climax, my thighs damp with my juices.

My body is going hot and tight all over. I want to close my eyes, to rest, but all I can think of now is my favorite vibrator, packed away and out of reach, and the damn dream.

Bodies pressed close together, skin to skin, a little sweat. Yes, even in my dream I can smell the earthy scent of sex. Smooth hands touching me, skimming over my belly, between my thighs, clever fingers pinching my nipples, my clit, everything going hard and taut. Clever tongues on my skin, lapping at my wet slit…

*Oh, yes…*

The door swings open and I bolt upright. Audrey stands there, looking almost as flushed as I feel. My heart is a hammer in my chest.

"Whatever do you have packed into these little suitcases?" she asks as she drags them both through the door.

*My vibrator.*

"I'm sorry. I know they're heavy. I have a lot of books…" I trail off. I can barely talk.

She leaves them in the middle of the floor, flops down on the bed next to me, panting a little with exertion. She is close enough that I can feel the heat of her skin. And there's plenty of skin. She's wearing the bikini top and a pair of short white shorts. Her legs are thin and long, her bare feet in rubber flip-flops, the toes painted a glossy red, which seems incredibly erotic to me for some reason.

I look up and find her watching me. Not looking at me. *Watching me,* as though my staring at her toes is fascinating to her.

"Thank you for bringing my luggage, Audrey."

"Sure. I wanted to spend a little time with you, anyway,

before everyone gets here. I wanted to have you to myself for a while."

She smiles at me, as though she's my best friend. My sister. We've talked online, but we've never been close, not the way I am with Viviane. But in person, she's different. Warmer. Charming.

She takes my hand in hers and gives it a squeeze. "This will be just like summer camp. We can make popcorn and hang out on your bed, talk about…everything. Our movie-star crushes. Our dreams. We can talk until the sun comes up, and fall asleep on the floor like a litter of puppies."

I smile at her. Impossible not to. "That sounds great."

"You're going to love it here. This is my third year. I always come back. We all do. You will, too. I'll personally make sure you have a wonderful time." She's smiling again, and I notice once more the dimple in her left cheek.

"So, you know everyone in the group?"

"Oh, yes, I know everyone."

It sounds as though she's intimating something more.

Audrey leans over, lifts her hand to take a strand of my hair, curls one end around her fingers. She's looking at it with curiosity, examining it, as she seems to do with everything. And as she crosses her arm over her body to get to my hair, her breasts push together, beautiful, golden-brown cleavage.

"You have the prettiest hair," she says, but all I can think about is the dark crescent of areola peeking from the edge of her floral swimsuit top. I am still damp from thinking about the dream, but everything in me goes liquid and hot.

God, I have to get ahold of myself.

I've never been attracted to a woman before, not really. Oh, I've thought about it, dreamed about being with a woman, and there are always women in my orgy dream. But I've never met one I was specifically attracted to. Until now.

Audrey gives my hair a small tug. "What's on your mind, Bettina?"

*Shit.*

"I…nothing, really. I'm still a little dazed from traveling. I'll wake up after dinner, I'm sure."

"If not, just go to bed early. I'll come and tuck you in."

Pulling a little on my hair, she leans in and brushes a kiss across my cheek.

My body burns.

I'm sure it was completely innocent, that she's just being friendly. But Audrey oozes sex. I've heard that expression before, but I've never come upon anyone like her. That must be it, just her natural aura of sensuality, and my leftover dream state. Because I've never really wanted to have sex with a woman, have I? Never yearned to touch a woman's skin, to take her lush breasts in my hands, into my mouth. To have her touch me with her soft fingers.

I pull in a long breath, force my pulse to calm. Tell myself that I do not want Audrey. Not like that.

Why does that feel like the biggest lie I've ever told myself?

# CHAPTER TWO

It's time for dinner and I leave my cozy little cabin with some trepidation. Already it feels like some sort of refuge to me. I can see the ocean from my windows, smell the scent of the sea, the scent of summer, even with the windows closed, although I opened them all up and left them that way until right before I slipped into my sandals to go up to the main house.

I unpacked my suitcases, put my clothes away in the small closet, set my laptop and a small pile of books on the little table and tucked my vibrator away in the drawer of the nightstand, I felt immediately at home, all of my things fitting perfectly.

I have the strangest sense of being secure here, protected, of fitting as perfectly as my belongings do, as though this place was made just for me. But there is also this sort of strange tension that makes me all loose and shaky inside. Maybe it has something to do with what happened with Audrey earlier. Even though nothing *happened*. Except that I am beginning to think I want it to.

God, I don't even know what I'm thinking!

I shut the door behind me and make my way back up the gravel path. Everyone is on the patio, which is dominated by a long table covered in a white cloth that flutters in the small breeze coming off the water. The table is already set with big bowls and platters of food, dishes in bright blue and yellow and stark white. There must be half a dozen bottles of wine on the table, along with baskets of bread, glass carafes with what I think is olive oil and balsamic vinegar. Everyone is still in casual clothes: Viviane in her jeans, Kenneth in his shorts and Hawaiian shirt, Patrice in cropped cargo pants. And Audrey in her shorts and bikini top, with a sheer white blouse hanging open, moving in the breeze like the tablecloth.

Audrey spots me first and, smiling, comes to take my arm possessively in hers as she leads me to a chair.

"I'm claiming Bettina tonight," she announces, then, turning to me, whispers in my ear, her breath warm and tickly, "I always sit with the newest arrival. It's a tradition."

Why do I feel as though she's paying me special attention?

Maybe I need it that badly.

Everyone sits, with Viviane at one end and Kenneth at the other, and Patrice across from Audrey and me. Sid circles the table, stopping to grin and wag his stump of a tail at each place, hoping for table scraps, perhaps. I reach down and give his big head a scratch before he moves on.

The open wine bottles are passed around, and I fill my glass with a California Chardonnay, cold and crisp, and take a sip. Audrey chooses a Cabernet, I notice.

"Let's make a toast," Viviane says. "To our newest summer-retreat member, Bettina Boothe."

"Hear, hear," Kenneth says.

Everyone raises their glasses. Audrey winks at me as her glass clinks mine, smiles, dimpling. She has gorgeous teeth, almost perfectly straight except for one on the bottom row that's the slightest bit crooked.

Why am I noticing everything about her in such minute detail?

I am all nerves again, suddenly. Too aware of that delicate female flesh next to me.

"Bettina, what did you bring with you to work on over the summer?" Patrice asks.

"Oh, well, I'm halfway through a book about a girl who's orphaned and raised in these awful foster homes. But I've been stuck..."

"Ah, the sagging middle," Patrice says, nodding her head sagely. "That's always the time to up the stakes. Make something exciting or tragic happen."

"I usually blow something up," Kenneth says, grinning.

He has a kind face. I think I'll like him much better than Patrice. I don't know how to get past my intimidation with her.

"Well, this entire story is a bit tragic," I tell them. "I need to...think about it some more."

"This is an excellent place to think," Viviane says.

"Yes, I believe it will be."

If only I can think of something other than Audrey's smooth, gold-touched skin, the citrus scent of her hair.

"What about everyone else?" Viviane asks. "I'm working on a contemporary romance, an older woman, younger man story. Forbidden fruit and all that. Absolutely sad and desperate love." She sighs happily.

Patrice gestures with her wineglass. "Mine is a murder mystery with a dark twist."

"They always are," Audrey says, sipping her wine slowly. I can see the ruby liquid pool on her lower lip through the dome of the glass before she swallows.

"True. But that's why we're all together, isn't it?" Patrice says. "We each understand the dark side of a story. The darkness in people. In the world. That's what brought us all together."

"Who started the online group?" I ask, suddenly realizing I don't know.

"You don't know about Angela?" Audrey asks.

"Angela?"

"Angela Moore," Viviane says, her voice low. She casts a furtive glance at Patrice. I don't know what it's about.

"I know the name. She wrote those really intense psychological thrillers, didn't she? Whatever happened to her?"

"She died," Patrice says, her tone flat. She picks up her glass and takes a long swallow, then another.

"Angela was Patrice's partner," Viviane says quietly, watching Patrice. But her features are as impassable as ever.

No, looking closer, I can see the clench of her jaw.

"I'm sorry," I say, feeling completely inadequate.

"It happens," Patrice says, reaching for a thick chunk of sourdough bread from the basket. She picks up the bottle of olive oil and makes a small puddle on her bread plate, then adds a few drops of the balsamic. "Let's not sit around like a bunch of mourners. It's been five years already. I'm perfectly fine."

"Of course you are," Viviane says, her eyes going soft. After a moment she reaches for a large wooden salad bowl, serves Patrice, then herself. "So, Leo should be here soon, and Jack."

"It'll be nice to have the boys here," Audrey says, turning to wink at me.

"You do like the boys," Patrice mutters, forking a piece of lettuce from her plate.

"Yes, I do, Patrice," Audrey says, her tone a little forceful, tense. She swigs her wine again, drinking it down fast.

Why are they baiting each other? Or is it only the sort of family banter that goes on in most people's houses?

I wouldn't really know. My family never had that. No siblings, just me and my parents, who were never really quite there. Living with two professors is an isolating existence for a kid. We spent dinners with everyone's heads buried in a book. Which is, perhaps, why I'm so lacking in social graces myself. And that is one reason why I've made this trip. To learn this stuff. But they're all talking again, and the tension at the table is dissipating.

"I thought we should have a Mary Shelley night," Viviane is saying. "You know, sit up all night drinking wine and writing the darkest stories we can come up with."

"And that's different from what we always do how?" Kenneth asks, laughing.

"I know, but it would be more of a formal arrangement. Maybe we can write our own versions of *Frankenstein,* each in our own genre? Oh, I'd love to write Frankenstein's love story. He's always been such a tragic figure."

"He's a monster, Viv," Audrey says. "He's meant to be tragic."

"Yes, but even a monster deserves love. Look at *Beauty and the Beast.*"

"You're such a romantic," Patrice accuses.

"Yes, I am." Viviane smiles at her and pats her hand. Patrice frowns, but as she looks away I can tell she's trying to hide a small smile behind her napkin.

Dinner passes with the same sort of meandering conversation, wonderful food, perhaps a bit too much wine. When it's over we all help take the empty plates into the big kitchen, but Viviane shoos us out, not allowing anyone but Patrice to help her clean up. Kenneth settles into a chair on the patio with a pipe, Sid sitting in a lump beside him.

"Bettina, why don't we go down to the beach," Audrey says, taking my hand. Hers is small, birdlike, the bones so delicate I feel as though I could easily crush them.

"Oh, I don't know. It's so dark."

"There's plenty of light from the house, and from the porch light on your cottage. And you haven't been yet. Come on."

"Okay. I guess it'll be…fine."

"We'll just take this with us."

She grabs half a bottle of red wine from the island counter and heads out the back door. I follow her around the house, down the gravel path between my cabin and the other one, which is dark, empty. A half-moon hangs in the sky, its silver glow reflected in the water, helping to light our way, and it's not nearly as dark as I'd thought it would be. Audrey is a black silhouette in front of me as we make our way over the dunes, her white shorts standing out, catching the moonlight.

She stops and plops down on the sand, and I sit next to her, a foot or two away, and stare out at the water, like swirls of ink, the foam barely visible in the night. The sound is awesome, exhilarating, as the waves rumble and crash. The ocean feels kinetic, powerful.

So does my awareness of Audrey next to me, her long, bare legs stretched out before her.

"I love this place," she says to me.

"I think I'm going to."

I'm more relaxed than I should be. Too much wine. Or maybe just enough. Audrey takes a swig from the bottle, then hands it to me. I sip more carefully. It's the Cabernet, a little strong and rich for me, but I like it. I kick off my sandals and dig my toes into the dark sand. It's damp beneath the surface, a little cold, but it feels good on my heated skin.

"Tell me about your life, Audrey."

"What would you like to know? I'll tell you whatever you want. Anything, my darling Bettina."

She's a little drunk. But then, so am I.

"Tell me about your family."

"Really? Wouldn't you rather hear about my sordid sexual history?"

I laugh. "Maybe after."

She sighs, takes a long pull from the bottle, hands it to me, and I drink as she begins to talk.

"They live in Richmond, Virginia."

"That's where you're from?"

"Yes, originally, although I've lived all over. It's a staid, solid place, Richmond. Big banking town. That's what my daddy does, banking. That's what every good citizen of Richmond does. That's one of the reasons I was so fucking desperate to get out. You can imagine how well I fit in there."

"So, you're not close with your family?"

Audrey laughs, a short sort of humorless bark. "My mother is the second wife. I have two half brothers and a half sister, but they want nothing to do with us. No, they're just worried that Daddy will die and leave all his money to my mother, which he probably will. Daddy dotes on my mother, and she dotes on him. Which left very little room for me. They come a few times a year to visit Daddy. I always try to be gone then." She takes another long sip from the bottle of wine while I sit, quiet, not knowing what to say. "Actually, I try to be gone most of the time. It's better that way. Especially for me. I got tired of being invisible."

"God, me, too."

Audrey turns to me then, and I can see her eyes glittering in the moonlight. "Are you invisible, Bettina?"

I nod. "Yes." It comes out as a whisper. My heart is pounding.

She stares at me for a long moment. "*I* see you." Audrey lifts a hand, strokes my hair from my face, her gaze hard on mine, her dark, elegant brows drawn together. "We understand each other, you and I. I knew right away we would."

I am warm and shivery all over. I lick my lips, which have gone dry in the breeze coming off the water. I have an odd sensation of being grounded to the earth, suddenly. And my attraction to Audrey is part of it, although the knowledge that we share this bit of our histories is part of it, too.

"I do understand," I tell her. "My parents haven't been aware of my existence since…maybe ever. Or maybe only vaguely, as though I'm at the edge of their consciousness. It's better not to be there, not to have to feel that. Easier."

"Yes, exactly. I don't want that in my face every day. I don't want to have to feel that exclusion. I can get that shit anywhere in this world."

"But you…you never do, I'm sure. Not from anyone else."

"Why would you say that?"

She looks truly puzzled.

"Because," I start, having had too much to drink to censor myself, "you are the most amazing person, Audrey. Fascinating. And I don't mean that in any sort of patronizing way. Not like some zoo animal to stare at and study. But you make me want to…be with you. And I think everyone must feel that way."

She smiles brilliantly, leans over and kisses my cheek. Her lips leave a hot, damp imprint on my skin. I want to lift my hand, press my fingers there, but I don't do it. Instead, I cross my legs, trying to ease the sudden ache there.

I really shouldn't have drunk so much wine.

"Sweet Bettina," she says, pulling her hand back to swig from the bottle once more. The wine is nearly gone. "But it's not true, you know. The world at large rejects me. Always has."

There is pain behind this simple statement. I want to make her feel better. But I don't know how.

*Yes, you do…*

God, what am I thinking? She is not flirting with me!

Is she?

"We should get back," she says. "I want to get up early tomorrow and hit the beach before I write."

"Oh, okay. Sure."

She stands, and, taking my hand, helps pull me to my feet. I'm a little dizzy with the wine. And she pulls me in, her arms going around me. The wine bottle is still in her hand and it presses, hard and cool, against my back. And against the front of my body, her breasts are warm. My nipples harden instantly, my sex going damp. She hugs me tightly, briefly, then lets me go.

"Come on. Time for bed."

*Yes, please…*

I follow her silently over the dunes, my legs working against the sand, my muscles fatigued. We reach flatter ground, the sand turning to gravel, and then we're at the door to my cabin.

"'Night, Bettina. See you in the morning."

She waves and is gone, disappearing down the dark path to the main house.

I stand there, stupefied. I realize I'm barefoot, the gravel biting into the soles of my feet. My sandals are on the beach somewhere. I should go get them, but I don't.

What had I expected? Wanted? I don't even know.

Shaking my head, I step onto the small porch, open the blue door. Inside, I turn on a bedside lamp, then go into the bathroom to wash my face. But the splash of cold water doesn't help. My body is on fire.

I know what will help.

I strip my clothes off as I walk from bath to bed, pull open the nightstand drawer and grab my flesh-colored vibrator. In moments I am on the bed, naked, my legs spread wide, as the cool night air plays over my skin, seducing me, taunting me. My nipples are two hard points, red and swollen.

I turn the phallus on and lower it between my thighs. I often tease myself, let the buzzing instrument play around my pussy lips, lovely, light touches. But I am already so turned on I hurt. I go right for my clit, turning the vibrator up high and pressing down hard.

God, it feels good, that humming going through my system, a sharp, stinging current. Desire builds, my entire sex engorged, painful. I need to come so badly.

I press harder, moving it slowly from side to side, rubbing my hard little clitoris with the textured head of the vibe, closing my eyes and thinking of her.

Her face. Her lush red mouth like sex itself. And her saying to me, a wicked smile on her beautiful face, "I can make you come, Bettina."

So hot, those words. And I imagine her lowering her face between my legs, her wet tongue lapping at my wet slit, her fingers sinking into me.

*Oh, yes…*

I spread my legs wider, welcoming her. And she pulls my clit between her lips, sucking hard, her fingers pushing into me. My hips arch into the vibrator, and my climax is shattering, like a hard current in my pussy, my belly. My thighs are shaking, I'm moaning. And in my mind is her face, her wicked mouth.

She's smiling at me as I come, saying, "I told you so."

★ ★ ★

Mornings on the beach are different than they are anywhere else. There is the slow process of coming out of my dreams to the muted roar of the surf, the gray, fog-dimmed light coming through the windows as soft as a whisper.

I stretch, trying to remember my dreams, as I do each morning, but today they are nothing more than a dimly lit memory of my parents at a dinner table piled with books, a flash of hearing a baby crying as I ride a train. And Audrey.

I have to stop thinking of her. I tend to be obsessive. I know this about myself. I don't like it, but I haven't been able to change it.

I want to go back to sleep, to lose myself, but it's too late. I'm wide-awake.

Throwing back the covers, I get out of the warm bed, slip my feet into my fuzzy blue slippers and pad to the window. The beach is lonely in the morning, but peaceful. I watch as a gull swoops in, low over the waves, nearly skimming them, then is joined by another. The water is a chilly gray this morning to match the early sky. I shiver and reach for my soft, gray knit robe, which I left draped over the chair last night.

*Last night…*

Last night I made myself come over and over, my trusty vibrator held between my aching thighs, sweat pouring off me by the third climax, every muscle in my body tensed and hurting.

Maybe I should start writing erotica.

*Fuck.*

I push my hair from my face, my fingers tangling in the tight curls, snarls left over from my late night on the beach.

*Stop thinking about her!*

I shake my head as I make my way to the shower. Ridding myself of my robe, I step under the hot spray. The water is soft here, like silk gliding over my skin. And it is everything I can do simply to take a damn shower, wash my hair. Not to slip my hand between my thighs, pinch my clit, plunge my fingers into my pussy, get myself off again.

I have spent far too much time alone, Terry is right about that.

This is ridiculous.

I hurry through the rest of my shower, pull on some clothes and shut the cabin door behind me. The morning air is still gray and cool, though the sun is beginning to cast its golden rays through the cypress trees, and my damp hair grows cold around my shoulders. But I don't mind. I need to cool off. Literally and figuratively.

I move around the side of the house and step tentatively through the kitchen door. Immediately I am hit with the lovely, rich scent of coffee. Viviane and Patrice are sitting in the chairs by the fireplace, a low fire burning. The room is warm, the acrid scent of the fire mixing with the coffee. Nothing has ever smelled so inviting.

"Good morning, Tina," Viviane singsongs, waving me in. "Get yourself a cup and come sit."

"Good morning," I answer, following her gesturing hand to where a coffeepot sits on the tiled counter, a row of cobalt blue and red mugs lined up next to it. I pour, find sugar and cream next to the mugs, a spoon to stir. I like my coffee sweet. I like it to be dessert. A bad habit, I know, but it is one of my little indulgences. That, and endless hours of orgasms, apparently, alone in my bed.

*Stop it.*

I take a moment to calm myself, pretending to taste test my coffee, but it's already perfect. I breathe in the steam from the mug, exhale, then turn around.

"'Morning, Patrice."

She nods silently. I decide not to care, and go to sit on one of the woven-leather chairs. It's more comfortable than it looks, the brown leather straps cradling my butt.

Viviane is in a pair of hot-pink sweatpants and a black thermal top with a skull and crossbones on the front. She looks adorable. Patrice is wearing khakis and a sweatshirt with a kitten on it. She looks…odd. I never expected "cute" to be her thing. But I am constantly surprised by what I don't know about people. I always question if I'm reading anyone right.

I am questioning how I'm reading Audrey. I wish there was someone I could ask. But Terry says I have to learn to trust my instincts, to trust myself.

"Did you sleep well, Tina?"

"What? Oh, yes. I love the sound of the ocean. It lulls me."

That, and being completely worn-out from coming so much, like some sort of nymphomaniac.

"I find it irritating," Patrice says, frowning. "I always wear my earplugs when I'm here."

"It's not for everyone," Viviane soothes.

Kenneth wanders in then, looking rumpled and sleepy in his plaid cotton robe tied loosely over a pair of shorts and a T-shirt, Sid following at his heels.

"Ah, there you are, Sid," Viviane says. "Traitor." She turns to me. "He always sleeps in Kenneth's room."

"Don't worry, I'll hand him back over at the end of the summer. He won't even miss me."

"Ha! We'll both miss you, as always."

Kenneth looks pleased as he pours himself a cup of coffee and wanders out to the patio.

"Is Audrey up yet?" I ask, then immediately wish I'd kept my mouth shut.

"She usually sleeps until noon, that one," Patrice tells me.

"Oh, she does not, Patty!"

Patty? Only Viviane could get away with that.

Patrice just huffs and sips her coffee, staring into the fire.

"She'll be up by ten, I'm sure," Viviane says. "I was think-ing we could all do some brainstorming on the beach today. Do you have a pad of paper with you? If not, I have piles of legal pads. I always stock up for the summer."

"Yes, sure. That sounds great. I could use some brain-storming."

"Good. Just throw your suit on. I'll bring a blanket and towels and something to drink. Don't worry, it'll warm up soon. Okay, who's ready for breakfast?"

"Kenneth always is," Patrice remarks. "Might as well get started."

"Can I help?" I ask.

"We can handle it. You relax."

Viviane smiles at me, and she and Patrice get up and start pulling things out of the big brushed-steel refrigerator: eggs, milk, bread, a side of bacon. Soon the kitchen is filled with the aroma of food cooking, the bacon snapping on the flat grill built into the stove. I feel helpless and sort of foolish sit-ting around doing nothing while they do all the work, but too shy to insist on helping.

I watch Viviane and Patrice work together, and it's almost like a dance as they move around each other. They don't talk much. Viviane is humming quietly, and Patrice is absorbed in mixing eggs, cheese and mushrooms into an omelet, taking charge of the pan, flipping it like a professional chef, and I am surprised by her once more.

I get up only to refill my coffee mug, and when I pass her, Viviane gives me a quick hug. She is so sweet.

As I take my seat again, I have to wonder why her touch is so different from Audrey's. She is every bit as beautiful, in her own way. But my body responds differently, with nothing more than a warm fondness. A feeling of security. It's different with Audrey.

Everything is different with Audrey.

And as though she's sensed me thinking about her, she shuffles into the room on bare feet. Her hair is tousled, her face a bit pale in the morning light. Her eyelashes are so dark against her skin, it makes her eyes blaze, that pale, hazy blue a sleepy glow from beneath her half-closed lids.

"Hangover, Viv," she mewls, slumping into the chair next to me.

She is wearing a white cotton baby-doll chemise, her tanned legs looking long under the short hem, her pink cotton robe open, doing nothing to hide the fact that the nightgown is nearly see-through. I can see the rosy circles of her nipples beneath the fabric, the dark strip of her pubic hair. And I go hot all over, my pussy drenched.

I sit up and take a long sip of my coffee. The newly poured liquid scalds my tongue and I cough.

"You all right, Bettina?" Audrey asks me.

"Yes, sure. I just…I should have waited until it cooled down."

*I* need to cool down.

"Poor baby," Audrey murmurs, taking my cup and blowing into it. After a minute she stops, takes a sip. "It's better now," she says, smiling at me. She takes another sip. "Mmm, this is good. Like candy." Then her pink tongue darts out and she licks the rim, smiles again at me before returning my coffee to me. "You like your sugar, don't you?"

"All writers do," Viviane says, carrying another mug of coffee over and handing it to Audrey, along with a couple of aspirin. "Drink up, babe. You'll feel better."

"Thank you, Viv." She takes the mug and squeezes Viviane's

hand, flashing her one of her dazzling smiles, despite her hangover.

Audrey flirts with everyone, it seems, not just me. Maybe I've imagined that spark of chemistry between us. What would I know about it, after all? I've never felt attraction to a woman before. Or from one. I've never felt this intense chemistry with anyone.

There are reasons why.

Viviane lets Audrey and me help set the table on the patio, and Kenneth joins us as we all sit down to eat. The food is wonderful and plentiful, comfort food, and I eat too much. I feel lazy after, sitting in the morning sun. Everyone else seems to, as well. We all lounge around the table, drinking gallons of coffee, picking at the big bowl of fruit.

They're talking about past summers at this house, and although I wasn't there, I feel that lovely sense of camaraderie, can enjoy it with them. They talk a bit about Jack Curran, who will arrive at some point in the next week or two. Jack is a mystery to me. He participates in the online group in fits and spurts. I know he travels a lot, that he lives in Portland, which isn't far from Seattle. I am familiar with his work. But otherwise, he's a vague figure I know little about.

"Leo is coming today, by the way," Viviane announces.

"Oh, I can't wait!" Audrey is effusive, her hangover disappeared at some point during the meal. She turns to me. "Bettina, you know him already, though, don't you? Isn't he from Seattle, like you?"

"He is. He's a friend of my best friend at home. Calvin is a comics artist, too. That's how he and Leo know each other, but I've never actually met him in person. We've only talked online. He introduced me to the group."

"I'm glad he did." Audrey is smiling at me, and under the table she reaches over and pats my thigh.

Her palm is warm on my skin, even through my cargo shorts. It's all I can do not to pull away. Or to spread my thighs to invite her touch.

"So am I," Viviane says, smiling at me. "More coffee, anyone? No? Then why don't we go down to the beach. I'll clear the table and meet everyone down there."

"Let me help you, Viviane," I volunteer, and she smiles and nods her head.

"Sure."

Everyone wanders off, and Viviane and I carry plates and platters back into the kitchen, making several trips. She rinses the dishes and I load them into the dishwasher.

"Thanks for the help, doll," she says.

"I'm glad to help. I wanted to earlier…I feel like being allowed to help is part of the initiation."

"And so it is." She smiles, then begins to hum again as she washes the pans and hands them to me to dry with a thick dish towel. "How is it going so far for you, Tina?"

"Everything is so wonderful. I find myself wishing I'd met everyone sooner, that I'd come here sooner. Maybe my hermit tendencies would never have become so…exaggerated if I'd had someplace like this to come to."

"I'm glad."

"I think even my discomfort with Patrice is good for me, challenging me in a way I've needed, maybe. It's good for me that I have to deal with those feelings in order to be here, if that makes sense."

Viviane nods in understanding.

Maybe even my uncomfortable attraction to Audrey is good for me. It makes me think. She makes me *feel*. For the first time in a long time. For the first time ever, really.

I know what it is in my past that has done this to me. I know my distant parents haven't helped. But it's time for me to take charge of my life. Isn't that what Terry and I have been talking about for over a year? That I need to get over what's happened to me, the tragedy that is my sterile family life. The real tragedy of what happened when I was fifteen that my parents don't even know about.

Maybe I need a female touch to allow myself to feel. Maybe I need something really different to force me to break beyond those physical and mental boundaries I've erected to protect myself.

And maybe I've imagined all this mutual chemistry, that it's only a sort of immature girl-crush most girls experience in high school or college.

*Please don't let it be all my imagination.*

God, I can't believe I am even thinking these things. That I want Audrey to touch me, to kiss me, to fuck me in whatever way women do. But God, I do. I *want,* in a way I never have before. And it's scary and exhilarating and I need to go back to bed with my vibrator again.

Instead, I pull in a deep breath, focus on the sound of Viviane humming, carefully dry the pots and pans. Try to act normal.

But all I'm really thinking about is Audrey's tanned skin, her lips, so red and absolutely ripe-looking. And the ache between my thighs pulses like the rhythm of the ocean beyond the front doors, primal and insistent and a part of *life,* moving and breathing on the earth.

# CHAPTER THREE

The beach is a long sweep of pale sand with a rocky outcropping some distance to the south and another to the north. A few houses are scattered on the edge of the dunes, some small cottages, some enormous places made all of glass, taking advantage of the spectacular view. The old cypress and eucalyptus trees grow in spots almost to the shore, and the sand is dotted with clumps of ice plant. It's low tide and seaweed lies in dark, curling strands at the edge of the water, waiting to be carried back out to float on the sea. I can smell the salt, tangy and fresh and energizing. I can feel the power of the waves as they surge in, then out.

Why does it feel sexual to me?

Everything does.

We sit on colorful Mexican blankets, our legal pads in our laps, discussing our books, making notes, drinking the iced green tea Viviane has brought with her in a pair of huge thermoses. The sun is warm, but not too warm; it feels good on my shoulders, bared by my tank top, and on the tops of my bare feet. Everyone is relaxed, eager. It feels a bit like it does when we do this online, except better, everything clearer than it is when we're all madly typing to each other, trying to get our thoughts out as fast as our fingers will fly across the keyboard. And it's wonderful to see everyone's expressions as we talk about our ideas, that true reaction you don't get unless the person is sitting right in front of you. Another small epiphany for me.

Audrey is in her bikini, with an oversize, pale blue linen shirt thrown over it. A long, fine silver chain lies over her breastbone, making her look even more delicate. She manages to look incredibly sexy and casually put together at the same time. Some people have that gift. It's not one of mine. I feel sloppy if I'm not careful about how I put myself together, maybe because my hair is so utterly out of control. But today I feel so good I hardly care.

If only Audrey weren't sitting next to me, her bare, tanned skin tempting in my peripheral vision as her loose shirt flaps in the breeze. I am eternally damp, my senses on keen alert, in a constant state of mild arousal that I find difficult to ignore for more than a few minutes at a time. It makes me uncomfortable, but also adds to the energy of the day.

The sun is high in the sky and it's getting to be a bit too hot when Viviane announces it's time to break for lunch. Everyone gets up and brushes the sand from their clothes before starting up the dunes toward the house. Audrey hangs back, standing to look out at the sea.

"Everything okay?" I ask her.

"Perfect." She turns to smile at me, and I bask in the warmth of that smile.

I am being ridiculous again.

"It's hot, isn't it? We should go for a swim before lunch," she says, her eyes gleaming like two sky-colored crystals in the sun, challenging me as she slips the big blue shirt from her shoulders.

"I don't have my suit on."

"So? Swim in your underwear." She leans in until I can smell the citrus scent of her hair, and says in a low, faux-sexy tone, "You *are* wearing underwear, aren't you, Bettina?"

I laugh, trying to cover how her voice, her silly question, is making me hot all over. "Of course I am."

"Come on, then."

Suddenly her hands are tearing my tank top over my head, and desire throbs between my legs, in my breasts. Even worse when she kneels in the sand and unbuttons my cargo shorts, dragging them down my legs, revealing my pale pink cotton panties that match my bra. I am so soaking wet I'm afraid she'll see it, smell my desire. But she just tosses my clothes on the sand and grabs my hand, pulling me with her into the waves.

The water is a shock at first, and I gasp.

"Cold?" Audrey asks.

"It's freezing!"

"Oh, it's not so bad. Come on, Bettina."

She drags me in deeper, the water swirling around my stomach.

"I can't!"

"Sure you can. I'll help you."

She wraps her arms around me, presses belly to belly, and it does warm me, but not only in the way she intended. But do I even know what she intends? I can't figure it out. All I know is that her body is keeping mine warm. That my nipples are hard and aching against hers, my pussy clenching and unclenching. Empty. Hungry.

Audrey pulls me farther into the cold water, and I taste the salt on my tongue as a wave splashes against our shoulders. But she doesn't let me go.

"Better?"

"Yes. Better." I smile at her.

She smiles back, leans in, touching her lips to mine. And it is more shocking than the cold ocean. Just the merest contact, her soft lips pressed to mine, and oh, God, I think I could almost come just from this. But how is that possible?

She pulls back, and I can barely hear her over the roar of the ocean, the roar of desire in my ears. "You really are beautiful, Bettina."

She smiles again, sunnily, and releases me. I nearly fall back, into the swirling water, but manage to catch myself. Audrey is laughing as she dives into the water, comes up with her hair streaming, looking like a mermaid. She grins at me, splashes me playfully, and I splash her back, my brain working at a thousand miles an hour, trying to figure it out, trying *not* to figure it out and just enjoy whatever is happening.

I spend far too much time dissecting things. And trying to dissect this, whatever it is, will drive me crazy if I let it.

We swim and splash, diving under the water, coming up salty and sputtering, until I'm shaking, my lips beginning to go numb.

"Okay, now it's cold," Audrey yells over her shoulder as she moves through the water, back onto the beach.

She sits on the sun-warm sand and wraps her arms around herself, shivering, as she watches me follow after her, the waves dragging at my tired limbs. I collapse on the beach beside her. She lays her arm around my shoulder, pulling me in close to her side.

"Your turn to keep me warm," she tells me.

And just like that, I am on fire again, my body burning with desire.

"Audrey..."

"Hmm?"

She is pushing her wet hair from her face with her free

hand, but her eyes are steady on mine. She's smiling a little, just a quirk at the corner of her full mouth, her dimple sweet and tempting in her cheek.

I swear I see the same desire in her eyes I feel flooding my system, her features going soft. She leans into me, her smile widening as she tilts her face to mine. And it is one of those magical moments, and I'm sure I'm not imagining things this time. Heat arcs between us, and she is going to kiss me again. But I have to say something this time. I have to ask her.

"Audrey—"

"Hey, girls!" Viviane is shouting from the top of the dunes. "Leo's here. Come say hello!"

Audrey jumps to her feet. "We're coming!"

I don't really know what I wanted to say to her, anyway. *Fuck.*

I grab my cast-off clothes, pulling them on over my sodden underwear and bra, and we trudge back up the beach.

"You'll love Leo," Audrey says to me over her shoulder. "He's a doll. I'm so excited!"

Why do I feel as though I suddenly no longer exist for her? That I am merely part of the background? Or am I being overly sensitive? It wouldn't be the first time.

We reach the patio and everyone is there, including Leo Hirogata.

Leo is a few inches taller than I am, slender, with golden skin and pretty, black eyes as dark as his black, spiky hair. He's good-looking, if a bit androgynous. He's wearing a T-shirt with the cast of a popular Japanese comic book I recognize as being one my friend Calvin has shown me. Audrey goes straight to him and throws her arms around him, planting a kiss on his mouth. It's more than a friendly peck; it's several moments before she pulls back, her dazzling smile directed at Leo. My chest knots up.

*Don't be ridiculous.*

But I *am* being ridiculous. I can't seem to help myself. It's as though our time on the beach never happened. Or maybe what happened means nothing to her. Maybe it only meant something to me because my perceptions of people are so fucked up. Because I'm so fucked up.

Eventually everyone has said hello to Leo, and he sees me standing at the edge of the group.

"Hey, you must be Bettina. We finally meet."

"Yes, hi, Leo. It's nice to meet you."

"How's Calvin doing?"

"Calvin? Oh, he's fine. Fine. Just…you know. Doing his comics."

Why can't I speak like a normal person?

"Awesome. Too bad he isn't part of this group. Man, he'd love it here. I love it here. So glad to get out of the Seattle gray."

Leo turns to grin broadly at Audrey.

"Well, we're all glad to have you here, Leo," she says, taking his arm in both her hands, sort of wrapping herself around him. "Why don't I take you up to the house and help you get settled. Do you need something to drink?"

"Yeah, I could use a Coke or something."

Audrey smiles at him once more, brilliantly. "I'm really glad you made it, Leo. Come on, I want to see your new comics."

I see Leo blush, color staining his cheeks. His black eyes are sparkling. Audrey will do that to a person. I should know.

"Sure," he says. "I'll show you what I've been working on the last few weeks."

Audrey pulls on his arm and they go into the house. I am left feeling oddly lost, and cold and sticky from my swim. I slip out to go back to my cottage and change.

Once my clothes are off, though, and I'm in the shower with the hot water pouring down on my bare skin, I am all a confused mass of lust and hurt. *Need.*

I need her. I don't understand. I didn't want this. And as strange as it seems, even to me, I slip my hand between my thighs, over my soaking-wet slit, my hardened clit. Desire builds, higher and higher. I rub harder. But I can't keep the images straight in my head: Audrey, her kissing me, the ocean moving around us, cool and fresh. Her kissing Leo.

*Goddamn it!*

I turn the shower off, grab a towel and head to my bed, where I don't even bother to really dry off before pulling my vibrator from the nightstand and sitting back against the pillows, my knees bent, my thighs wide. I push the vibe right into my pussy; I am so wet I don't even need any lube. It sinks right in, the buzzing carried through my system, a current of pleasure, hot and electric. I squeeze my eyes shut and see her face, feel her lips.

*Audrey.*

I see her kissing Leo, see the beauty of his mouth. And suddenly, he's kissing me, too, while Audrey lowers her face between my thighs, her tongue snaking out to lick at my clitoris, to spear into my body.

I am shivering with need, tensed, waiting.

More, as Audrey takes my breasts in her hands, and my own hand reaches up as I take my nipple between my fingers and squeeze. A shock of desire, hot and pulsing.

*Audrey.*

And Leo's mouth on mine, his tongue hot and pressing into my mouth. Her tongue working between my thighs, so damn good, and the vibrator deep inside me, buzzing against my G-spot. And I am coming, crying out, my hips arching.

Pleasure is hot and sharp in my body, spearing into me over and over.

I pull the vibrator from my sex and turn it off. My legs are shaking. I feel empty.

What is it I want? I don't know. I don't fucking know.


That evening we have dinner at a restaurant in the small town of Goleta. The decor is classic Mexican: gaily painted ladder-back chairs with straw seats, red-and-yellow tablecloths, colored lights hanging all around the high ceiling, making small splotches of blue and red and green against the pale adobe walls. The salsa is hot enough to really burn, but fantastic. We order pitchers of margaritas, and even Patrice drinks too much before the food arrives.

Audrey sits between Leo and me, and she is subtly flirting with him, and with me. And with the waiter.

The waiter bothers me the most, for some reason. Maybe because he isn't one of us. Maybe because he is so incredibly good-looking, with his sleek black hair and flashing brown eyes. He's tall and slim, but with broad shoulders, and classic Latino good looks: high cheekbones, a chiseled chin with a dimple in the center, beautiful smooth brown skin. I'd be attracted to him if I weren't so busy resenting him.

I am being completely ridiculous.

I know that, and yet I cannot stop.

The food is some of the best I've had, but I am constantly distracted by what Audrey is doing: the way the fork disappears between her red lips, the graceful gestures she makes with her hands when she's talking. The way her eyes sparkle, the way she pushes her hair behind one ear when she's flirting with Leo or the waiter. Or with Kenneth, Patrice or Viviane. Or me.

I keep reflecting back to that kiss in the ocean, asking myself what it meant. If anything. And I have to wonder if all of this self-doubt has as much to do with Audrey as it does with just *me*.

Terry has talked to me about taking myself too seriously. I was the one who brought it up, initially, as a sort of half joke, but Terry addressed it as though I was being perfectly serious, and I've come to understand that maybe I was.

God, if Audrey could see the shit going on in my head she would definitely tell me to lighten up. And she'd be right.

I decide to lighten up.

I turn back to my nearly empty margarita glass and sip the sweet–bitter liquid through the straw. It's cold on my tongue, sliding down my throat. I'm more than a little buzzed, but so is everyone at the table, except Viviane, who's driving. Audrey is laughing at something Leo has said, leaning into him, shoulder to shoulder. I try to tune in to what they're laughing about, but it's too late; I've missed it. I smile, anyway, as though I get it.

"Has anyone heard from Jack?" Patrice asks, and I see Audrey stop laughing and turn her head, attentive, eager to hear the answer.

"Not yet," Viviane says. "But you know how he is. He lives life at his own pace. He'll just show up without notice, like he always does." She pauses to eat a tortilla chip covered in salsa, wipes her mouth carefully with her cloth napkin. "It doesn't matter. I'll be glad to see him, whenever he arrives."

Patrice and Kenneth exchange a glance, but I have no idea what the meaning of it is. Audrey just looks excited, and Leo looks a bit disappointed that she's no longer paying him any attention. She's leaning across the table now, toward Viviane.

"I hope it's soon," she says. The light of the candle in the middle of the table is reflected in her black pupils. It makes her look as if her eyes are glowing with some kind of fire. Maybe they are. "It's been too long."

Viviane nods her head and smiles, but there is something vague and distracted in the way she does it. What is going on here? But another pitcher of margaritas arrives, and everyone is drinking and laughing again. Audrey flirts with the waiter while Leo visibly pouts, then she shifts back to him once more, but she keeps an arm around the back of my chair in an almost possessive manner.

I'm really a little drunk by now and I don't care about anything as much: what Audrey is doing, what it might mean. Or the tequila has made it easier to pretend this is true, anyway.

The drive home is short. We're all quiet, a bit sleepy from the alcohol. Kenneth's soft snores accompany the classic rock on the radio. Audrey's head is resting on my shoulder, and my body is in a warm simmer. A bluesy version of "Ain't No Sunshine" comes on, and I find myself quietly humming to it, thinking of Audrey. She's like the sun, bright and shining and dynamic like no one I've ever met before, making you feel lighter. And when her brilliant light is turned away, it leaves you feeling empty. I feel it now. And I've seen Leo affected in the same way. What is it about her?

I'm anxious suddenly to get back. To get into my bed in the cozy cottage, to crawl beneath the covers and read. To sleep away this strange anxiety I can't seem to escape, gnawing at the pit of my stomach. My odd need for Audrey's attention, her touch, her scent.

Obsession is a strange thing. I've read about it over and over in the novels I have always devoured, as vital to me as food. But I've never experienced it myself, until now. I don't think it's a healthy thing. It doesn't feel healthy. It's excruciating in between those moments when the object of my obsession is focused on me. But in those moments I feel so amazing, as though I am lit up from inside with some powerful force.

Audrey shifts, her face turning toward mine. She mumbles sleepily, and I can't hear what she's saying, but I can smell her margarita-scented breath, and it is sweet, tempting. If we were alone I might dare to kiss her, to press my lips to hers. To open her up and taste. But I can't do it here, wedged in the car with the others. I squeeze my thighs together to ease the ache there, a beating pulse of desire. It doesn't help.

Finally we reach Viviane's house and spill out of the SUV, everyone wandering off to their rooms. Audrey gives my hand a fleeting squeeze, and I hold on a moment when she tries to pull away. She stays there for several seconds, long enough to smile at me, her smoky eyes watching me. I am burning for her, her hand hot in mine. But what can I do about it? I want to send her some mental message: *Come with me.*

Her brows draw together, as though she almost hears me. Then she says, "Good night, Bettina." She squeezes my hand again and pulls away.

In my cottage I turn on all the lights. My heart is pounding, and I am far more awake than I should be. It's late, I'm at least halfway drunk, and I should just put myself to bed. But if I do, I know I'll only lie there and think of Audrey.

Instead, I plug in my laptop, open the manuscript I'm currently working on. It's a sad story of abused children. My stories are always sad. I'm okay with that. I think I use my writing to work out some of my own issues, even when the particular issues I write about are different from my own. The feelings are the same. Abandonment. Loss. Fear.

I manage to do some editing, write a few paragraphs, but I can't concentrate, and eventually I shut my computer down and get ready for bed. I take a little comfort in my bedtime ritual: brush teeth, floss, wash face, braid hair. I love ritual, love the familiar. It comforts me. I pull on my short cotton nightgown and get under the covers, turning out the light.

Outside, all other sound is obliterated by the surf crashing on the shore. There could be a stampede of elephants out there and I wouldn't hear it. It is almost as if the sound of the ocean insulates me from the world. I love this idea. I only wish it could insulate me from the thoughts inside my own head.

They are all of Audrey.

I have been in a mild state of arousal all evening, and it's no different now. I force myself to do some yoga breathing, to calm my beating heart. I don't want to masturbate tonight. I don't want to give in. But when I turn over to lie on my stomach, even the mattress pressing into my mound is too much for me, and I can't help but grind my hips into the bed.

*Audrey…*

Her lips are so damn soft. And tonight she would taste of citrus and tequila as my tongue slides inside…

With a groan, I give up, flop over and pull my vibrator from the nightstand drawer. I coat it in lube. I want it fast and easy tonight. Lying back, I open my legs wide, slip the vibe into my pussy, gasping. No time for any complicated fantasies tonight, just her face, her mouth, as I thrust my hips, taking the vibrator in, then sliding it out, rubbing it against my G-spot while I pinch my clit between my fingers. And soon I am coming, my body shivering with waves of pleasure. Still trembling, I slip the vibe from my wet slit, my body still tense, needy. I press the vibrator to my swollen clit, harder and harder, desire building once more, cresting, my hips pumping. And I come again, more fiercely this time, crying out, challenging the roar of the ocean with my pleasure.

It's not enough. And even though I am panting, breathless, my muscles tense and aching, I do it again, holding the vibrator to my clit, shoving two fingers into my pussy, pumping, deeper and deeper. And once more I'm coming, shaking, my body almost too weak now to ride it out. But I do.

After, I am exhausted, too tired to come again, even though I want to. I want to work this need out of my system. I want to work Audrey out. But I know damn well that's not going to happen.

Finally, sleep claims me, and I dream of Audrey, of being mermaids in the ocean, our hair streaming, our mermaid tails twining as we fuck in some lovely, mysterious, sea-creature way, her arms around me as we float out to sea.

It's Sunday, and Patrice and I get up early and go to the small Goleta farmer's market with Viviane to buy produce for the week. Everything is so beautiful, the colors of the fruits and vegetables laid out in orderly pyramids or piled in enormous tubs. There are flowers everywhere. We're all quiet as we browse the aisles. I feel as though I can't quite wake up today. I slept deeply after all those orgasms last night. Maybe the alcohol helped.

We buy steaming lattes from a vendor and taste peaches and strawberries as we move from booth to booth, and there is a quiet camaraderie between us, even with Patrice. She is enjoying herself, her face more relaxed and open than I've ever seen it as she spies a particularly beautiful cluster of tomatoes red on the vine, a ripe honeydew melon, a bunch of purple grapes gleaming in the morning sunlight.

On the way back to the house we stop at the grocery store for supplies, and I wander off to buy a bestselling suspense novel I've heard a lot about. One of Jack's books is there, too, his latest thriller. I always love seeing books on the shelf from authors I know. Except that I don't really know him yet.

In the car we talk about unimportant things: movies we've loved, movies we've hated, the transvestite with a day's growth of beard we spotted at the farmer's market, bits and pieces of publishing industry news. It strikes me for a moment that what Viviane has told me about Patrice is true: that her bark is worse than her bite, and I'm glad I'm getting to know her. I think she may have some of the fears that I do, and I wonder if some of the things I feel are more universal than I thought. It makes me feel a little narcissistic, as though all this time I thought my pain was so unique, that I've spent too much time focused on *me*. But there is also a sense of relief, of community with the human race, which is something I don't feel often.

Back at the house it's chore day. The guys have been cleaning off the patio furniture, preparing lunch, and the rest of the afternoon is spent doing laundry, writing on the patio, then everyone in the kitchen making dinner together. The evening is cool and cloudy. Kenneth has built a fire in the double-sided fireplace that opens on both the living and dining rooms, and we eat inside.

The change in weather seems to have gotten to everyone, and they all retire to their rooms soon after the meal, leaving Audrey and me alone on the big sectional sofa in front of the amber glow of the fire.

"What should we do now? Are you tired?" she asks me.

She is sitting only a few feet away, Viviane having just vacated that spot. There is no way I'm going to bed while she's still here. She is sitting with her legs crossed, her long cotton skirt spread around her. She's wearing a white thermal top with her bohemian print skirt, but somehow it looks great on her. And she's not wearing a bra, her full breasts outlined by the soft, clingy fabric, her nipples dimly visible if I look hard enough.

"I'm not tired," I tell her truthfully. No, my insides are warming up, alive, simply being alone with her.

"We should have our slumber party," Audrey says, her eyes

sparkling in the firelight. "Do you want popcorn, or maybe just some wine?"

"Wine," I decide. "I don't know why, but being here makes me want to drink wine. Like I'm in the Italian countryside or something."

Audrey grins at me and we get up and head into the big kitchen without turning on the lights, but we can see our way around by the firelight coming through the doorway from the dining room. Audrey opens a bottle of Cabernet and I grab a large bar of dark chocolate from the well-stocked pantry. Viviane always has plenty of chocolate on hand; it seems to be a universal staple for writers.

"Are we going back to the living room?" I want to be alone with her, but I can't seem to say so.

"Let's go to your cottage. I don't want to wake anyone up. Do you have some nail polish? We can make it a real girls' night."

"I do, but it's pink. Don't you usually wear red?"

"I don't mind. Come on."

We go outside, and the air is chilly, making goose bumps rise on my skin. Or maybe it's knowing I will finally be alone with her.

Once inside my cottage, I turn on the lights and head into the bathroom.

"I have some polish remover, too," I call over my shoulder. I look through the drawer where I've placed most of my toiletries, everything lined up in neat rows, and come up with the polish remover, a file, some cotton, and bring it back into the main room.

"Perfect," Audrey says, and I feel unaccountably pleased.

She opens the wine and pours it into two glasses she brought with her from the house. I arrange all the nail supplies on the table and sit on the edge of the bed.

"I'm not very good at this," I tell her, taking a long swallow of the wine. It's rich and dark on my tongue. I swallow some more.

"Oh, I'm sure you are," she says, her tone throaty, flirtatious.

But that's Audrey, isn't it? I shouldn't read too much into it, no matter how much I want to.

"No, really. I'm not that much of a girlie girl. I don't wear much makeup. Keeping my toes painted is one of my few nods to being female."

"Don't sell yourself short, Bettina. You're very female," she says, sipping her wine, watching me over the rim of her glass.

A small flutter starts in my stomach.

*Don't be foolish. This is just Audrey being Audrey.*

I take a breath, forcing my pulse to steady. I drink some more of my wine, finishing off the glass. It helps a little.

"Can I do your toes?" she asks me as she refills both our glasses.

I am not going to say no.

"Sure."

"Here, scoot up and sit on the bed against the pillows."

She shakes the polish, and I wait with my breath held in my lungs as though I am waiting for her to bend over me, to undress me, kiss me.

*Stop it.*

She leans over my toes and strokes the old polish off with a ball of cotton. I can feel her fingertips around the cotton ball. I drink some more of my wine, trying not to watch the way her hair falls around her face, like dark satin.

"So, tell me what kind of guys you like," she says to me.

I laugh uncomfortably. "What?"

"We can't have a slumber party without taking about boys!"

"I've never actually had a slumber party before."

Audrey pauses to look up at me. "You're kidding."

"Nope."

"Pardon me for saying so, but that's a little weird, Bettina."

"I know. I've had a weird life, I guess, but not in any sort of interesting way. I've just missed out on a lot."

"Well, it's an awfully good thing that I came along then, isn't it?"

She's teasing me, but it's true, I think.

"Yes. It is."

She grins at me, and I smile back, and she empties her wineglass before bending her head to her task once more. I swallow the rest of my wine in a few gulps. It goes down easy, and my body relaxes.

"So. About the boys," she prompts.

"I don't know if I have a type. Guys are so…they're a mystery to me. I don't like that I never seem to know what they're thinking."

Audrey laughs as she opens the bottle of polish and begins to paint my nails. "I can tell you what they're thinking. They're thinking they want to get in your pants."

"Yes," I say a little too quietly.

She looks up then. "Hey. Are you okay?"

How does she seem to know something is going on with me from nothing more than a drop in my tone? But she does.

I shrug, lie. "Sure. Yes. I'm fine."

"But…?" She arches a brow, clearly waiting for me to answer.

"But…I've had some…less than stellar experiences with men."

"Welcome to the club, hon."

She doesn't say it sarcastically. She means it.

"What happened to you, Audrey?" I ask quietly.

She shrugs, goes back to painting my nails. "Same old story most girls have, I guess. Date rape."

"Jesus, Audrey."

Another shrug. "It happens. I was at a frat party with a friend. I wasn't actually in college yet, but I went to the parties all the time." She is stroking the polish onto my toes in short, even streaks of pink. "He was so cute, and I liked him. That part really bummed me out. Disappointed me. But I grew up that night, you know?"

"Maybe. But I don't get how you can sound so casual about it. Wasn't it awful? It must have been."

"Oh, it was." She bites her lip for a moment as she applies a second coat of polish to my toes. I wish she'd look up at me, that I could see her eyes so I'd know what she really feels about what happened to her. "And that wasn't the only time. Happened to me again a few years later, and that time it was my boyfriend. He just didn't want to hear the word *no*. But it's part of life. I don't let it get me down." She's quiet a moment, studying her handiwork. "I don't let anything get me down."

"I don't know how you do that. I wish I could."

"I refuse to give anyone that kind of power over me. It's as simple as that." She looks up finally and her eyes are blazing. She is not as unconcerned about what happened to her as she claims to be. She gets up, brings the bottle of wine back with her, fills our empty glasses. "You shouldn't either, Bettina."

I shake my head, drinking more wine, letting it warm my limbs. "I don't know. I don't think I can do that. I can't think of it that way. I'm not a strong person, Audrey. I'm not like you."

"We are all a lot more alike than we think we are," she says. "Tell me what happened to you, Bettina, because I can tell something did."

I shake my head again, but I take a long swallow of my wine and tell her. "It was a friend of my dad's, another college professor. They had one of those cocktail parties people in academia seem to have all the time." Hard lump in my throat, but I continue. "I was hiding away in my room, listening to music. He came in, said he was looking for the bathroom. But I'd seen him watching me before, and I knew he'd come looking for me. He was a little drunk."

"But not enough that he didn't know exactly what he was doing," Audrey says, her voice low, dangerous.

"Yes."

"Asshole."

"Yes."

"How old were you?"

"Fifteen."

"Fuck."

"He didn't…I mean, he touched me, but he didn't…you know." I shake my head. I want to tell Audrey everything about me, just open myself to her, yet this is still hard to talk about. Even with my therapist. It's hard to think about.

"He's still a reprehensible bastard, Bettina! He probably would have done more if there wasn't a party going on in the next room."

"Maybe. I don't know."

"And it doesn't even matter. What matters is the intent. That he meant to do whatever he wanted to you. That he made you a victim. That he took your power from you."

Why does she seem more disturbed by my experience than by her own? More disturbed than I am myself? She puts her wineglass down on the table and moves up to sit next to me.

Her mouth is set into a grim line, her forehead creased. Her eyes are dark, glittering.

I just nod my head, the extent of her anger seeming to drain some of my own.

"Look, Bettina. You can't let this guy control who you are. Do you understand? You cannot let him win."

"I haven't, not entirely. It's affected me. But I haven't allowed that one experience to dictate who I am. I've still dated, had sex. I just haven't…really had intense passion for anyone. But maybe I haven't met the right person. Or maybe I haven't been ready. I don't know."

She is so close to me I can feel the heat coming off her skin. How can I feel this way talking about what happened to me, about that night that scarred me. Fucking impossible. But I can't help it. And this moment is all about Audrey, about opening myself to her, not about that asshole, as she says. Maybe this is what she means. And I realize I feel an enormous sense of relief, even more than I did when I told my therapist about the incident. Maybe it's knowing that she's been through it, too. I feel closer to her, some sort of kinship.

"Good," she says, nodding. "You can't let that experience define who you are. You can't let it control what you do."

"I don't think I have. Not entirely. But these guys…it's never been…important to me. I've never really been into it. I do better with my vibrator," I tell her, then feel heat creep into my cheeks.

She smiles wryly. "Don't we all? Nothing to be ashamed about, hon, we all do it. No one knows your body better than you do." She pauses, licks her lips. "Except maybe another woman."

I nearly jump out of my skin, my pulse racing. Her words have switched a gear in my brain so suddenly my head is spinning.

"Do I shock you, Bettina?" She's watching me, her gaze steady, her voice low. "I don't think so."

I shake my head. I can't speak.

"I turned to women after that first experience," she says. "I needed that softness." She reaches out and strokes my hair from my face, and I go hot all over, desire a thrumming pulse between my thighs. "Don't you ever need that?" she asks, her tone so low I can barely hear her. "Don't you ever crave that gentle touch? That safety?"

I swallow hard. "Yes. I think...I do."

And it's true. Somehow, I feel that it might be healing for me. I imagine her soft hands on me, and I am back to that simmering state of lust instantly.

"Do you want that with me, Bettina?"

It comes out on a whisper, my throat closing up, tight with need. "Yes."

She smiles. "I was hoping you'd say that." And she leans in and kisses me.

# CHAPTER FOUR

Audrey's mouth is soft and silky as butter, her tongue sweet with the wine. And I sit frozen for several moments, my body blazing with need, paralyzed with it. Then my hands come up and I bury them in her hair, as I've been wanting to do since I first saw her, I realize from a distance. She sighs into my mouth, and we slip back together on the bed.

Her body is delicate next to mine, but her kiss is powerful, taking me over. I feel as if I am in some sort of dream state. This can't really be happening. But my body knows it's real. My nipples are so hard they hurt, my sex pulsing, damp, and I arch into her without thinking about what I'm doing.

Her arms are around me, and she holds me as tight as any man, tighter maybe, her full breasts crushed against mine. I can feel the hard points of her nipples, and I shift until our nipples are aligned. Desire flares like heat lightning in my belly, spreads outward, until I am weak with it.

I have a moment of panic: I don't know how to do this. My heart is a hammer in my chest. I freeze.

Audrey pulls back and whispers to me, "Don't worry, Bettina. I'll take care of you. I'll show you how. Trust me. Trust yourself."

Her voice is soft, breathless, and I know that she wants me, *know* it in a way I wasn't certain of until now. And it gives me permission to want this as much as I do. To want it, and to have it, and to simply let it happen.

She straddles me, her slender legs on either side of mine. Her weight is nothing on my body. Her heat is everything. Her skirt is pooled around her waist, and as she settles onto that small band of bare skin between my jeans and my sweater I realize she's not wearing any underwear. She is slick and hot against my stomach. A shock goes through me, making me moan.

Audrey smiles a little as she pulls her top over her head, and her breasts are full and naked, the nipples dark pink and as hard as I know my own must be. I want to take them into my mouth, suck them. I want to do it so badly I'm shaking.

"Beautiful Bettina," Audrey whispers, reaching out to take my hair between her fingers. "I love your curls. They're wild. There's a wild part of you, Bettina, just waiting to be let out."

"I don't know…"

"Oh, yes. You just need someone to help you free it."

I don't know what to say.

"Come on. Take your sweater off for me," she tells me. "Let me see you."

I have to pull in a hitching breath before I drag my sweater over my head. I feel clumsy, as though my hands are half-numb. Audrey is still sitting on me, her sex wet against my belly. She leans over me, kisses me again, and it is soft and moist, her lovely mouth on mine, her tongue slipping between my lips. And I think back to the dream I had, about us being mermaids together, and fucking in the ocean. And what's happening right now is every bit as dreamlike to me. Mystical.

She kisses me harder, beginning to pant into my mouth, and my body heats with desire. A low humming has started in my veins, in my pussy. I can hardly stand it. I pull my mouth from hers.

"I need to be naked with you, Audrey."

"Yes, I need it, too. Let's get you undressed."

She sits up and pulls me with her, her hands hard on my shoulders. She unzips my jeans quickly, and I lift my hips as she helps me wiggle out of them. She tosses them on the floor.

"Cute," she says, hooking her fingers in the waistband of my underwear, which is peach-colored cotton with a little white lace trim. Then her smile turns a bit feral as she drags them down over my hips, and I am almost naked, finally. "Take off your bra, Bettina."

I reach behind my back and undo the clasp, and my breasts feel heavy as the fabric falls away.

"Oh."

It is a small, breathy sound of admiration from her, and I flush. My breasts are small but well shaped. One of my best assets, I think. And glancing down I see that my nipples are swollen, a pale pink darkening by the moment. I arch a little, silently begging for her touch, and she leans over me once more and strokes the hard tips with her fingers. Her touch is soft, gentle, her hands impossibly hot. So different from a man's.

"Ah, God."

"You like this, Bettina?"

"Yes…"

"Do it to me. Touch me."

I take her breasts in both hands, pressing just a little, testing the fullness of her flesh, and she sighs. She takes my nipples between her fingers and pulls them out in long, sweet strokes, and I do the same to her. And all the time her blue gaze is on mine. I watch as her eyes cloud, go darker, like a storm coming over the sea. Her nipples are going harder and harder beneath my touch, as hard as mine. It's like looking at some sort of reflection, as though my pleasure is mirrored in her, intensifying everything. And I am growing wetter and wetter, my sex filling until the pulse beat of desire is painful.

"Tell me what you want, Bettina," she says.

"I want...I want to touch you. Everywhere. But I don't know how."

"Just think about how you want me to touch you. To kiss you. To lick you."

Quick flash of my dreams, of a feminine mouth between my thighs, and I hold back a groan. But I nod, understanding. I pull on her skirt, and she lifts up on her knees and slips out of it before pushing me down on the bed once more and straddling my prone body.

Her sex is shaved, beautifully naked, the lips pink and tender looking. And her clitoris is swollen and longer than mine, peeking from between those soft lips. I reach out and touch that hard little nub. She moans, smiles down at me. Encouraged, I slip my fingers along her slit, and it is all wet, lovely heat. Incredible. I shiver, desire a steady thrumming in my body, my own sex filling, swelling.

"Come on, Bettina," she says, her hips arching toward me. "Really touch me."

I slide the tip of one finger inside her and feel her clench around me, so hot and tight. I push a little deeper and she lets out a long, slow breath. It's like nothing I have ever felt before, not even like my own body. Her pussy is so soft and slick as I add another finger and push a little deeper. I want to explore her, with my hands, with my mouth. But my own need is so great I can't really control myself, what's happening.

"Audrey, please…"

Another quick smile from her, then she is on me, my fingers slipping from her as she slides over my body, her weight pressing me down into the mattress. She spreads my thighs with her hands. One last smile up at me before she dips her head.

Another shock as her tongue flicks out, catching the tip of my clit, and I gasp.

"Oh!"

She uses her fingers to spread my pussy lips wide, and traces her tongue up and down my slit. It's very much like a man doing these things to me, except more gentle, more in tune with my desires, instant by instant. And the nearly excruciating knowledge that it is *her* doing this to me, her face between my spread thighs, *Audrey* licking my pussy in long, slow, lovely strokes. I am soaking wet, needy, writhing in moments. Then her tongue dips into my aching hole, wet and pressing, pushing inside me, and my whole body comes up off the bed.

"God! Audrey!"

She really goes to work then, licking and licking, my pussy, my clit, until I think I might lose my mind. Pleasure is like a knife, cutting into me over and over as I watch her dark head moving between my thighs. I can hardly believe it, that this is happening, that it's *her*. And I can barely hold my orgasm back. When she pushes her thumbs inside me, taking my clit into her mouth and sucking so hard it hurts, I come, shattering, lights flashing in front of my eyes, dazzling me.

"Audrey! Oh…"

She keeps licking me, and my climax shudders through me, and I don't know if it's ever going to stop. But eventually it does.

Usually after an orgasm I am languid, spent, but I am more eager than ever to have her under my hands, my mouth.

I sit up and she rolls onto her back on the bed, as though she's anticipated my need, or maybe simply her own.

"I want to do this right," I tell her.

"You will."

Her eyes are gleaming, fevered, her cheeks and her breasts flushed. I bend to take them in my hands once more. Her flesh is impossibly soft, lustrous and golden. Her nipples are larger than mine, dark and swollen. I pinch the tips lightly, watching her squirm. I pinch harder and her dark lashes flutter closed as she moans.

"Ah, yes, that's good, Bettina. Suck them, please. Come on."

I bend over her, and I can smell sex on her, smell her desire, smell the scent of my climax all over her. I pull in a deep breath, my body simmering again already. Holding her left breast in my hand, I knead the flesh a bit before pulling the tip into my mouth.

"Oh, that's good," she breathes.

I curl my tongue over her nipple. It's hard and soft all at once. I graze it with my teeth, take pleasure in the way she squirms. Then I suck. And she is all soft flesh and hard nipple, everything hot and fragrant. And I am going warm all over, my sex pulsing, needing to come again. But I will make her come first.

I slip one hand down between her thighs, and she opens for me. Her pussy is soft, swollen, smooth and slippery. I move my fingers down, over her slit, and she spreads even more. I find her hole, rubbing at the edges, slipping the tip of my finger in, then out. I cannot believe how hot and wet she is.

"Come on, Bettina. Come on."

I suck her nipple harder, letting it slip from my lips at the end, and she gasps. But I have to see her, have to watch my fingers inside her.

I shift so I can see better, and move one of her thighs, until she is spread wide on the bed. Her sex is pink and glistening with her juices. And I am fascinated simply watching my fingers stroking that lovely, wet flesh.

"Oh, you are killing me," she groans.

But I can't help myself. I play with her a bit longer, just stroking her pussy lips, her hole, over and over, until she is writhing and panting.

Finally, I slip my fingers back inside, hard and all at once, and she clenches, going tight all over, but mostly it's her pussy grabbing on to my fingers. And my sex is pulsing with need, hers and my own.

God, I need her.

"Audrey, I need to…I need to fuck you. How do I do it?" I am desperate, lost suddenly.

But she sits up and drags me down on the bed and straddles me again.

"I'll fuck you, baby," she says, making me shiver.

I have never heard anything as purely erotic as Audrey saying these words to me.

She pulls one of my legs over hers, yanking me until our bodies are right up against each other's. Her sex is hot on mine. Soft. Wet. Jesus.

Then she starts to move, a slow undulation of her hips, her hands digging into my buttocks as she holds me tight against her. And she is fucking me. And it is like nothing I have ever felt before.

She grinds into me, and soon I am moving with her, creating a rhythm, pussy to pussy, wet heat to wet heat. So slick, her swollen lips against my flesh, rubbing my mound, my hard clit. Desire builds, hot, electric. And we are gasping and pumping our hips against each other.

"Oh, baby," she moans. "I'm going to come, baby. Come on. Come with me."

I am so fucking wet, slipping against her, and I feel her clit, feel how hard and hot it is. She reaches for me, her hands covering my breasts, her palms scorching hot against my nipples. And as she pinches them I explode. There is no other word for it. I'm coming so damn hard, my body clenching in hard jerks. I feel a liquid gush between my thighs, and I don't know whether it's her or me. Then she's tensing, shaking, her hips arching hard into mine, hurting me. But I don't care.

"Fuck!" she yells, then collapses on top of me.

We are both panting hard, my sex, my body, still pulsing. My head is buzzing. I can't think. I don't want to think.

I want Audrey to tell me everything is okay. That I did things right. But I didn't *make* her come, and it bothers me. Worries me.

I've never had this sort of concern with a man. Of course, men are easy; they always come. And none have ever really been important to me. I know that sounds harsh, but I can't help it.

Audrey lets out a deep sigh and rolls off me, but her head is pillowed on my shoulder. It feels nice. I turn my face and smell sex and the citrus scent of her hair, and faintly, the ocean air. Or maybe it's that ocean scent of female arousal, of female come. And suddenly I want to taste her, to know that scent, that female flavor.

I want to do it. But I don't know how. I don't even know how to ask if it's okay.

My body is heating again, my breasts going tight, my sex filling with the pressure of desire. But more than that, even, is this *need* to put my mouth on her. To make her come.

I roll onto my side and she is staring at me.

"That was awesome," she says, making me smile. Making me feel a thousand times more confident. "I told you that you'd know what to do."

"Did I?"

"Yes. Absolutely."

She reaches out and smooths her palm over my side, my breast. "Your nipples are hard again. They're the prettiest shade of pink. Just like your nail polish. We probably smudged the hell out of it."

I laugh until she tweaks my nipple between her fingers, and my laugh turns into a low moan.

Audrey grins. "You need more, Bettina?"

"Yes."

"So do I."

"I want to go down on you," I tell her.

"Oh, yes, please. Come here."

I assume she's going to roll onto her back, but instead she pushes me down flat, turns and straddles me, so that her pussy is right over my face. It's really beautiful up close. I've read of people describing a woman's sex as looking like a flower, an orchid, and it's true. I do nothing more than stare for several moments, fascinated, turned on simply looking at her. Then her hand slips between my thighs, stroking my slit, and I open my thighs wide.

"Bettina," she says, her voice low, breathy as she moves down, lowering her body over mine. "Come on, baby."

I stroke her with my fingertips, making her squirm. Then I grab her hips and pull her lower, guiding her, and let my tongue flick out over her wet, pink flesh. She does taste like the ocean: dark and damp and a little salty. And she is so slick under my tongue, the taste of her, her scent, her arousal making me hot, pleasure rolling over me in undulating waves.

I use my hands and my mouth on her, fingers and tongue and lips, exploring, experimenting with touch and taste. And her fingers are deep inside me, fucking me, but not too hard. I thrust my tongue as deeply into her as I can, and her hips are moving as I fuck her with my tongue, using the same slow, even rhythm she is using with me. I reach around and massage her clit with my fingers, and she is slippery with her juices, with my saliva.

"Suck my clit," she tells me, and I do, taking that hard nub into my mouth. Audrey gasps, pants, and I suck harder.

"Oh, baby, yes!"

Her hips are bucking now, and she's hard to hold on to, but I suck and suck. Her fingers are pushing hard into my pussy, her thumb pressing onto my clit. I'm shaking with desire, with the need to come, but I am too into her body, her response to my hands and my mouth. Suddenly, she grinds down onto my face and I suck hard, holding her, and feel a warm, liquid rush on my lips, my tongue. It is sweet and salty, a mermaid coming into my mouth.

It's too much for me, and I come again, my body exploding, shaking with pleasure, hers and mine. We clench and unclench, thighs tensing, then finally, relaxing.

"That was so good, Bettina," Audrey says, her voice rough, low.

She shifts, falls down onto the mattress beside me, leans over and kisses me, licks my lower lip, bites it gently.

"Was it…I mean, was I okay?"

"You were great." She's smiling, her eyes half closed. "God, I could sleep for a week, couldn't you?"

But I am wide-awake, my body humming with energy, my mind going a thousand miles an hour, and I know sleep is far from claiming me.

"Mmm…gotta sleep," she says, kissing my cheek. "Okay if I stay here with you?"

"Of course."

I don't want her to leave. My heart is thudding with emotion, confusion. And as she immediately drifts off, her breathing shallow, I get up and turn off the lights, then come back to bed and lie next to her in the dark.

Audrey curls against me, one hand on my hip, and her skin is warm against mine.

What does this mean, if anything? Does it mean Audrey has feelings for me? Or simply that she's attracted to me? How do I feel about her?

God, I wish I weren't being such a girl. But at least I finally know what it's like. Maybe that's all I need to know. That I can feel this. That I can become attached to another person in some normal way.

I turn to watch her sleep, and in the light of the fog-shrouded moon and the stars coming through the sheer curtains, I can just make out her silhouette. I reach out and stroke the silk of her hair, and she shifts closer, mumbles something I can't make out. It doesn't matter. None of it matters, maybe, and it is a huge relief. It's enough just to feel like this. Just to *feel,* for once.

I listen to the gentle sound of her breath, to the hollow thunder of the ocean, to the sound of my own heart beating in my chest, and finally, I sleep.

I wake early—seven-thirty—and she is gone.

My heart thuds, but I command myself to calm. She is probably simply being discreet. I'm not ready to answer anyone's questions, certainly. It's better this way.

I turn onto my side and try to go back to sleep, but I can't stop thinking of her, of what happened last night. It was erotic and beautiful and I can't feel any guilt over it. I'm not even certain why I think I should.

*Go back to sleep, Bettina.*

I cover my head with one of the down pillows, shutting out the sounds of the sea, but I am too much in my own head.

Is she sleeping in her own bed now? Will she come back to me tonight?

Maybe the not-feeling thing was better than this torturous doubt.

I sigh, flop onto my back, inhale the fragrance of her left all over my bed.

*Audrey.*

And along with it, the stale wine, the ocean scent that is ever present here.

I lie there for maybe an hour before I give up, get out of bed and get dressed. As soon as my clothes are on, I take to the beach, walking along the shore in the early gray fog.

Why is the beach such a lonely place, yet so comforting at the same time? It's as though there is a certain stability about it. The ocean will always be here, on the earth, despite the dire warnings of scientists. It's too enormous, too powerful, to ever be entirely defeated.

I roll up my cargo pants and wade into the frigid ocean, standing right at the edge of the waves as they roll onto the shore. My feet sink into the soft sand, the water making the tiny granules fill in the spaces around my toes, beneath them, then surging back out, taking the sand with it. I loved to do this as a child. I've always loved this sensation. It's like moving while holding still. Magical.

The ocean is pure magic to me: powerful, graceful. Frightening. I have some deep understanding that it holds all the secrets of the earth. It knows my secret now. That I am half in love with Audrey.

I stay for a very long time, staring out at the horizon as the sun rises in the sky, cutting through the fog. The day will be warm; I can feel the heat building already. I slip my zippered sweatshirt from my shoulders and walk back toward our part of the beach. Sitting in the sand, I dig my toes in, enjoying the dampness beneath the cool surface.

I don't want to think too much more about last night. Don't want to dissect it any more than I've already done. It is what it is. I'll know more when I see Audrey.

I want desperately to see her, but I force myself to calm, to try to internalize some of my more sensible ideas about how I should be handling all this.

I can't have been out here more than an hour, but already the group is making its way over the dunes, carrying blankets and hampers. All but Audrey.

"Bettina, you're up!" Viviane smiles at me. "Breakfast on the beach this morning, then we write. We've brought plenty of pads and pens. Or do you need to go back to your cottage to get anything before you begin?"

"No, this will be fine, I think I can work without my notes. Thanks."

I will not ask where Audrey is.

Maybe this will be good for me, writing, being with the others. Distracting. Constructive. I haven't written nearly as much as I thought I would. Luckily, my deadlines this summer are fairly loose, so I'm not under too much pressure.

Viviane and Patrice have made a simple breakfast of pastries and fruit, and brought thermoses of hot coffee, which I accept gratefully. We eat, drink our coffee, everyone chatting quietly about the beautiful weather, about nothing at all. Everyone is relaxed. I am partly a confused knot of tension, even as another part of me is in waiting mode, accepting that I don't know what will happen next.

We finish eating and Viviane passes the pads of paper around, Leo handing out the pens. I notice his black hair shining almost blue in the morning sun, the smooth golden tone of his skin. I recognize that everything is eroticized for me right now because of last night, that I don't really have any desire for Leo Hirogata.

We all sit on the blankets, facing the water, and become lost in our stories. It takes me a few minutes, but finally I am able to sink into my work, to shut the world out and write.

We've been there for maybe an hour when Audrey arrives and sits in the sand next to me. Seeing everyone working, she quietly accepts paper and a pen and some coffee from Viviane. She smiles at me broadly, and I feel warmed by that momentary attention, able to relax now. I can talk to her later. Then she is focused, scribbling away on her pad. I am able to do the same, and I actually get some good work done on character development for my current work-in-progress.

We write for several hours, and it's getting warmer, the sun rising over the ocean, tinting it in brilliant greens and blues. The gulls are squawking at each other, diving, skimming the silver crests of the waves, and a few of them sweep in close on gray wings while we eat a simple lunch of bread, cheese and fruit. This bit of beach is so gorgeous, and I'm happy here, with Audrey sitting close by. I feel a strange sort of contentment, mixed with a low thrum of excitement in my veins. I look up and Audrey is looking right at me, smiling.

She is so beautiful, I can hardly believe it. I smile back, broadly, foolishly, I'm certain. And she laughs a little, as though we are sharing a private joke. Perhaps we are. I laugh back, making Viviane look up from her notepad.

"Is someone writing comedy?" Viviane asks, one brow raised, a small smile on her lips.

"In this group?" Audrey says. "We're all far too dark and twisted, Viv."

"That we are," Patrice agrees, stifling a yawn with her hand. "Anyone else ready for a siesta? I've had enough sun and I didn't bring my hat."

"I'm done." Kenneth stands and holds a hand out to help Patrice to her feet.

They dust sand from their shorts, and Viviane rises, gathering up the blankets, Leo helping her, casting longing glances at Audrey from beneath his spiky black lashes, and I feel a little sorry for him.

But I can't think too much about Leo right now. I'm sleepy from our late night the night before, beginning to yawn, and an afternoon nap sounds perfect. We all move up the beach toward the cypress trees. Audrey keeps pace with me, lagging behind the others.

She bumps me with her hip and whispers, "Want some company?"

I turn and smile. "Yes, definitely."

She smiles back, then calls out, "You guys go ahead. Bettina and I are going to work some more."

Leo looks over his shoulder, his eyes narrowing, a frown on his face, and I think, *he knows*. But it doesn't matter, does it? It's no one's business.

We slip into my cottage. It's cool inside, the wood floorboards smooth on my feet when I kick my sandals off. The afternoon sun coming through the window is diffused by the curtains and the shade of the cypress trees. Audrey drops her pad on the small table and I do the same. Then she is on me, her arms coming around my waist, pulling me close. Her skin is warm from the sun, and she smells a bit of sunscreen, that coconut-and-beach scent. It smells amazing on her.

"I missed you," she whispers into my ear as she pulls the

clips holding my hair back, burying her fingers in the tangle of curls. "Did you miss me, Bettina?"

"Yes. I did miss you. I've been thinking about you."

"And what were you thinking?"

"I was thinking about last night."

"Ah. And what conclusions did you come to?"

"That I need to do it again."

Audrey laughs, deep in her throat, then she leans in and nips gently at my neck. I am wet, shivering, instantly.

"Bettina…"

"Yes?"

"I want to take a shower with you."

"A shower?"

"I'm feeling…dirty."

"Oh…"

I feel foolish, but I am not about to refuse. Audrey steps back and strips her clothes off in seconds. She stands there, naked, glorious, looking at me. "Well? Get naked, girl."

I smile—I can't help myself—and take my clothes off, letting them drop in a small pile at my feet. I can't believe how erotic it is, simply standing naked together on the sun-warmed wooden floor, the light slanting in, casting everything in gentle gold and white.

"Come on," she says, taking my hand and leading me into the small bathroom.

I lean in and run the water in the shower, and we step in together. She pushes me under the water and it flows over me, just warm enough on this hot afternoon. She moves in, joining me under the spray, until we are both wet all over, then she grabs my bottle of shampoo, pulls my hand up and squeezes some into my palm.

"Wash my hair, Bettina? And I'll wash yours."

"Yes. Sure."

There is an innocence to what we're doing, just being wet, washing each other's hair. Except that I am on fire, my body burning with lust. And when her sudsy fingers go into my hair, massaging my scalp, my sex clenches with need.

Audrey is standing behind me, her hands in my wet hair, and I feel the tips of her breasts brush against my back. They're hard, warm. Then she moves around me and pulls me under the water, and I close my eyes as she rinses my hair clean. And as the water cascades over my face she is kissing me, and everything is wet: our lips, my skin, my pussy, tight with need.

She arches into me, until our mounds are pressed tightly together, our breasts crushed, soft flesh to soft flesh. Her tongue is sliding over mine, and she tastes like water, clean and pure.

Finally, she pulls back and says to me, "Spread your legs, baby."

I look at her, and she is more lovely than ever, the water sliding down her tanned skin. I smile, do as she asks.

Audrey reaches around me and takes the shower sprayer from its hook, and my smile broadens. I lean into the tiles of the shower, and watch as she slips to her knees in the bottom of the tub.

"Wider, baby, that's it."

She uses her soft fingers to part my aching pussy lips, then aims the spray of water right at my clitoris. I am moaning in seconds, my body pulsing with pleasure. She leans in and licks at my hard clit, the sensations amazing: her mouth and the water at the same time, everything so warm and slippery.

"Audrey…I'm going to come!"

"Come on then, baby."

She sits back on her heels, her dark hair streaming down her naked back, and aims the sprayer at my clit once more, using her fingers to massage the lips of my sex. Pleasure is warm, undulating, a serpent in my system, spiraling higher and higher. And I come, softly, my legs shaking, my moans a breathy plea for more.

I shiver for long moments, then Audrey stands and wraps her arms around me, kisses my mouth.

"My turn now," she says.

I am still shaky, but I get down on my knees, and she raises one leg and rests her foot on the edge of the tub. She is wanton, her legs spread, and I can see her pink sex, wet and open, and another surge of pleasure goes through me. I use my fingers on her first, playing with the swollen folds, then slipping inside.

Her head falls back, and she whispers, "Oh, yes."

Holding the sprayer in one hand, I let the water play over her clit, a hard pink nub between her naked pussy lips, and I use my other hand to impale her: one finger, then two. She is wet inside, slick, and she is squirming, panting, as I work her, her hips arching into my hand.

"Oh...oh!"

Then she is coming, her hips jerking hard, her pussy clenching around my thrusting fingers. And she is more beautiful to me than ever.

We stay in the shower for a long time, quiet, sated, washing each other, our soapy hands slippery on each other's skin. When we finally get out we are both pink all over from the heat. From coming, maybe.

"Come on," Audrey says, "let's take a nap. I'm so sleepy."

"Yes, me too. Let's sleep. I just want to curl up with you."

She takes my hand and we climb onto my bed. And I am thinking vaguely how different this is, being with a woman, just as she'd said. It's softer, and perhaps I have needed this.

Because I do feel healed, somehow. And it's not just Audrey's magic, but the *femaleness* of it. Of her, of us together.

We are curled up together, naked, on top of the blue-and-white quilt, like a pair of kittens. That sweet. That innocent. And we sleep in the gentle afternoon sunlight, the ocean soothing us, like a mother's lullaby neither of us can remember.

# CHAPTER FIVE

We're on the beach again, all of us, writing, brainstorming our way through blocks, drinking cool iced tea from the big thermoses Viviane always brings. The ocean is our constant companion, the waves rolling onto the beach, then receding, as though it can't make up its mind.

I am a little in dreamland today, but I'm comfortable here, with these people who have quietly become my friends in the last ten days, or at least familiar to me. After a week with Audrey she is still as much a mystery to me as her body is familiar. And yet, I feel that I know her, and she knows me, perhaps because we have shared our secrets. I've shared some of my fears, but I know she still holds a lot back from me.

We have established a pattern already, a way of life here. Another set of rituals in which I find comfort. Not only Audrey and me, but the entire group. I've come to be familiar with everyone's little quirks: the pure sweetness that is Kenneth, the glimpses of softness beneath Patrice's sharp exterior, Leo's odd, dark sense of humor and awkwardness, Viviane's mothering tendencies, such a contrast to her cool and glamorous rock-and-roll exterior. And I find myself wishing this would never change, that we could be here at Viviane's house, in this summer, forever.

But nothing lasts forever, isn't that what they say?

It starts with Audrey yelping as she jumps to her feet. She is racing across the sand toward someone, but all I can see from where I'm sitting is a silhouette against the sun. Audrey launches herself at the figure, her arms and legs wrapping around him. And I know who it is: Jack.

Her weight makes him stumble back, and they fall over together onto the sand. I can hear their laughter. And I can see him now, or what little of him is visible beneath Audrey's veil of hair as she lies on top of him in the sand. He's tall, with one of those long, wiry builds. His hair is dark, curly, a little too long. Then they are kissing, and jealousy is a hard pit in my stomach. I feel nauseous.

"That must be Jack," I say stupidly to the others.

Viviane has an odd half smile on her lips. "Yes, that's Jack."

Kenneth is getting up then, a grin on his face as he calls out, "Hey there, you two! Let the rest of us say hello."

He ambles off toward Audrey and Jack, and Leo follows. Patrice glances at Viviane briefly, and I wonder once more what it might mean, but vaguely. I'm distracted by Jack's arrival, by Audrey draped all over him.

Leo drags Jack and Audrey to their feet, and Kenneth pulls Jack into a bear hug, then Leo does one of those hand-shaking, slap-on-the-back things men do. They all come back to where we're sitting, and I see him for the first time. Jack.

He's even taller up close, with broad shoulders. His face and his arms are tanned, and there's a heavy, black tribal tattoo peeking from the left sleeve of his black T-shirt, with some sort of lettering beneath it. His mouth is lush and wide. Great bone structure, with a little dark stubble growing along his jaw. But his eyes…they are a shifting dark and pale green with touches of gray, like the sea itself. Amazing. Compelling. And I am furious with my response to him: heat, desire like a punch in the stomach.

I do not want to like this man Audrey is so excited to see. Who kisses her in front of everyone as though he has some right to.

Maybe he does.

I feel my cheeks go uncomfortably hot, and my fingers clench.

*Fuck.*

That hasn't occurred to me.

Obviously there is something between Jack and Audrey. What does that mean for me? Is whatever has happened between Audrey and me over? It occurs to me that I may have intruded on a relationship I didn't know existed.

I hate this idea. It makes my time with Audrey seem tawdry, rather than beautiful and enlightening, and I am so upset suddenly, my vision blurs with tears. I turn out to face the sea, let the power of it drain some of the tension from me before the others see.

I don't want to see Audrey in Jack's arms, but after a few moments I have to turn and look, have to greet him so I won't seem rude. But he's smiling at me. He is watching me in that same sort of careful way Audrey has, his gaze seeming to pierce me. My cheeks go hot again.

"This must be our shy Bettina," Jack says, his voice deep, resonant, a little husky.

He grins and it's impossible not to smile in return; he is so sincere, so friendly. Audrey is clinging to his arm, her eyes alight with excitement, and I can see why. He is letting her, but not really paying attention to her as he takes my hand in his, his grasp warm and dry, his palms a little rough, as though he works with his hands. He seems so…elementally male to me. And his touch makes me go warm and liquid all over.

Whatever is wrong with me? It must be some leftover from last night, a lingering sensation of desire in my system. Or maybe somewhere in my subconscious I'm worried that being with Audrey means I'm a lesbian, even though on a conscious level this doesn't concern me at all. I've never been one to be concerned with labels, for myself or anyone else.

Maybe I am simply losing my mind.

He is still holding my hand, those ocean-green eyes on mine. His smile is slow and languorous, as though we have all the time in the world to stand here and shake hands. Finally, he lets go, and he is absorbed by the group as we walk back to our spot. But I notice that Viviane stands back, watching as Kenneth jokes with Jack, the two of them laughing. Leo is practically dancing with excitement on the sand, and even Patrice seems entranced by him, sticking close to his side, touching his arm as they talk.

Audrey pulls Jack down onto the blanket and feeds him bits of pastry with her fingers. He is smiling at her, laughing and sucking the sugar from her fingertips, and it is purely erotic to me, watching them together, even as a knot forms in my stomach.

I don't know who I am more jealous of: Audrey or Jack.

*I am an idiot.*

Somehow we get through the rest of the morning as we all settle in to write. There is the occasional murmur as someone either loves or hates whatever they are working on. And sometimes when I glance up, Jack and Audrey are smiling at each other, or she is pouring coffee for him.

They are too beautiful together. Perfect, really. I feel more the fool than ever.

The sun is high overhead and it's really getting hot. I wipe the sweat from my forehead and put my pad down on the sand.

"It is getting warm, isn't it?" Patrice remarks. "I'm going back to the house."

"Good idea." Viviane sets her pad down beside her, stretches her arms over her head. "Why don't we all go back. Maybe have our usual afternoon siesta before lunch."

"Excellent idea." Kenneth nods and stands.

Leo gets up, then Jack, who pulls Audrey to her feet as though she doesn't weigh anything. She doesn't. I remember her body laid out on mine just last night. What is that old-fashioned saying? Bones like a bird.

We pack up and everyone helps to carry everything back to the main house, leaving the blankets and the wicker hamper in the sitting area off the kitchen.

"I'll put this away later," Viviane says. "By the way, Jack, the red cottage is yours."

"Thanks, Viv. I'll grab my stuff from my car. I could use a nap."

He flashes her a smile that would melt ice. Pure white teeth. He has a dimple in his left cheek, just like Audrey. I'm not sure why this bothers me so much.

Maybe because they really are so perfectly matched.

Jack goes out through the back door, and as I rinse the morning's coffee mugs and load them into the dishwasher, I can't even pretend not to watch out the kitchen window as Jack opens the door of a big, black truck. Audrey is right behind him. The door hides most of their bodies, but I can see from the position of their feet, their heads through the dusty car window, as she sinks into him. I can tell they are body to body as he leans in and kisses her. A mug slips from my hands, crashes into the bottom of the steel sink, chipping.

"Damn it."

"Don't worry, doll," Viviane comforts. "I have more."

I turn and give her what I'm sure is a washed-out smile.

"Hey." She takes my chin in gentle fingers. "Why so sad?"

"I'm not sad." I try to turn away, but she holds me firmly.

"Everyone's gone to nap. You can tell me."

"I don't…I honestly don't know. I mean…God, that's a lie. I do know." I bite my lip. "It's Audrey."

"Ah." Viviane drops her hand. "Honey, there is something you should understand about Audrey. She's full of passion and brilliance, and is more lovable than she knows. Oh, she throws herself at everyone, it's in her nature. And we all bask in her blazing light while she's focused on us. Then she finds someone else to dazzle. Don't take it personally. I know that feeling. She makes you her best friend and then she disappears. Jack is a bit the same, that dazzle. And Jack always distracts her."

"Yes."

"But?"

"But…it's complicated."

"Ah."

I look up at her. "What do you mean, 'ah'?"

"It's none of my business." Viviane picks up a dish towel and begins to dry a mug, but her gaze is still on me.

I fidget, my fingers twisting together. I don't know what to say. This is not something I'd planned to talk about. Hell, I haven't even had time to really think about it myself. But if I can't tell Viviane, who has been so good to me, I can't tell anyone.

"Viviane." I pause, waiting for her to put the cup down and really look at me. "Something has happened, with Audrey."

She nods, her shoulder-length black hair swinging. The sunlight makes the purple streaks blaze like fire. "Okay."

"That's it? Just 'okay'?"

"You're both big girls. I've been with other women before. I'm hardly going to judge you."

"No, I never thought…I didn't think you would. I just don't know how to talk about it yet. I don't know how to even think about it."

"You don't have to tell me anything, Tina. I shouldn't have pressed you. I'm sorry, babe. I'm just concerned for you, that's all. I don't want to see you hurting. But you do your thing. No one has to report in around here. Okay?"

"Okay. Okay."

"We're all a little tired today. Too much sun, maybe. Why don't you lie down for a while."

"Yes, I'll do that."

She drops the towel and gives my hand a quick squeeze. "Dinner is at seven. Skip lunch, if you like. Or come up and help yourself whenever. There's plenty of sandwich stuff. I'm going to let everyone do their own thing this afternoon."

I nod and watch her walk out of the kitchen, then turn and do the same, heading through the front door, then making my way over the short gravel path to my cottage. The sound of laughter stops me short, and I stand for a moment, listening to Jack and Audrey in his cottage.

I do not want to hear this.

I move past, swing the blue door to my cottage open, and retreat inside. I strip my sandy clothes off and lie down on top of the crisp blue-and-white quilt, and let the ocean drown out the sounds of Audrey and Jack together. But my heart is beating in my chest in an uneven rhythm, as though something inside me has chipped, just like the cup I dropped into the sink. Only I am not so easily replaced. And I hope, not so easily forgotten.

I feel more invisible than ever.

★ ★ ★

I was certain I would lie awake in my bed, straining to hear Audrey with Jack. Or Jack with Audrey. I'm still not clear on which scenario bothers me more. Ridiculous. But I must have fallen right to sleep feeling sorry for myself; I don't remember. Now I'm awake and stiff from having slept in a bad position, facedown in the pillows, on top of the covers. The room is growing dark, and it's chilly and damp. I'm still wearing the same clothes I put on this morning. The cuffs of my pants are crusted with sand and salt. I roll over onto my side and stretch, yawning, my eyes focusing on a few grains of sand scattered over the quilt, barely visible in the fading light, but if I narrow my eyes I can see that some are dark in color, some nearly clear, like tiny bits of crystal.

I am still trying not to listen, but I do, anyway. All I catch is the usual dull roar of the surf and the thoughts racing through my head: What is the nature of Jack and Audrey's relationship? What does it mean for me? Was I nothing more than a few hours of pleasure for her, if even that? Is this something she does all the time? Maybe they have an agreement about her sleeping with women?

Why do I care so damn much?

Part of it, I think, is that being with her was ultimately as much about connecting with her on some deeper level as it was about the chemistry. Which was, undeniably, intense. It still is.

Maybe I just need to be happy with this experience and move on.

Right. Because all my years in therapy have shown me how great I am at moving on.

I sigh, roll into a sitting position. I'm hungry, but I don't feel like going up to the house, seeing anyone. I don't want to see Audrey and Jack there, happy together. I don't want to *not* see them there and imagine them still together in his cottage. In his bed.

I am all fucked up.

Maybe I should leave, just go home, back to my old, un-complicated life. But I don't really want to leave this place. I want to stay here and get over these feelings.

I just want to stay here.

Moving into the bathroom, I strip down and step under the spray of steaming water. It makes me feel a little better, initially. A hot shower always does. The heat and the water are soothing, safe, somehow. I've had a number of dreams over the years of being in a big shower, always beautifully tiled in brown and green, filled with steam and fragrant soap and the hot water coming down on my skin. I have no idea what it means, except that I'm always calm, serene.

It's also one of my favorite places to masturbate. I could take the shower sprayer in my hand and aim it right at my clit. It works every time, makes me go off like a rocket, just as I've done in this very place with Audrey, over and over. But I'm too tired, too *something,* and for once I don't even want to get myself off.

Masturbation is a great pastime for a lonely hermit like me. Like I have been, anyway. I came here so I would learn not to be such a hermit. I have no idea if it's working, or if I'll go back to being myself once I'm home. Or maybe the group is simply small enough that I can be okay here.

Except that I am no longer okay.

I shut the water off and get out, simmering with resentment, suddenly. This trip had a purpose! And it was not to sleep with Audrey, to fall for her. To be undeniably, exquisitely, painfully attracted to her goddamn boyfriend.

I pull drawers open, find my skin creams, my dental floss,

my lip balm, slam the drawers shut. I have no right to be so furious. I know that. But it doesn't matter.

Terry would say that even though my feelings are valid, my response is not necessarily appropriate to the situation. But Terry isn't here and I have to handle things on my own, like a big girl. And my stomach is rumbling now; there is no way I can avoid going up to the house.

*Fuck.*

I get dressed, pulling on a pair of jeans and a long-sleeved T-shirt, comb my hair out and go.

The house is bright with lights, and I can see through the windows everyone gathered in the kitchen. I feel a terrible sense of isolation for several moments, as though standing there looking in on the warm, friendly scene from the outside is symbolic in some way. But I have to get over this stuff.

Moving inside, I force myself to walk into the kitchen. There's an old Janis Joplin song playing on the radio and Viviane is singing to it, really belting it out, her voice strong and raspy. Really awesome singing voice. I looked up some of her old songs online as soon as I found out who she was: Viviane Shaw of Crush. But hearing her sing in person is something else. It's too bad she gave it up, but I understand her reasons: the lifestyle, the drugs that eventually killed Malcolm, her husband and guitarist. But she's so into it, her body moving, her throat working, even as she stands at the center island chopping vegetables with Patrice, who has a small smile on her face, her birdlike eyes sparkling.

Leo is dancing a little to the song in uncoordinated, jerky motions, a huge smile on his face. He's wearing an apron and looking faintly ridiculous as he mixes something in a big bowl, and Kenneth is snoring in one of the leather chairs in front of the fireplace, Sid laid out at his feet, snoring in time with him. Everyone nods at me as I enter the kitchen, as though it's assumed I belong there. I suppose I do.

A nice thought, and it warms me a little.

"Can I help with dinner?" I ask.

Viviane nods her head in time to the music and hands me a knife and, with a small push, guides me to a wood chopping block on the island. A bunch of the gorgeous tomatoes she brought home from the farmer's market is laid out there. Viviane is still singing, and I smile as I begin to cut up the tomatoes, the knife biting through the plump, red flesh. They smell fresh and slightly acidic, and my hand stings where I have a small paper cut, but I don't mind.

Leo has joined in now, his voice surprisingly good, if a little high-pitched. He has a huge grin on his face. Viviane sidles up next to him, and they sing the rest of the song together, their voices harmonizing nicely. Patrice and I applaud when the song is over, and our applause is joined by more from the back door as Audrey and Jack come in.

They look fresh and beautiful and the slightest bit ruffled, as though the evening breeze has caught their hair. Or as though they've just gotten out of bed, rumpled from sex.

*Stop it.*

But it's hard. Their eyes are shining a little too brightly, their cheeks a bit too flushed, and I know that expression. I have it myself after sleeping with Audrey.

My body goes warm, remembering. And just looking at them, Audrey's bohemian beauty, Jack's grace, the power of his long, lean muscles, makes me sort of melt all over. Longing is like honey in my veins, making me feel soft and weak. I don't like it. Except that I do.

Unexpectedly, Audrey comes up behind me, draws my hair aside and kisses my cheek. But before I can even look up, she's moved on, hugging Viviane from behind, her arms wrapped around Viv's tall figure as they sway together with the music, and I have no idea if the kiss actually meant anything.

Jack is hanging back, a smile on his face, and God, his mouth is beautiful. I have never wanted to kiss a man more than I want to kiss Jack Curran. And I'm still having a hard time separating out my crush on Audrey from my attraction to him. Is it all tied in? Or is it that I simply don't trust my feelings about anything? How can I trust them when I've been half-numb most of my life, and suddenly I'm feeling…all of this?

Emotion and chemistry and sexual yearning that's nearly painful.

My stomach is in knots. I try to swallow the anger, the confusion, and simply accept things the way they are. But how are they? I still don't know. I turn back to my tomatoes and give them a good hard chop.

"Whoa, easy there, girl," Jack says. And before I can respond he is standing behind me, one arm around my body as he covers my right hand, helping me grip the knife. His skin is hot, even hotter than Audrey's. "You'll add your fingers to the salad if you're not careful," he warns.

"Gross," Leo says, laughing.

I am frozen. Jack's body is so damn solid behind me. He smells like fresh laundry, which is suddenly utterly sensual to me. I hope I'm not visibly shaking, but my insides are trembling. On fire. He steps away and I can breathe again. I can breathe enough to realize in some logical way what an intrusion of my personal space that was, from a man I hardly know.

Yet I want him to do it again. Want him to press up against me, want to know every plane and curve of muscle in his body, instead of this teasing little taste.

I want him. *Want* him!

I suppress a small groan and, more carefully this time, go at the tomatoes once more.

Somehow I get through the rest of dinner preparation, and we sit at the big indoor dining table. The lights are low, and a fire burns in the big fireplace, the acrid, ashy fragrance mixing with the scents of the food. We're having a Tuscan pasta dish along with the big salad and baskets of crusty Italian bread, and wine, of course. A beautifully simple meal that we eat leisurely. I love these long meals. They feel luxurious, eating and talking, lingering over the wine. Viviane serves bowls of sliced melon with crisp almond biscotti for dessert, and I watch from the corner of my eye as Audrey feeds Jack bits of the succulent melon with her fingers. I can't help myself. Her fingers disappear between his lush lips, then slide back out, and it looks sexual to me, like fucking, all wet, pink flesh.

I need to calm down, but it's not happening, is it? And worse yet, Jack talks through the meal, and he is smart and funny and kind, and utterly charming.

"Kenneth, how is Gracie doing? And the girls?"

"They're all fine. Diana is off to college in the fall and they're all after me to get her a car. Since when does an eighteen-year-old girl need a car?" But he's smiling as he says it. Kenneth adores his wife and daughters.

"I had a car at eighteen," Audrey breaks in. "It was a beat-up old Honda Prelude." She tears a piece of bread, bites into it, chews. "That car ran forever. Had a million miles on it."

"Yeah, at eighteen I was on my fifth car. A '79 Camaro. Powder blue." Jack's eyes are dark in the firelight, gleaming. "I loved that car. But there was always another one I had to have. I sold it for a classic El Camino with dual exhaust. That baby had flames on it."

"Awesome," Leo says.

Leo sort of fan-worships Jack, I can tell already. Which is

maybe why he doesn't seem to resent Audrey paying attention to Jack the way he did when she was focused on me.

"How's the horror novel coming, Leo?" Jack asks.

"It's coming. It's really different from doing comics. The story is still there, but I have to keep reminding myself to execute it on the page, that I don't have any images to tell the story."

"It'll come to you, don't worry. Your stuff is good. Solid. But talk to me if you need any help."

"Sure. Thanks, man. Maybe we can hang out tomorrow?"

"Yeah, let's do that."

Jack smiles at Leo, and it's warm and sincere, and I want to hate them both. All of them and their easy conversation with this man who is more kind than I want him to be. And all the while Audrey fawns over him, looking at him adoringly.

She looked at me that way in bed.

*Fuck.*

I stand and begin to clear the dishes, carrying them into the kitchen. I am annoyed to find Jack joining me.

"Want some help?"

I don't, but it would seem stupidly ungracious to say so.

"Sure."

He disappears, returns with another armful of dishes, Sid trotting at his heels. The dog finds his bed near the fireplace and is immediately snoring again.

"You want to wash or dry?" he asks, setting a pile of plates on the counter next to me.

"Wash, I guess."

"You're not much of a talker, are you, Bettina?"

I blow out a long breath. "No, I'm not."

He reaches around me and I step to one side as he pulls the garbage can out from beneath the sink and begins to scrape the plates into it. I run the hot water, filling up the sink and adding dish soap, watch as the bubbles rise, reminding me of the foam that crests the ocean waves.

"But you talk to everyone else," Jack says quietly.

"I…" But I don't know what to say. It's true.

"Bettina, I know I just got here, but have I done something to offend you? Maybe said something online?"

"No. Of course not."

"Because I can be a self-centered son of a bitch sometimes, I know that."

I look up, and his expression is teasing, a small smile on his lush mouth.

I want to kiss him.

*Fuck.*

"Bettina, look…" He moves right up next to me, and I can feel the heat of his body again. His eyes are a deep mossy-green now, his lashes thick and as black as his hair. "You should know that Audrey told me what happened."

"What?" My cheeks go hot. "She…told you? What did she tell you?"

"She told me about the two of you being together this last week. That you've slept together."

"And you're so calm about it?"

"Why wouldn't I be?"

He looks truly puzzled, and I don't understand.

"Because she's your girlfriend! You don't mind if your girlfriend sleeps with other people?"

"First of all, Audrey is not anyone's girlfriend, and in particular, she isn't mine. Second, if she's going to sleep with other people, I kind of like that it was you."

I'm so flustered all I can do for several moments is stare at him.

"Wh-what does that mean?"

He smiles, all too-good-looking charm, his mouth wide and soft. He has the most incredible bone structure, his dark stubble outlining his strong jaw. Despite myself, my confusion, my small bit of outrage, I am melting again.

"The image of you two in bed together makes a pretty picture in my mind," he says, his voice low. "I'm sure it was even more spectacular in person."

I feel my mouth open in a small o. I have no idea what to say to this. The idea that he's fantasizing about Audrey and me together. The idea that Audrey told him about us! The still-fresh painful confusion over her leaving me in the dust for Jack.

His smile fades. "I'm sorry. I see that I've offended you."

He takes a step back.

"What? No. It's just that Audrey…I mean…God, I don't know what I mean."

I look away, pick up a dish towel from the counter and dry my hands.

He moves back in. "She's confusing, I know. Believe me, I know. It's the same every summer, every time the group meets for our winter retreats."

"What do you mean?" I still can't make myself look at him. I stare instead at the pile of plates stacked on the counter, the bubbles popping in the sink.

"When Audrey is focused on you, it's overwhelming, even for someone like me. I should be used to it by now. But it's like she has some sort of ADD. As soon as someone else comes along, you're invisible."

"She's so happy to see you."

"She always is. For a few days. A few weeks. Then it's some-one else. A waiter. Another writer who drops in. Poor Leo last summer, and it really made his head spin for a while."

"Leo? I couldn't figure out why he stares after her like some lost puppy. I thought it was just that everyone seems to want her attention. Actually, I thought before I got here…I mean, I got the impression from talking to him online, and because he's friends with my friend Calvin, that Leo was gay."

"He is."

"Oh. But…never mind."

"Yeah." He gives a low, rough laugh. "She's like that. She has that magic. But you'll find after a while that her magic is as temporary as she is. You get over it."

I look up at him once more. He seems taller than ever, standing right next to me. "Do you?"

He shrugs. "Sure. Every time. And every time I see her again, I fall under that spell. But I let myself do it. I give myself permission to."

I pause for a moment, thinking, watching him. He's put his hands in his pockets, and shifted his weight from one foot to the other. Something going on with him, but it's hardly my business to ask.

"So…what did you mean when you said 'even for someone like me'?"

He shrugs, a graceful ripple of muscle moving beneath his plain white T-shirt. "I'm not exactly the relationship guy myself. I'm always amazed that being with her has any repercussions for me. I'm always surprised that I'm not immune."

"I don't get when people say that."

"What?"

"That they're not relationship kind of people. I think it's… just a stage people go through. I mean, I haven't been that person, either, but it's not what I want. It's nothing I've aspired to. I think saying you're perfectly happy being that way is a cop-out."

Where has all this honesty come from, suddenly? Maybe it's that this whole Audrey thing has opened me up, and now

I find it hard to lock my emotions back down tight. I don't want to. That's what I'm trying to say, but whether for his benefit or my own, I don't quite know.

He's quiet a moment, still watching me, and I am still melting a little beneath his green gaze. Then he says, "So, you do talk to me."

I can't help but smile. "Apparently."

"Good." He smiles back, a slightly crooked quirk of his lush lips. "I hope you'll keep doing it."

I'm embarrassed now. Blushing. And when he reaches out and touches a fingertip to my chin I go hot all over. Blazing.

"I like you, Bettina," he says, his smile widening, and I am flustered into silence again.

I'm saved from having to answer and no doubt saying something foolish by Patrice and Kenneth carrying the mostly empty platters and bowls of food into the kitchen.

"You don't have to do the dishes, Bettina," Patrice says, scolding, but I know she doesn't mean it; that's simply her way.

"Saves me from dish duty." Kenneth chuckles, going to his favorite lounging spot by the fireplace, next to Sid's dog bed.

And just like that I am drawn into the warm embrace of the group once more. I realize I am feeling separate less and less, that this place, these people, are working. That Terry was right about me coming here. That my earlier thoughts about leaving just because of this thing with Audrey are ludicrous. I don't need to sabotage myself like that. I need to be here.

Jack has nothing to do with it.

Of course he doesn't.

# CHAPTER SIX

A week has gone by since Jack's arrival. It's been torture. It's been lovely.

I've been really getting into my book, the words flying onto the page. And I've been getting closer with everyone. I've come to know Kenneth's warm humor; he really is the sweetest man. I've talked video games with Leo, become familiar with his quirky sense of humor, something I should have expected from someone who creates horror comics. He's a bit strange, but also delightful, in his way. I've even become more comfortable with Patrice. And Viv is becoming like a big sister. I am dying to talk more with her about Audrey, and about my unexpected feelings for Jack, but something in the way she looks at Jack when she thinks no one is paying attention has made me pause.

I have hardly seen Jack. Or Audrey. They spend a lot of time in his cottage with the red door, or walking on the beach together. I want to know—too badly—what they say to each other when they're alone. I want to know the way they touch each other. I spend every single night in my bed with my vibrator, or getting off using the showerhead. Orgasm after orgasm, and yet I am more lit up each and every moment than I have ever been in my life. Maybe all that coming just makes it worse. But I cannot help myself. I really can't.

Sometimes I hear them, a few cries and moans over the roar of the surf. I keep my windows open every night, during the regular afternoon naps we all take, hoping to catch some sound, to see them.

Oh, yes, I have stared out my window at the sheer curtains fluttering in the breeze of Jack's open window, dying for even a small glimpse of the two of them, naked bodies pressed together. I feel like a pervert. But I can't stop myself. I have even stood at the window with my vibrator clutched in my hand, pressed to my hard and needy clit, peering through the dark and pretending I can see them fucking.

I am all kinds of messed up. Out of control. I know that. But some part of me wonders if maybe it's time for me to lose some of my tightly held control. That's one of my issues, after all. And how is this hurting anyone?

Part of it is simply that I want them, both of them. I don't know who I want more.

I've been fantasizing about being with them. Audrey. Jack. At the same time. All three of us, arms and legs in a sweaty tangle. And as I sit on Viviane's patio, all of us writing quietly in the late-afternoon sunlight, I am thinking of exactly this scenario: Jack and Audrey in bed, and I am there, between them. Naked flesh, the press of body upon body, hands everywhere, mouths, tongues…

"Oh, yeah!"

I start as Leo yells. Press my damp thighs together beneath my light cotton skirt.

Viviane laughs. "What was that, Leo?"

"It's all working. Coming together. I found a plot hole and suddenly the entire book is gelling."

"I love when that happens." Viviane sighs. "Good for you. I wish mine were going as well. I seem to be stuck on this same scene. It's been two days and I can't get past it."

"Maybe we can help," Patrice suggests.

Viviane begins to explain where she is in her book, what the issues are, but I can't concentrate. I am in a state of acute arousal, my vivid imagination having wandered a bit too far. I blink, take in a breath, smooth my hair from my face. And find Jack looking at me.

Not just looking, but watching closely. His eyes are a deep, dark green, the bits of gray like silvery flint. Gleaming. And his mouth has gone sort of soft around the edges. He's looking right at me as he tilts his head. His lips part, as though he's about to say something, then he glances to his right, at Audrey. And she's watching me, too, that same expression in her eyes. And suddenly I understand what I'm seeing there. At least I think I do.

*Desire.*

It goes through me like a shock. My gaze flits back and forth between them, and they exchange a brief glance. And I know that we all feel it, we all know exactly what's going on. And I am on fire, lust burning in my veins like molten honey, hot and sweet and fine.

I lick my dry lips, cross my legs. I'm soaking wet.

I watch as Jack runs a hand over his hair, swallows, his throat working. Audrey puts a hand on his arm, but neither takes their eyes off me. It's as though there is some spell in the air, some bizarre connection between the three of us.

Is this really happening?

"Hey, there!"

Viviane stands as two women step onto the patio, one a tall blonde with spiky hair, the other petite and dark, both of them dressed as Viviane dresses, in jeans and rock-band T-shirts.

I don't know where they came from; I didn't hear a car pull up. But I wouldn't have heard a freight train with Jack and Audrey looking at me the way they were.

Viv hugs the two women, then says, "Everyone, this is Toni and Layla, some friends of mine from L.A. They're having dinner with us tonight."

Everyone greets them, and we gather up our laptops, our pads of paper, our writing day over. The sun is lowering in the sky, the trees casting long shadows as we all go into the house to begin preparing dinner. Jack is beside me at the island, cutting up vegetables for the salad. And even though there is a good two feet between us, I swear I can feel the heat of his big body. Audrey is flitting around the kitchen. I'm too distracted to tell what it is she's doing. But every time she swings by me I feel a rush, as though my blood is rising up to stretch toward her. Ridiculous, I know, but that's how I feel.

We sit down to eat in the dining room, all of us crowded around the long table. Toni and Layla seem nice, but I'm having a hard time keeping track of the conversation. I'm seated at a corner of the table, with Audrey on my right, and her knee keeps bumping against mine. She looks up now and then, a small smile on her lips, as though we share some sort of secret. And we do. The secret of our desire. Hers, mine and Jack's.

I have no idea what this means. But this is too lovely, this secretive casting of yearning glances between us. Jack is sitting across the table from us, talking to Kenneth, but I catch him watching us from the corner of his eye.

I am trying hard not to tell myself that it's only Audrey he wants. That I am nothing more than some sort of added-on bit of fantasy for him.

*Please don't let it be so.*

By the time dessert arrives, an enormous bowl of homemade

tiramisu, I am anxious that Jack and Audrey will go off together after dinner, leaving me alone with this pounding ache between my thighs, abandoned to my lonely vibrator once more. I can't stand to think about it.

Dinner is endless, and I try not to resent Viviane's guests. They're awfully nice, and I feel like a total bitch. I just want this to be over. I can't think of a reason to excuse myself, and I won't, anyway, as long as Audrey and Jack are still at the table.

The conversation has moved to Viviane's band days as she and her friends reminisce about her life on the road, about her husband, Malcolm.

"You should have seen her then," Toni announces. "She was a wild thing."

"She's still a wild thing," Kenneth says, laughing.

All I can think of is Audrey in my bed, between my thighs, her dark, silky hair a wild, tangled mass, her lips damp with my juices when she raises her head to look up at me after I come.

"Ha! Hardly," Viviane says. "I live up here in Santa Barbara, hidden away like some old woman. I'm surprised I don't have a hundred cats."

"You'll never be an old woman," Jack says kindly. There is real warmth in his eyes. It makes me like him even more.

Viviane glances away. "Thanks for saying so. But I'm afraid it's true."

"No, it's not, Viv. Don't be silly." Layla, who is sitting next to Viviane, puts a hand over hers, shaking her dark head.

I find myself wondering if I detect some chemistry between them. Or is it just that everything seems to have some sexual content to me lately?

I really have to get a grip.

Or I have to get laid.

And as I think this, Audrey puts her hand on my thigh beneath the table and strokes. Upward.

I am not imagining this.

She leans in a little, reaching for the breadbasket, which is on the table in front of me, and whispers, "Meet me in your cottage in an hour."

I pull back, look at her. She's smiling innocently, as though she hasn't just invited me to have sex with her. I am burning. Uncertain.

She blinks, raises her eyebrows. "Yes?"

I shiver. Nod. "Yes."

*God, yes!*

I spend the rest of the meal and kitchen cleanup drinking too much wine too fast. It goes to my head, but I'm already dizzy, anyway, with lust. Dizzy and anxious and wondering if Jack will be upset. And wanting him there.

I feel selfish. Ungrateful. At least I'll have Audrey tonight.

Finally, Audrey leaves the house, and I wait a few minutes before following her. I move over the lit patio, walking down the darkened path to my cottage. The moon is bright overhead, silver light peering through the drifting fog. My body is nearly vibrating with the most exquisite anticipation I have ever felt in my life.

As I approach my cottage I can see a light already burning dimly.

Audrey.

I open the door, and she's there. In my bed. Naked.

So is Jack.

My heart stops.

I know that's just an expression, but I swear it comes to a stuttering halt in my chest.

Audrey smiles, holds out her hand to me. "Join us, Bettina."

"I…what's…I don't understand."

Oh, but I do. It's just too much for me to absorb, my every fantasy come true, suddenly, and I don't know what the hell to do with it.

But they do.

"We don't mean to startle you," Jack says, his voice low and a little rough. "We just…wanted to be with you. Do you want us, Bettina?"

I swallow, hard. The sheet is covering his lap, but his bare chest is all firm, lean muscle and tanned skin, with just a sprinkling of dark hair in the center, and a narrow line below his navel. My mouth is watering. And beside him Audrey is all delicate golden flesh, her dark hair flowing over her shoulders, covering part of one full breast. Their nipples are dark and dusky, nearly the same color. My sex gives a good, hard squeeze.

"Yes," I whisper.

Jack smiles then. So does Audrey. But I am frozen. I want this so much, I can't breathe, can't move.

"I'll help," Audrey says, rising from the bed.

She comes to me and pulls my shirt over my head, unzips my peasant skirt and pushes it down my legs. I feel vaguely self-conscious, but then Jack is there, too, sitting on the end of the bed, running his fingertips over my belly. Desire is like a knife, cutting deep, and it is as though I am bleeding lust, just seeping from my pores, from my mind, my breasts. And my pussy is as wet as it's ever been in my life.

When I look down at Jack's hand, I can see his cock standing erect between his thighs. And it is every bit as beautiful as the rest of him, a long, hard shaft, perfectly formed, the head dark and swollen.

Hands all over me as they remove my bra, slide my cotton panties down my legs. Being naked feels so right; it's exactly what I need. To be naked. To be touched. I am shivering so hard I can barely stand.

"Come, baby. Get on the bed," Audrey says, taking my hand.

Jack's hands are on my hips, and I am planning to sit on the side of the bed, uncertain as to what I should be doing, but he helps me settle onto the mattress, laying me back on the pillows.

"We know this is your first time," Audrey says.

Jack nods. "Just lie back. We'll do everything."

I moan softly.

*Yes, God, do everything... Everything!*

My nipples are already so damn hard they hurt. And when Audrey brushes her fingertips over them, I feel absolutely scalded. But it's so, so good. I arch into her touch, needing more. But there's too much going on; things are happening too fast for me to keep track of it all. My body is filled with sensation as Audrey leans in and takes my nipple into her hot, wet mouth, and sucks. And Jack is just stroking my body: my belly, my thighs. His hands are warm, incredible on my naked skin. My sex is pulsing, aching, soaked. Pleasure shimmers over my body, arrowing deep inside.

*Someone fuck me, please...*

I don't care who it is. I just desperately need one of them to be inside my body, so I know this is real.

Audrey is still working my nipples, going from one to the other, and my hands are buried in her dark, silky hair, holding her there.

I hear Jack whisper, "Beautiful Bettina. Skin like satin," as he runs his hands over my flesh. "Come on, Bettina. Open for me. Yes, that's it."

Then his hands are gently pushing my thighs apart, and I let them fall open. There is nothing in me that wants to resist. I feel wanton. Beautiful for the first time in my life, because Jack has told me so. Odd that I believe him. But I do. I don't care about anything but that he finds me beautiful, that and my need, the desire burning me up inside.

His palms are sliding up my thighs, and I lift my head a little to watch him. And find him watching me, his green gaze on my face. His mouth is lush and loose, desire softening his features. He licks his lips, and a jagged bolt of need shoots through me.

He says, his voice low, the words coming out slowly, like satin, like water, "I'm going to go down on you, Bettina. I can't wait. To feel you on my tongue. To taste you. I bet you taste like sugar."

I moan, unable to speak.

He smiles, and brushes one fingertip over my mound. I arch, squirm.

Audrey lifts her head to kiss my cheek, my lips, briefly. "Oh, this is going to be so good, baby."

She shifts, until she is lying next to me, her naked body pressed against my side, and she loops one leg over mine, her wet sex open against my thigh. She feels like damp velvet, and I want to touch her, to press my fingers into her hot and eager hole, but I can't move.

"Kiss me, Bettina," she says, lowering her mouth over mine.

Her tongue slips inside, twines with mine. And she is sweet and demanding all at the same time, her lips lush and soft. Lovely. As she kisses me harder, Jack slides his fingers along my wet slit, and I groan into Audrey's mouth.

"Ah, beautiful," Jack murmurs. "Just keep kissing her, Aud. Just like that…"

Then his fingers are brushing my pussy lips once more, parting them, holding them open. And I cannot believe how this feels: Audrey's wet mouth on mine, her tongue pushing inside, and Jack's fingers as they slide over my sex. Everything is so wet, so slick, like the ocean thundering outside. Like the desire pouring in a steaming tide through my body. And when Jack pushes his fingers into me, I almost come off the bed, Audrey's weight on my right side the only thing holding me down.

A small chuckle from Jack, then I feel his warm breath between my legs. I tense, waiting, and as his tongue flicks at my hard clit, Audrey moans, lifts her head, biting her lip, her white teeth coming down on that plush, red flesh. Raising my head, I can see that Jack has his fingers buried in her pussy as he begins to lick mine. I fall back on the bed, out of my head with lust. Sensation overload. I am paralyzed by it: Jack's hot, licking tongue on my clit, Audrey grinding into my thigh. I can feel Jack's hand there as he moves in and out of her.

I can no longer lie still, just taking it. I reach up and fill my palm with Audrey's full breast until I find her nipple. Taking the swollen tip between my fingers, I tug. She closes her eyes, moans. I know she loves this, this rough play with her nipples. I pinch and she groans, low in her throat. And all the time Jack's mouth is on me, licking in long, slow strokes, torturing my sex with pleasure. And it's too good, too exquisite, almost more than I can take.

But I will take it. And want more.

I arch my hips into Jack's mouth.

"Please, Jack."

"Your pussy is so damn wet," he murmurs, pushing the tip of one finger inside, making me squirm. "Pink and wet. Like a flower in the rain."

Then his mouth is there once more, his tongue sweeping

over my clit, his fingers pushing into me, thrusting, fucking me. My hips move, pumping in rhythm with Audrey's against my leg. And he is fucking us both with his fingers, his tongue like a hot lance on my pulsing clit. And Audrey is moaning above me, panting, about to come.

I reach up, bury my fingers in her hair, drag her face down to mine.

"Kiss me, Audrey," I demand, surprised at myself, but too far gone with need to really care. All I know is what I want, what I need, desire cutting into me like some sweet-edged knife.

Jack pauses to whisper, "Fuck. Yes."

Then he goes back to work, licking my clit, his fingers pumping. I pull Audrey in, and her mouth opens to mine. Her tongue is hot, sleek, like Jack's tongue working my clit. Pleasure is rising, hard and fast, and I am shaking all over with it. Too much is happening; I can barely hold on. It is only Audrey's slim body against mine that keeps me rooted to the earth. Because Jack is sucking my clit now, sucking, sucking, his fingers thrusting deep, into me, into Audrey.

She tenses, groans into my mouth, then her body is writhing, twisting, as she comes, her juices pooling on my leg, hot and sweet. Jack sucks hard on my clit, flicks his tongue over the tip, and with Audrey still coming, panting, my body explodes, pleasure hot, searing. I cry into Audrey's mouth, against her tongue, and she kisses me harder while the fire of my climax rages through my system. My pussy is on fire, hot and pulsing, sending pleasure deep into my belly. I grind hard into Jack's face, his fingers, as my climax shudders through me. It is endless, a force of nature.

Finally, Audrey goes limp, her face buried in my neck. I am still coming in small waves, and Jack is relentless, his sucking mouth on me, his fingers moving inside me. Until I, too, am weak, exhausted, the final quivers of pleasure shimmering, then fading away.

Jack rises up, kneeling back on his heels. His cock is hard and proud between his thighs. "My two beauties," he says, smiling, desire darkening his eyes. "I need to fuck you now. I want you both."

"Yes…" I can barely speak. "I need you, Jack."

Audrey rolls off me, onto her back. "I want to watch you fuck Bettina," she says. "I want to see her come again."

She spreads her legs, and her hand goes between her thighs as she slips her fingers into her shaved pussy. Her gaze on Jack's, she pulls them out, wet and shining, brings them to her lips, and sucks her fingertips. He moans.

"Come on, Jack. Fuck her while I watch. While I get myself off again. You know how I love that."

I don't even care about the implication that they've done this before, taken another girl into bed with them. No, what's important is that I'm here with them now. That Jack is going to give me what I desire most.

He's smiling at me, his teeth straight, gorgeous, as he reaches into the pillows and pulls out a condom, slips it onto his beautiful cock. All around us is the sea-scent of female come, mine and Audrey's. And it seems to urge me on, to be a part of the driving need in my body. When Jack reaches for me, I go to him, love the feel of his strong arms snaking around my waist. He pulls me closer, right into his arms, and the hair on his chest softly scratches my naked breasts.

Jack whispers into my hair, "Oh, yes, have to have you, Bettina. Have to fuck you."

I am shivering all over, hearing him say these things to me. Nothing has ever been hotter. My nipples are going hard once more already, my sex pulsing. I can hardly wait. I arch my hips into him, feel his erect cock against my thigh, and he lays me down on my back, his body draped over mine. And it is so damn good, his velvety skin on mine, his cock hard and strong pressing against my belly, and his scent, the scent of fresh laundry and male skin and the sharp edge of desire.

"I want to turn you over, take you from behind," Jack says. "Do you like to be fucked that way, Bettina?"

"Yes…"

I'll do whatever he wants, frankly. As long as I can feel him inside me. I spread my legs wider.

"Ah, nice," he says.

Then he wraps his big hands around me and just turns me over, as though I weigh nothing. And I love the feeling of being taken over. I love to look up and see Audrey beside us, watching, her blue eyes gleaming, her hand between her thighs. Her face, her breasts, are flushed. She is too beautiful.

"Come on, Jack. Just do it." Her voice is breathless.

Jack pulls my hips up, until I am on my knees, and he brushes my hair aside. He leans in and places a kiss on the back of my neck, making me tremble. Anticipation is like some wild aphrodisiac as the heat of his body closes in on me. Then his fingers part my drenched pussy lips and I feel his cock poised at the entrance to my body. I surge back, and he laughs, a low tone, and I feel it like the stroke of his fingers on my pussy lips. He is stroking, stroking, exquisite torture. But I want him, now.

"Don't tease us, Jack," Audrey says, and I moan in agreement. "See? You're killing us both. Come on, Jack. I want to see you slide inside her."

Another chuckle from him, then the swollen head of his cock pushes into me, making me gasp. He's big, which I don't normally like. But I'm so turned on, so soaking wet, I can take anything right now. And I just want him, in a way I've never wanted anything in my life.

"Jack, please," I beg.

"Tell me what you want, Bettina."

"Jack…"

"Tell me."

"I want you to fuck me. Just do it. I want it hard. Please."

"Ah," he moans, "you are perfect, my girl. My beautiful girl. Push back onto me, take me in. Yeah, that's it."

I do as he says, surging back, opening myself, my pussy swallowing his cock into my body, and pleasure washes over me. My knees are going weak, but Jack's strong arms are wrapped around my waist, pulling me against him as he buries his cock inside me.

"Jack!"

"Oh, nice," Audrey murmurs.

I look at her, and her fingers are deep inside her pussy, working, in and out, as Jack begins a gentle rhythm. She is focused on the two of us, watching Jack pump into me, and the pink flush is rising on her breasts, her nipples two dark red points. I want to touch them, to pull them into my mouth. But I am too paralyzed with the pleasure of Jack's cock moving inside me. Even thinking about doing it drives me higher. And watching Audrey fuck herself with her hand is so damn erotic, making everything more intense.

When Jack reaches around to play with my clit, another stab of pleasure goes through me, and I have to close my eyes, shutting everything out but his cock thrusting deep into me, his clever fingers rubbing my clit.

I want him to fuck me forever, but I know I can't hold back much longer. My eyes flutter open, and Audrey has let her legs fall wide. Her sex is open to me, pink and wet, her fingers pumping, her hips arching. And Jack is hard inside me, pushing deeper.

"Come, Bettina. I know you want to," he says. "I can feel it. You are so damn wet, so tight. Come. And Audrey will come with you, won't you, Aud?"

"Yes, I'm ready. Come on, baby. Come for us."

And I do, my body trembling as waves of pleasure wash over me. My pussy clenches around Jack's cock, over and over. And Audrey is crying out, her hand working between her spread thighs, her head falling back onto the pillows. And I am coming so damn hard, coming and coming.

"Oh, God…"

Jack is panting, thrusting into me. "Yeah, that's it, beautiful girl, come on. Come all over my cock. Yeah…"

Then he tenses, cries out, and fucks me harder than ever, driving the last of my orgasm on as he comes. And as my body goes slack, Jack's still-hard cock inside me, Audrey's lambent gaze on mine, it is as though I'm in a dreamworld. Something all about touch and scent and the desire still pulsing like an ever-restless heat in my system.

Jack rolls off me, pulls me into his body, and Audrey curls up on my other side. It is such a lovely contrast: his hard, sculpted body and Audrey all soft and silky skin, her long hair tickling my shoulder a little. We are lazy with spent pleasure, the cooling evening air lovely on my heated skin.

As I catch my breath, I glance from Jack to Audrey and back again. Their eyes are closed, both of them. And I begin to think.

I don't want to. I don't want to know if this will happen again. If tomorrow things will go back to the way they were before, with Jack and Audrey together, and me alone. I don't want to know.

*Fuck.*

*Stop it!*

Yes, I need to calm my mind and just enjoy the post-orgasm buzz in my veins, the heat of their bodies against mine, the sheer beauty of each of them, separately and collectively, which is nearly overwhelming.

Audrey sighs, turns onto her side, murmurs, "When do you think you can do it again, Jack?"

He laughs, reaches over me to smack her smooth bottom, making her yelp. "I'll get to you soon enough, I promise. Give me a minute to recover."

"Hey, I didn't get mine yet." Audrey mock pouts.

"Contrary to popular belief, I am not Superman," Jack says. "Although I try."

"And we appreciate it, don't we, Bettina?"

I can't help but grin, happy again, in the moment. "Yes, we do. But we'd appreciate it more if you'd do it again."

"You two are dangerous together," Jack says, grinning.

"We try," Audrey purrs, then reaches for me, brushing her fingers over my breast. My nipple goes hard beneath her touch. "Maybe we can keep each other busy while Jack takes a few minutes. He can catch up with us later. What do you think, Bettina?"

I smile, cover her hand with mine, urging her fingers to my nipple, and she tugs. "I think that's a brilliant idea."

I can't believe my body can become aroused again so quickly, so thoroughly. But it does. As Jack watches, Audrey lays her body over me, her breasts pressed against mine. She is unbelievably hot: her skin, her mouth as she lowers it to my throat, her tongue making lazy circles. There is something about the unrelenting pleasure, about the way my body has been heated and sated over and over again. I am really out of my head now. And I don't care.

Audrey slides her thigh between mine, and her sex is slick and warm on my leg, and mine against hers.

"Oh, too nice," Jack says quietly. "Can you make each other come for me?"

Audrey moans softly and kisses her way up my neck. "We can do anything you want, can't we, Bettina?"

I nod, bite my lip as she lowers her head to take my nipple into her mouth. "Oh, yes."

And it's true. I would do anything for them. For Jack.

And it strikes me, even as Audrey moves down my body, her tongue leaving a trail of wet heat all over my skin, that it is Jack I really want.

Is it just that I'm afraid, once more, of what being with Audrey means? Or is it Jack himself?

But I can't think now. Audrey has reached the apex of my thighs, and with Jack watching, his eyes glittering like shadowed emeralds, she pushes her tongue inside me. I gasp, arch into her mouth, pleasure swarming me.

Is this really happening?

Jack moves in closer, his palm stroking my belly. "Oh, yeah. Come, Bettina. Into her mouth. Come while I watch, both of you. Turn around, Audrey."

She lifts her head, smiles and moves around until her sex is over my face. I reach behind me, prop my head with a pillow, and pull Audrey's pussy to my mouth. She is wet, the scent of her desire, of her come from a few minutes ago, fresh and salty on my tongue. She's moaning, her hips pumping as I push my tongue in and out of her, using my fingers to tease her clit.

"Jesus," Jack murmurs.

Audrey is working my pussy like crazy, using her tongue, her fingers, thrusting into me, sucking on my clit, and I'm doing the same to her, both of us in a frenzy of desire, needing to come again. And I am acutely aware of Jack watching us,

catch a glimpse of him kneeling on the bed beside us, stroking his lovely cock from the corner of my eye. And Audrey is
grinding down onto my face now. I push my fingers deeper,
hard into her dripping pussy, and she comes, her sex squeezing my probing fingers as she cries out. Almost instantly, I'm
coming again, too, my hips arching hard, pleasure shivering
through my system.

After, I am nearly numb. Audrey slides off me, and Jack
grabs her and turns her onto her stomach on the bed. And
as I catch my breath, he spreads her legs and slides his cock
inside her. He begins to move, a fast, hard rhythm, fucking
her furiously, his fingers digging into her hips.

I am barely conscious, but it's so hot, watching them together. My body is alight with need once more, but I am too
far gone to do anything about it. I lie there and watch, their
bodies coming together, slick with sweat, the acrid scent of
sex heavy in the air.

But no matter how arousing the scene before me is, I am
distracted by the thoughts going through my mind.

It's not me Jack is fucking. And I want it to be. Only me.

But I got myself into this situation. And I am the outsider.
Just as I always am. And no matter how I'd love to think I am
an equal in this trio, that's simply not the truth. I would love
to be able to lie to myself, if even just for tonight. But I can't
do it.

Reality is like the harsh light of day, blinding me. I cannot
pretend that either of them is really mine. I don't understand
still that I want them to be.

Audrey. Jack.

Jack.

*Fuck.*

# CHAPTER SEVEN

I wake up warm, my body reflecting the heat of Audrey's sleeping form beside me. I'm glad she's there. Disappointed that Jack is not.

I don't know when he got up and left; I slept so heavily, and my limbs are still thick, weighty, my eyes scratchy, as though I slept drugged. Maybe I did. Drugged with endorphins, those happy opiates the brain releases during orgasm. I had enough orgasms to put anyone to sleep. I don't even know how many.

My sex gives a squeeze when I turn to look at Audrey. Her lashes are long and sooty on her cheeks, her skin flawless. Her mouth is pouty, innocent. I love knowing it's not, knowing what that mouth can do to me. I try to distract myself with these lovely thoughts, but I keep coming back to Jack.

Why did he leave us in the middle of the night? Maybe it's that he likes to sleep alone. Some people do. I used to prefer it. Until now. Maybe it's his way of disconnecting, as it seems to be for so many men. As it is for me, usually. But I want him here.

I feel oddly alone, suddenly, even with Audrey still dreaming beside me, all soft, naked skin as she curls into my side. I don't understand it. My body is as sated as it's ever been, and yet I feel the low hum of arousal at the same time. I am full of contradictions this morning.

Turning my face to the window, I peer through the sheer curtains. The sky is clear outside, a crisp blue at only 8:00 a.m., which means the day will be warm. I'll welcome the heat today. It'll warm me up inside, maybe chase away some of this ridiculous melancholy. I should be happy; I know that. But I'm not.

I silently repeat my little therapy mantra: my response is not necessarily appropriate to the situation.

Is it?

I don't even know anymore. All I know is this sense of wanting, yearning. For Jack.

*You cannot have him. May as well accept it.*

When have I ever wanted anyone this way? Not even Audrey, with all her charm, her pull. No, the whole thing with Jack is different. Really irresistible. And a little insane. I've known this man for a week. I've just had sex with him, yes, but is it really anything more than that? I am being ridiculous.

This is going to make me crazy. Jack is going to make me crazy. But I don't want to stop.

She sighs then, a quiet rush of air from between her lips, and her eyelids flutter open. Her eyes are that deep, smoky blue, her fringe of black lashes almost startling in contrast. So beautiful. But she doesn't seem happy this morning, either. Her dark brows draw together and her mouth is more pouty than usual.

"Good morning," I say, treading carefully, not sure where else to start.

"Morning."

"Jack is gone," I tell her.

"Yes. He usually is." She yawns, stretches, lifting her arms overhead, the sheet slipping down to reveal her bare breasts. "Don't take it personally. It's just his way." She sits up then, looking at me, an odd expression on her face. "You'll stay with me though, won't you, Bettina?"

A small thump of sympathy in my chest. "Yes. Sure."

She smiles then, if a little wanly, and reaches for me, dragging me to her, kissing my cheek. "My sweet Bettina. Don't go anywhere, okay? Just...stay with me today."

Her arms tighten around me, and I can feel her heart beating.

"Are you okay, Audrey?"

"What? Yes, of course." She kisses me again, pulls away, smiles at me, but her eyes are shadowed now, that frown back between her brows. "Bettina, you like me, don't you?"

"Of course I do."

"Really like me?"

"Yes. I really do. I wouldn't be here with you otherwise."

What is going on with her? Why this sudden insecurity from the girl I thought was all cocky self-assurance?

"Tell me you like me better than Jack," she says, childlike. And she looks like a child, so small and delicate.

"I..." The truth is, I don't know what to say to this. "I barely know Jack. We've spent several weeks together, you and I. You're the first woman I've been with. That means something to me."

It's true. But I haven't given her the whole truth. I can't do it. She is too worried this morning. She seems fragile to me for the first time since I've known her.

She pulls me in and hugs me hard. "Good. That's good."

I wonder if I've hurt her, sleeping with Jack, even though she seemed all for it last night. I had the impression it was her idea. But what if she was only doing it because she knew Jack wanted it?

I wish I could ask, but I can't. Maybe I don't really want to know.

I sigh, settle into her embrace, bury my face in her neck, and she seems happy with that. And frankly, I am happy with that: her scent, her silky flesh, her long hair like a veil over my face.

We sit still together for a while before my body begins to heat once more, and I kiss her neck, trailing my tongue over her skin, moving up until I can capture her lips with mine. She's sweet, sleepy still, but soon we are full-on making out, kissing hard, hands all over each other: belly, breasts, thighs. We're both panting, and I'm on top of her, legs tangled, pressing our mounds together in the way she's showed me. Only a few minutes of rubbing and I'm coming against her slim thigh, pleasure surging through me, wave after wave. And I keep thrusting my hips, until she's coming, too, crying out, her hands digging into my shoulders.

My body is humming with climax, my limbs warm and weak, and I roll off her. She immediately pulls me into her side, whispering to me, "Stay with me, Bettina. You promised."

"Of course I will," I tell her, wondering if it's true.

As I was coming I was thinking of Jack. His face, his hands, the scent of him still in my hair, and hers. The feel of his mouth between my thighs. His cock inside me.

No matter what, it's really Jack I'm thinking of. I can't help it.

The early-afternoon sun is high overhead, its golden rays warming my skin, fighting the damp, misty spray from the ocean. The day is gorgeous, clear, just as I thought it would be, and Audrey, Viviane and I are in our bikinis, all of the guys in swim trunks. Only Patrice is covered up in her usual khaki shorts, a lightweight white T-shirt and her hat as we sit together on the colorful Mexican blankets Viviane brought down from the house. Our sandals are scattered on the sand, along with a couple of small coolers holding ice and drinks. There's a striped umbrella stuck into the sand at one corner of the blanket, and Patrice has taken up residence under it on a low beach chair.

Audrey is sitting next to her, her dark hair in two long braids over her narrow shoulders. She's been silent all day, writing studiously on her legal pad, hardly looking up. I don't know what she might be thinking.

We showered together earlier, quietly, both of us a bit meditative, and there was no sex, for once. Maybe we were both sated after our quick orgasm this morning, after our little orgy last night. My sex feels full now, wonderfully used. But when I think about last night, which I seem to be doing every ten minutes, my body begins to pulse once more with desire.

I can barely stand to look at Jack, in his blue-and-white tropical-print board shorts, his tanned torso so beautiful to me, all long, lean muscles, his abs a tight six-pack. I know what his flesh feels like now, tastes like. I can still feel him beneath my hands, my tongue.

*More…*

But I have no idea if there will be more. If last night was some sort of fluke. If it will go back to being just Jack and Audrey. Or just Audrey and me, which would be nice, lovely. But Jack is the one I want. Too much.

It's not only physical, although the chemistry is nearly overwhelming, for me, anyway. But he's a good person. Smart, driven. A really great writer.

I really do need to stop. I've been warned, after all, about what kind of person Jack is. A free spirit. If anything more happens, it will be some friendly and rather fantastic sex, and that's it. Why am I even hoping for more? It's so unlike me.

Maybe that's why I can't stop thinking about him. He is the first man to affect me in this way. Ever. But perhaps I should attribute it more to my own personal growth than Jack himself. I've met nice guys before, hot guys.

*Never anything like Jack.*

Okay. I really *do* have to stop now.

I pull in a deep lungful of sea air: salt and water and fleshy seaweed, closing my eyes against the sun. When I open them, there's a shadow cast across the blankets. I look up to find a very beautiful man standing at the edge of our group. Skin like chocolate. Gorgeous. His bare chest is perfectly smooth beneath his open, white linen shirt, flapping in the breeze. Perfectly muscled. He's wearing low-slung cargo pants rolled at the cuffs. He looks like a Ralph Lauren ad. And his eyes are the same dark brown as his skin, tilted a bit at the corners. His smile is dazzling as he greets us, his voice tinged with an English accent.

"Hallo. I'm Charles Denny. I'm your neighbor for the next few weeks, the next house down. I wanted to introduce myself."

Everyone is introducing themselves to our new neighbor. We all recognize him; a well-known independent-film actor. Talented. Really great-looking. Spectacular.

Audrey has definitely noticed. She stands up, her body sleek in her bathing suit, her breasts pushed together in the halter-style top, the bright turquoise fabric showing off her olive skin, lighting up her eyes as she raises her sunglasses.

Her smile is even more radiant than his. "Charles Denny. Well, well. So nice to have you on our beach."

She extends her hand and he grasps it in his, and I can feel the sparks fly between them, instant, fiery. And just like that,

I understand perfectly that the rest of us have ceased to exist for her. Me. Even Jack. And I remember what Viv has said to me about her, and Jack, as well, about that intense focus Audrey can aim at a person. I remember what it feels like to be the object of her desire, as recently as this morning. But now I know I won't have to keep my promise to her. Oh, no, she won't need me anymore today.

Everyone chats with Charles a bit, recommending places to eat in the area, discussing weather conditions. Audrey has remained on her feet, her hips swaying slightly as though in invitation. She is all lovely, oozing sex appeal, and no one can resist. It makes me want to sleep with her again, simply watching her, despite my obsession with Jack, who is trying to pretend he is entirely unconcerned, scribbling away on his pad of paper. But he is too focused on it, not at all his usual friendly self with Charles, who seems awfully nice and down-to-earth.

"Charles, how long will you be here?" Viviane asks.

"Through the end of August, I believe, unless something changes with the production schedule on my next film."

"What are you working on?" Leo asks. I can see him looking Charles up and down, his steady gaze frankly admiring. I'm sure Charles is used to it.

"A small film about Rwanda. We shoot in Africa. It's a brilliant story, the best project I've had offered to me."

"Wow. Africa," Audrey says, her voice breathless, adoring. "Have you ever been before?"

"No, never."

"It'll be quite an adventure. But I'm sure you've had plenty of adventures on other shoots already."

He smiles, his dark gaze glued to Audrey. "A few, yes. Maybe I can tell you about them sometime."

"I'd love that," she says, flashing that dimpling smile at him.

Oh, yes, these two are smitten. And who wouldn't be? They are both almost too beautiful to be believed, with their gleaming smiles, their flawless skin. I feel almost ashen next to them. Insignificant. I glance at Jack; his gaze meets mine, and we exchange a look, acknowledging that we are both out of the picture. And I can almost believe he's feeling the same way about it as I am. But how is that possible? He is one of them, the beautiful people. And he isn't any more interested in a long-term relationship than Audrey is.

I want him to be jealous like this over me.

*Ridiculous.*

"I hope to see you all over the summer," Charles says.

"You don't have to wait," Audrey purrs. "Let me show you the beach."

His smile widens. "I'd like that very much. If I'm not disturbing you."

"Not at all." Audrey looks at Leo. "Take my work back to the house for me?"

"Sure," he answers.

Then she hooks her arm through Charles's and they walk off, toward the house Charles is staying in. It's a redwood-and-glass structure that sits back a bit from the shore, right next to our cottages, Jack's and mine. I look at him, and his dark brows are drawn together as he watches Audrey and Charles wander down the beach, talking, laughing.

"Well," Viviane announces, "I think I've had enough of this sun today. Anyone else?"

"Yes, plenty for me, too," Kenneth says, and Patrice agrees.

"I guess I'll go back up if everyone else is," Leo says. "I could use a sandwich, anyway."

"Me, too," Viviane says. "You coming, Tina? Jack?"

"I'm going to stay a bit longer, I think," I tell her.

"All right then. I'll leave the blankets for you. Jack?"

"No, I'll stay a little longer, too."

I look at him, but his expression is unreadable. My heart hammers imagining he's staying to be with me.

*Don't be stupid.*

We sit quietly while the rest of our group trudges up the dunes toward the house. They're gone for several minutes before Jack gets up, staring out at the water.

"I'm going to take a walk," he announces.

"I'll come with you," I say, then immediately wish I'd kept my mouth shut. I'm not in the mood for rejection.

But he doesn't turn me away. Instead he says, "Yeah, come on," holding a hand out toward me, helping me to my feet.

His hand is warm and large in mine, and I can't help but remember that heat on my skin. I shiver, feeling empty when he drops my hand and begins to walk in the opposite direction Audrey and Charles have taken. I follow, feeling a bit too much like a kicked puppy.

We're several yards down the beach before Jack stops and turns to me, his face clouded.

"Well, that was classic Audrey," he says, and I am surprised at the vehemence in his tone.

"Yes, I gathered that."

"I have no idea why it even bothers me anymore. Why it ever has."

"Maybe because it doesn't feel good to be dropped like that, no matter the circumstances, your own feelings. Or lack of them."

"I never said I lack feelings for Audrey," he says, his tone defensive.

"I'm sorry. I didn't mean—"

"No. Shit." He runs a hand through his dark hair. "I know

what you're saying. I'm just annoyed. More at myself than her, maybe."

"I just meant that even though you're not into the whole relationship thing…I mean, that's what you said, right?"

"Yeah. Right."

"Well, it doesn't mean that being rejected is going to feel good."

He nods, looking at me. "I'm sorry. You're probably not thrilled right now, either."

I look away, out to the sea, the water swelling, surging. It still looks like something entirely sexual to me. "No," I say quietly. "But I'm okay."

"Are you?"

I turn to him, and am surprised to see the concern on his face. His eyes are such a brilliant green, with flecks of silver gleaming in the midday sunlight. I have another moment of being absolutely stunned by the beauty of them. I hate myself for it a little. I don't want to be so damn fascinated with him. With a man who has no desire for anything other than the free and easy sex I am sure is readily available to him anywhere he goes.

People like him, like Audrey, are sort of spoiled in that way, I think.

"What is it?" he asks, his eyes narrowing.

"What do you mean?"

"Your face went dark." He reaches out, brushes a few stray curls from my cheek and I can't help that my heart lurches in my chest. That I can feel it low in my belly. "Just clouded over like the fog coming in."

I laugh roughly. "Oh, you are a writer, aren't you?"

"Yeah, I am. A little poetry is allowed now and then."

He smiles, and I smile back, this time more sincerely.

"So, what is it?" he asks.

"You're not going to let this go, are you?"

"Nope."

He plops down in the sand and drags me down next to him, and I am momentarily thrilled at the touch of his hand on mine.

I sit for a few moments, my pulse racing, waiting for him to let go of my hand. But he doesn't. And he's watching me, waiting for me to answer him, I suppose.

"I…I don't know what to tell you, Jack."

"Tell me what's on your mind."

"I thought it was only women who ever asked anyone that question."

"I'm interested."

"Are you?"

Damn it. I know right away I've weighted that question far too heavily.

He raises one dark eyebrow. "You're a little bitter about men, aren't you, Bettina?"

I shrug, leaning back to rest on my hands. "I prefer to think of it as being a realist."

He's quiet a moment. "That's sad."

"But true, nevertheless."

"I still think it's sad. That someone has hurt you, made you feel this way." He pauses, watching me. "I'm sorry. I'm not asking you to tell me anything. I'll shut up now."

He turns to the water, and I have a few moments to study his profile, which is strong and sleek, his jaw sharply chiseled, with just enough beard stubble to make him appear even more masculine. I'm sitting on his left, so I can see the shallow suggestion of the dimple resting on his cheek, and the tattoo that wraps around his left biceps. It's all black, the lines thick, dark, like a ring of thorns done in a very stylized manner. And beneath it are letters done in a beautiful, Gothic script.

I've seen it before, but I don't know what it says. It looks like Latin.

"'*Aut insanit homo, aut versus facit,*'" I read. "What does it mean?"

Jack laughs, turns to me. "It's from Horace. 'The fellow is either mad or he is composing verses.'"

I grin. "So, which is it?"

"Both, don't you think? None of us creative types are completely sane."

"Glad I'm not the only one."

"So am I."

"You like to be crazy?" I laugh.

"I didn't say that. But I'm glad I'm not the only one who feels like I'm losing my mind sometimes."

"The work does it, I think," I tell him. "Especially working under deadlines. Being creative on demand. Things were simpler when I was still writing for myself, before I had my first book contract."

"Were they? Were you less neurotic?"

"Hey! I didn't say I was neurotic."

"Just…crazy?"

I smile at him. I don't mind his teasing. And the truth is, I often think I'm both neurotic and crazy. Hence the need for therapy. But it does seem to be part of the creative process, for me, anyway.

"Do you think it's not healthy?" I ask. "That we're driven to create by our neurosis? Our craziness?"

He shrugs, his shoulders rippling with muscle beneath his tanned skin. "I don't know that it's a matter of healthy or unhealthy. It is what it is."

"That seems to be your attitude about a lot of things in life."

"Maybe. It makes life easier to deal with, anyway."

"Why does life need to be made easier?" I know what my own answer is, but I want to know what his might be.

He's silent for several long moments. Then, "Life is hard sometimes. And if you let it get you down, it'll beat you. Right into the fucking ground."

I am stunned. I'm not sure what he means, if there is something specific he's referring to, although I feel there probably is. But mostly I'm stunned by the raw honesty seeping through this brief remark.

I put my hand on his arm, and he flinches a little. He immediately turns to me and smiles, so I know not to take it personally. But his eyes are distant, a bit vacant.

"Jack? Do you want to tell me what you mean?"

"Not really."

"Okay."

"Okay." He turns to look out at the water once more, then he lies back onto the sand, his gaze on the sky, his eyes squinting in the bright sunlight. "It was my last year in college."

"What?"

I don't know what he's going to say, only that it's something important.

"That's when I learned what an asshole I was."

"Jack…"

"No, it's true. And it was a lot more true then. A chip off the old block, isn't that what they say? That's true, too, you know."

I shake my head. "I don't know that at all. I think we're each responsible for who we are, who we become."

"I *am* taking responsibility for who I am. I'm simply stating where I learned it."

"So, your father was not a very nice person I take it?"

"He was a nightmare."

"I'm sorry." I don't know what else to say.

"Yeah, well…" He trails off, and we sit quietly for a while.

The sun is beating down on my skin, but I don't mind it. I turn my face into the golden rays, close my eyes, breathe in the ocean, Jack's nearness.

"Come here," he says suddenly, pulling me onto my back on the sand beside him.

I lay there, looking up at the sky like an endless blue dome overhead, punctuated only by the reeling gulls. The sand is hot. It's soft and hard all at once beneath my back, and I can feel every vertebra in my back pressing into it. I don't know what to say, so I stay quiet, hoping he'll eventually open up to me a bit more. After several minutes in which I can hear my heart hammering in my ears, he does.

"My father cheated on my mother. All the time. That was his M.O. That was just…what he did. And when I was a teenager—and I mean just barely, like thirteen, fourteen years old—he would sit me down at night, sometimes after my mom went to bed, and he'd tell me…everything. Too much. I didn't know how to stop him. And frankly, a part of me didn't want to. It pissed me off, that he was doing this to my mom. But at the same time, there seemed to be something glamorous about it. He actually made me admire him for it, in some weird way."

"You were a teenager. A kid."

"Yeah. But even as a kid you should have some moral code."

"That doesn't mean you didn't."

"Maybe." His brows are drawn, scowling.

"But you were angry with him."

"Not enough to do anything about it."

"He was your father. What were you supposed to do?"

My stomach is starting to twist. There's pain in his voice. I don't turn my head to look at him, though. I don't think he'd want me to right now.

"That doesn't excuse any of it. It doesn't excuse what I did later." I stay quiet, waiting. Finally, he blows out a long breath. "I don't know why I'm telling you this."

"I don't know, either. But it's okay."

He's silent again, and I focus on the waves of heat shimmering over the sand, a watery mirage. A gull flies overhead, then another, and I watch them catch a current of air, spiraling upward together, their bodies dark silhouettes against the sun.

"So," he says, his voice low. "So…I became just like him. I cheated on all my high school girlfriends. The ones I had in college. I didn't even know why I was doing it, but I felt *driven* to do it. And I thought nothing of it. I was so damn cavalier about it. I never thought for one moment about the consequences. But this was only the beginning of me being an asshole." He takes a breath, then another. "In my senior year I met a girl named Sheri."

He stops again, and this time I turn to look at him. I swear there was a catch in his voice just now, and I am filled with dread for him. I know something bad is coming. He won't look at me. He just continues to stare at the sky, but I know he's not really seeing it.

"What happened, Jack?" I ask, keeping my voice down. I don't want to startle him, and I feel as though I might.

"Well, I cheated on her, too, of course."

"And?"

"And she tried to kill herself."

He says this matter-of-factly, his voice gone dead, dry. My breath hitches in my throat.

"Jesus, Jack."

"Yeah." He runs a hand through his hair, leaving his palm

on his forehead. "That's when I finally saw what I was. What my dad really was. That he wasn't some cool guy who got away with being bad, which in truth was my completely childish version of what he did, who he was. What I'd been telling myself in my head. I finally saw that we were both just these selfish assholes. That we were hurting people. And I couldn't fucking stand it."

"But you learned from it."

"Yeah. I learned that I would never do that to another human being."

"Why can't you forgive yourself, then?"

I shut my mouth so fast, as soon as the words come out of it, that my teeth clack together. This is *so* none of my business.

"I have. As much as I can."

"I'm sorry, Jack. I shouldn't have said that."

"No, it's fine. Fine."

But his fingers are gripping his hair, buried in the dark curls.

"And your father?"

"He died a few years after, in a car accident."

"Oh, Jack…"

"Don't. Okay?"

His tone isn't harsh; it's more pleading than anything, and I feel awful.

"Sorry. I'm sorry. I'll shut up."

"Fuck, Bettina, I didn't mean that. I just…I'm being an asshole again."

"No, you're not. You're not, Jack."

He's staring at me, watching me, a hundred shadows crossing his features. Finally, he says, "You're a good person, Bettina."

"Oh, I'm not so great."

"Why do you do that?"

"What?"

"Try to make yourself so small."

My chest tightens into a hard ball. "I don't."

But that's a lie. How is it he can see me so clearly, this man I barely know?

He reaches out and pulls me into him, and when I resist, he pulls harder, until I'm on top of him. His skin is everywhere against mine and my bikini is suddenly nothing, as though the two small scraps of fabric don't exist. And despite the seriousness of our conversation, I am burning for him instantly. Wet.

His eyes are dark with desire; I can see it as clearly as if they are reflecting my own. Maybe they are. Maybe it's only myself, my own need, I see in them. But whatever it is, I am lost.

And then he kisses me.

Totally, utterly lost.

# CHAPTER EIGHT

His kiss is hard, demanding. A little desperate. Or maybe that's my imagination, reading more emotion into what's happening here than there really is. But when his tongue slips into my mouth, I pretty much stop thinking altogether.

His hands are on my waist, making me feel small and female, and he's holding on to me so tightly it hurts a little, but I love it. Need it. To be possessed this way, by him. He shifts, and his hardening cock is against my thigh. And I'm getting so wet so fast, I wonder if he can feel it through my bathing suit.

I want him to.

*Jack.*

I want him to know how much I want him. I want him to feel my desire, for it to fuel his. I am craving that thing that happens when two people come together and it's really good, that thing that's happened between Audrey and me, between Jack and Audrey and me. But I want it to be about just Jack and me now.

All this is happening in the back of my head, not in words so much as pure, insatiable craving.

I grind my hips into him, and his tongue lashes into my mouth, tasting, pushing deeper. His hands move down and he grabs my butt, his fingers digging in just beneath the crease where the curve of flesh meets my thighs.

I moan softly, and he moans back, pulling me harder into him.

Then he pushes me back. I am left dazed.

"Jack…?"

"We can't do this, Bettina."

"Wh-why not?"

Hurt is flooding my body. Rejection. I am weak with it.

"Not here," he says roughly. "Come to my cottage, Bettina. Come into my bed."

I am so relieved, all I can do is nod. He leans up and brushes a kiss across my lips, then he stands, taking me with him.

We're both silent as he leads me back down the beach, but his hand is warm in mine. Every now and then he glances over at me and I can see the desire clear on his face. I can see that his cock hasn't gone down beneath the fabric of his swim trunks. And I am still wet, burning for him.

Soon we're back on our section of the beach, making our way up the dune, heading for the small stand of ancient cypress and our cottages standing side by side. We reach his red door and he pulls me inside. It's cooler than it is outside, but I can still feel the heat of the day in the still air, on the wooden floorboards, as I kick off my rubber flip-flops. Or maybe it's his warm fingers still gripping mine as he backs me toward the bed.

I have barely a moment to take it all in: the room that looks so much like my own cottage, except for the red-and-white quilt on the bed, his table covered in messy piles of notepads, old coffee mugs, his open laptop, a pair of wineglasses.

I don't want to think of him here, drinking wine with Audrey, so I don't.

The back of my legs bump the edge of the bed, the cotton coverlet soft on my skin.

"I want to undress you," he says, his hands already sliding the straps holding my bikini top from my shoulders. "I need to see you naked."

I nod, but he doesn't see; he's already leaning into me, his face buried in my neck, licking the tender flesh there as his silky hair strokes my skin, and I'm shivering with desire, my legs absolutely shaking.

He takes my top off and lets it drop on the floor and he pulls back, watching my face for several moments before dropping his gaze to my breasts.

"Ah, beautiful, Bettina. Beautiful girl."

And I feel beautiful. I don't feel like hiding anything from him.

Then he gathers my breasts in both his hands, and lust shoots through me, a shock of excruciating *wanting*.

"Jack…"

His voice is low, full of smoke. "I know what you need, girl."

Then he's down on his knees, and his hands are pushing my breasts together as his mouth closes in, his tongue lancing out at first one nipple, then the other.

"Oh…"

I bury my hands in his hair. It's so soft, the curls twining around my fingers. And even this smooth texture of his hair between my fingers becomes part of the sensation rippling through my system.

His tongue is wet, teasing. I arch into his mouth, pulling his head closer. He chuckles against my skin.

"What do you want, baby? Tell me."

"Jack…"

"Tell me," he says, his tongue darting out once more, then cruelly pulling away.

"I want…God, don't make me say it, Jack."

"Do you want this?"

His mouth meets my flesh, closing around my hard nipple and sucking.

"Oh! Yes…"

He pulls away. "Or this?" And he bites the tip of my nipple, making me groan.

"Yes, that, too."

He pulls back once more, kissing his way down my stomach, and desire is like a lead weight in my body. I can't move, his head, his silken hair, slipping from my fingers. His hands are on my sides, then my hips, and he pulls them forward with a sharp jerk, slipping his fingers beneath the edge of my bikini bottoms, and right into my slit.

"Ah, you're wet. So damn wet. You want me, don't you, Bettina?"

"Yes, please…"

"You want me to touch you. To push my fingers into that tight hole. To fuck you with my hand."

He does it, his fingers slipping right between my pussy lips, impaling me. I gasp, trembling with pleasure. He moves his fingers in, then out, pumping me, and I want to cry, it feels so impossibly good.

"Look at me," he demands, and I do.

His eyes are dark with desire, his mouth loose and lush. I can see the whiteness of his teeth between his parted lips.

"Do you like this?" he asks.

I like everything. I am nearly breathless, but I manage to answer. "Yes. Jack…"

"But you'd like my mouth even more, wouldn't you?"

"Oh, God, please…"

He smiles as he pulls my bottoms off. And with his gaze steady on mine, he parts my thighs and moves his face in between them. His hands are cupping my buttocks, and he pulls me in closer, just pushing his face into my soaking-wet mound. I cry out as his wet tongue meets my aching flesh.

I would fall if he weren't holding me up, his hands strong on my ass. And he's pulling me into him, over and over, his tongue lashing out at my clit, his fingers working my pussy lips. I am nothing but sensation, his hands rough on my skin, his tongue even rougher on my swollen clit. Sensation and the heady scent of my own juices mixing with the salt air and the fragrant undercurrent of old wood.

He is licking me, licking me, and I am pumping my hips into his face, shivering all over, pleasure driving into my body. And when my climax hits, my whole body explodes, fire and smoke and indescribable pleasure. I am blind, my body clench-ing: my sex, my belly, my hands on his broad shoulders.

"Jack! Oh… Oh…"

Finally it's over. I'm still shivering. He pulls away, his face slick with my wetness, and I feel it slide down the inside of my thighs. I don't think I've ever been this wet in my life. But I'm not done. And neither is he, thank God.

He pushes me down on the bed, onto my back, and quickly strips his trunks off. His cock is all hard, golden beauty, the head swollen and dark. My mouth waters. He kneels on the bed over me, his hand stroking my thighs, and I swear even this touch causes tiny rippling orgasms to run over my skin, or maybe just beneath it. And in his other hand are my tie-dyed bikini bottoms.

"You taste so good, I can't get enough of you."

He holds my bottoms to his face, inhales deeply, and I don't know why this turns me on, but it does. Maybe because I am still a helpless, shivering wreck, laid out on the bed, unable to move, my climax heavy in my body.

"Jack, I need you," I tell him, my voice a small mewling sound.

"And I need you, beautiful girl."

He lowers his hand, still gripping my bathing suit, and rubs it over his cock. My pussy clenches, hard. And as I watch, he begins a slow, thrusting rhythm, into his fisted hand, into my bikini bottoms, and it's almost as though he's fucking me. The sight of him is so damn hot, his rigid cock, the tip glistening with pre-come, his tight, tanned abs flexing as he moves, that lovely line from his hip to his groin.

"Fuck, Bettina," he growls, but I cannot stop watching his beautiful, pumping cock. "Do you want me to fuck you?"

"Yes."

"Tell me, girl. Tell me what you want."

I lick my dry lips, my body burning with need. "I want you to fuck me, Jack. Yes… But this is too good."

He laughs, his tone low and rough, and he throws his head back and gives a few good, hard thrusts, his fist going tight around his cock as he pushes into the bright fabric. "You are so damn hot, all that golden hair. Your skin. Christ, your skin, Bettina. I would come all over your bathing suit if I didn't want to fuck you so badly."

"Oh…"

Then he's on me, a condom produced from somewhere. Doesn't matter. All that matters is that he can't put it on fast enough for me. I need him inside me. *Need* him!

Finally he has it, the latex glistening on his hard cock, and I spread my thighs.

"Is this how you want it, my girl? Just like this?" Kneeling again, he moves in between my legs, pushing them farther apart with his big hands, draping them over his on either side.

"Yes. I just…I can't wait. Please, Jack. Just do it."

"Ah, I love this about you," he says. "That you fall apart like this in bed."

I bite my lip, wiping my hair from my eyes. "Jack…"

"Say it. I want to hear you tell me you want me to fuck you. I need to hear you, Bettina."

His cock is poised at the entrance to my body; I can feel the slick latex sheath resting between the lips of my sex, right at that wet, aching hole.

"I want you to fuck me," I tell him, my voice low, breathless.

"Ah, that's beautiful, baby."

He snakes an arm around the back of my neck, and pulls me up, holding me nearly upright. And with his other hand between my thighs, he spreads my pussy lips wide, and slides right in.

"Oh!"

Pleasure, raging inside me, pouring into my limbs, my sex, my breasts, hard and aching with need. Lust. Desire like a torch in my system. And then he begins to move, fucking me in a slow, steady rhythm, and I really think I am going to lose my mind.

My arms go around him, the muscles of his back rock hard beneath my hands. And I remember to breathe him in, the lovely, clean scent that is Jack, mixed with his sweat, my juices still on his lips. Then he's pulling me upright, holding me tight to his body. I can even feel the hard points of his nipples against the soft flesh of my breasts, that faint scratch of hair on my skin. I feel his heart racing, or at least, I like to think I can.

His mouth closes on mine, his tongue snaking between my

lips. And it is everything at once: tongues and lips, breasts and hands, cock and pussy, flesh and wetness and me coming again, hard and sudden. My body clenches, and a long, keening cry comes from my mouth and into his. But he only kisses me harder, fucks me harder, as I shake and shake.

"Oh, yeah, my girl, come on. Beautiful," he whispers to me.

His arms tighten around me, and he plows into my body, deeper, harder. I can barely breathe. His face is damp with sweat, and I lick it from his upper lip, drinking in the salt.

"Harder, Jack. Fuck me harder."

"Yeah…Christ, Bettina. I'm fucking you…fucking you… ah, baby…"

Then he's coming, his body jerking into mine, his pubic bone rocking hard into mine, bruising me. But I don't care. I know in some distant way that I'm moaning, small orgasm-like tremors shuddering through me. That I am whispering his name over and over. That I am incoherent.

But what really matters is that Jack is inside my body, the pleasure we are sharing, our sweat mingling. And still we rock together, his softening cock moving inside me, our hips coming together over and over. He's kissing my neck, sweet, openmouthed kisses, over and over. And when his hand comes up to push my hair from my damp face, I grab his wrist, take his fingers into my mouth and suck.

"Ah, that's nice," he murmurs.

I feel perfectly calm inside, as though he has put me into some sort of meditative state. And happier than I've been in a very long time. Maybe ever.

*Don't get used to it.*

But I am too suffused with pleasure, too weakened by it, to pay that censorious voice much attention. I am too in the moment, for once.

When I let Jack's fingers slip from my mouth, he wraps both hands around the back of my head and lays me down on the bed on my side, gently, as though I'm a baby, fragile, precious. He lies with me, facing me, and cradles me with one hand while the other moves over my body, down my side, back up again, sliding over my hip, up my spine. His touch is lovely, warm. And I am entirely comfortable, trusting, nearly in a dream state.

After a while he stills for a few moments. I am content to simply lie here with him.

"Fuck, Bettina," he says, his serious tone making my stomach lurch.

Have I done something wrong?

"Jack…?"

He turns his face into me and buries it in my hair, and suddenly I want to cry.

What is going on? With him? With me?

His voice is muffled. "That was spectacular."

"God, Jack."

This would be funny if it weren't so damn true. If I weren't so completely overwhelmed by the intensity of what just happened between us. And it is more than hot sex, although this is by far the hottest sex of my life. Hotter than what happened with Audrey: the two of us, then the three of us. This is more…personal. But I can't say any of these things to him. I don't want to say anything at all, to jeopardize what's just happened. Because I want it to happen again.

I want it not to be over. Not now. Not ever.

What the hell am I even thinking?

He's on his back now, his arm under my shoulder, my head pillowed on his strong chest. And I am in heaven, just like this. I'm afraid to move, to breathe, to break the spell.

I've lived my life in fear. But this is new, different.

I stay perfectly still and listen to the shallow cadence of his breath, his chest rising and falling gently beneath my head. I breathe him in, swallow down his scent, that fresh, clean scent, the earthy musk of sex, of come. And I close my eyes and allow myself, for just a few moments, to imagine being with him like this again and again. In my own bed at home.

*Don't be a fool.*

I draw air into my lungs, deeply, command my racing heart to calm, my imagination to stop leading me down this unrealistic path.

"Hey," Jack says, his voice rough, sleepy. Sexy.

"Hey."

His arm tightens a little around me. "How're you doing?"

"Good. I'm good."

"Yeah?"

"Yeah. Yes."

"Then why are you twisting your hair like you're trying to break it?"

"What? Am I?"

"Bettina." He pauses, turns to face me once more, his hand on my cheek making me want to cry for some reason I don't really understand. "You know who I am, right?"

I swallow. "You mean…that you're not a relationship guy? Like we talked about before? Sure. Yes. And I'm not really looking for that right now. It's okay, Jack."

"Is it? Because I don't lead anyone on."

"I know that. You've been perfectly honest with me. You've been clear. And I'm a big girl, Jack. I can handle this."

But even as I say it I'm not sure it's true.

"Okay. I just wanted to be sure you're okay with this. Because that was amazing. And I hope it'll happen again."

This makes me smile, and I latch onto it. Too much, I

know, but it'll do for now. It'll keep me afloat until I can get my head back on straight.

"I'd like that." I pause. "I'd like it to happen again right now."

He laughs, brushing a kiss across my mouth. "Mmm, give me a few minutes, and it will." He pulls my hand to his lips, kisses the back of it, making me shiver. "You're a little minx, you know that, girl? You'd never know it to look at you. But I like that it's hidden away behind that innocent face of yours."

"God, do I really look so naive?"

"Yes," he says matter-of-factly, making me groan. "But I like it. It makes you irresistible."

"I'm hardly irresistible."

"Ah, but you are."

I shake my head. "I'm not. I know what I am, and it's okay."

"So, what are you?"

"I'm…cute. Attractive. But not beautiful, or exotic. I'm not like Audrey."

"What do you mean?" His brows are drawn together. "Is that what you think?"

"Yes. I don't have her perfection. Her magic."

"Bettina." His hand is on my cheek, his thumb stroking, and he looks so serious. "You are beautiful. You're beautiful like *Bettina*. That's all you need to be. And it's pretty damn amazing." I begin to shake my head, but he holds my face in his hand, firm, unarguable. "There are different kinds of beauty, you know. Oh, I get that Audrey is hot. Sexy as hell. I know you know that. You feel it, too. But that doesn't diminish you in any way. Don't let it. Don't let anyone."

My pulse is hot, racing, my cheeks warm. And there's a

strange knot in my chest. It hurts and it's pleasant all at the same time.

"I'm trying not to let anyone do that to me anymore," I tell him, wondering where this honesty has come from, but not really wanting to hide anything from him. Except my intense fascination, the degree of my need for him. "That's old stuff for me. I think we can put our pasts behind us, Jack. If we try. And I'm trying to do that."

"Maybe sometime you'll tell me about it."

"Would you really want to know?"

"Why do you seem so surprised? Just because I'm not looking for a one-on-one relationship doesn't mean I'm a total dick. I'm usually friends with my lovers. Shouldn't sex be as friendly as possible?"

"Hmm. Yes, I guess so."

It sounds right on the surface, anyway.

"So, do you want to tell me?" he persists.

"Yes. But not right now."

"What do you want to do now?"

I smile, feeling sultry suddenly, in a way I don't very often. And slipping my hands between us, I stroke his cock, feel it harden beneath my touch.

"Ah," he says, his voice catching. "I like the way you think."

"Jack?"

"Yeah."

"Can I ask you to do something for me?"

"Anything about now, my girl."

"Will you…will you touch yourself for me?"

"You want to watch?"

"Yes, please."

He smiles, gives me a quick kiss, gets up on his knees, as

he was earlier, takes his swelling cock in his hand and runs his fingers up the length of the shaft.

My mouth goes dry. My sex goes wet.

"There's only one catch," he says, his voice going rough already.

"What's that?"

"You have to let me watch you, too."

"Now?"

"Oh, yeah."

I hesitate, swallow.

"Fair is fair, Bettina," he says, wrapping his fingers around his cock and squeezing. "Come on, baby. You can do it."

I sit up a little on the pillows, spread my thighs, slip my hand in between them, begin to rub.

"Jack…this doesn't…my own hand doesn't really do it for me. I can't come like this."

But I can't take my eyes off his cock sliding in and out of his fist.

"Don't think about it. Just do it. For me. And spread for me. Ah, that's it."

I let my legs fall open, watch as he licks his lips, and pleasure signals from my hardening clit, thrumming deep in my belly. I spread wider.

"Ah, I think you have a little exhibitionistic streak. And I like it. I love it."

His tone has dropped even further, and his hand is working his cock. I move my hand in the same slow rhythm, over my slit, which is wet and beginning that lovely, needy ache. Maybe it's more from watching him than it is from touching myself. Doesn't matter. I'm getting hotter and hotter by the second.

"Oh, yeah. Beautiful. My beautiful girl."

His hips are thrusting, slow, sharp thrusts, and he's squeezing his cock, the head going purple. I want to put my mouth on it, to kiss it. To curl my tongue around it. To taste the pre-come gathering on the tip.

I lick my lips.

"That's it, Bettina. Now pinch your clit between your fingers. Roll it. Yes…"

I do as he says, a thrill going through me. I love that he's instructing me. It's almost as though he's *doing* this to me. And maybe he is.

"Tell me more, Jack," I beg breathlessly.

"Ah…" He's smiling, his teeth white, glistening. He's so damn beautiful. "Use your other hand to touch your breast. Just slide it up over the curve, brush the nipple. Oh, yeah, it's getting hard. You have the most perfect breasts. Firm and smooth."

He's stroking himself faster now, and so am I. I can't believe how turned on I am, listening to him say these things to me. Pleasure radiates through my body like waves of heat.

"That's it, baby. So good. I can see how wet you are. I know just what that feels like, to have my hands on your wet pussy. My mouth. To push my cock inside you…just. Like. This."

Each word is punctuated with a rough stroke. He lets his head fall back, his eyelids fluttering closed, and he pulls in a gasping breath. Then his eyes open, his hand stills.

"Fuck, need to wait for you, Bettina. Come on, baby."

"I don't know if I can."

But truthfully, my body is unexpectedly poised at that edge. I keep my eyes on his cock, the swollen tip, the small pearl of pre-come there. I lick my lips, watching as he begins to stroke once more.

"Baby, I can barely hold it back," Jack says. "I want you to get off. For me. You can do it."

"Maybe…" My voice is shuddering, breathy.

"You can. Just stroke yourself, run your fingers over your clit. Harder. Yes, back and forth. And take your other hand and pinch your nipple. Christ, you're beautiful."

His hips are pumping once more, into his fisted hand, and as I rub my swollen clit, pinch my hard nipple, sensation floods my body in slow, lovely waves. I am imaging his cock is pumping into me. I can almost feel it.

"I need to fuck you again," Jack says. "Soon. But now, come for me. Come, Bettina."

"Oh! Oh…"

And shockingly, I do, that slow, liquid sensation filling me up, hot and urgent, taking me over. I'm shivering, pleasure flowing into me like water. Like the salty ocean pounding outside. And I am drowning in sensation, my pussy spasming, my gaze on his hard, thrusting cock, the muscles of his abs, his hips, working, straining.

"Ah, baby, yeah. Beautiful, beautiful girl," he gasps. "Yeah, I'm coming, baby…"

His come spurts out, thick and white and lovely between his fingers. And even as my body quivers with my own climax, I watch Jack coming, fascinated, awed.

He stops, staring at me. I'm a little shivery all over; with pleasure, with an odd edginess. I'm not sure what it is. Nerves? But I'm not nervous; far from it.

I pull in a deep breath, then another, watching him watch me, and all I want is his arms around me, his lips on mine.

"Jack. Jack?"

"I'm right here."

He leans over me and pulls me into his strong arms, and it feels better than even the sex, the orgasms. And I know what it is I was feeling, that little bit of panic.

It's emotion.

I want to tell it to go away. To stuff it down deep where I don't have to look at it.

I burrow in, my cheek pressed hard against his chest, listening to his heart beating. I ground myself in that, thinking about how alive he is. How alive I feel.

I lie there and simply listen to him breathe for a while. I'm tired, but too jacked up to sleep. I am trying not to think, but my mind is whirring away on its own.

How long will this last? If I fall asleep, will I wake up later to find him gone? Or will he send me back to my cottage alone in a little while?

Maybe it would be better to go now, just get up, find my bathing suit and get out of there.

I start to sit up, but he holds me down.

"What are you doing?"

"I thought…I was going to go."

"Go? Are you done with me so soon?"

"I wondered the same thing about you."

I am too raw to censor what I say right now. I just can't do it.

"Ah." He's quiet a moment. Then, "Do you want to stay here with me, Bettina?"

"Yes," I answer before I can stop myself.

"Good. Because I want you to stay."

"But for how long, Jack?"

"Do you need to know that now? Right this moment?"

"I…maybe not. No." He's stroking my hair. I don't want to think about how good it feels. How intimate. "Jack, I don't know how to do this. This casual, friendly sex thing."

"You've never had sex unless you were in a relationship?"

"Of course I have." I just don't know how to do it with him. But I don't say this. "I did with Audrey."

"You have to with Audrey," he says, and I am a little surprised at the bitter edge to his voice.

"Jack? Has she…has she hurt you?"

"No. Yes. Fuck." He runs a hand through his hair, which I am beginning to recognize as a sign that he's agitated. Or that he's talking about something he really doesn't want to. "It's different with Audrey. We've talked about that a little. She has that effect on you. On me. When I'm with her, anyway. Then she goes off wherever, with whoever, and I'm pissed for a few days. Then I'm over it. I know what I can and can't expect with her. The lines are crystal clear. And because of who I am, and who she is, I don't want anything more permanent with her. So it's okay, on that level. But I'm not some robot. I still have feelings, which are sometimes unreasonable."

I nod. "Yes. I understand that. I feel that, too. I wanted to be with her, initially. I wanted to be the center of her universe, because in those moments when I was, it was so powerful. Maybe I wanted some of her glamour, her shine, to rub off on me. Or maybe I just wanted to feel that intensity. I wanted more with her. But now I'm not so sure. And it's been confusing."

"Are you saying you wanted a long-term relationship with her?"

"I…no. I didn't really think of it in those terms. I simply wanted her. And that was new to me."

"You fell for her," he says, not really asking.

"In a way. But maybe not in any different way than you did. But it was more than just sex for me, yes. And I feel like I can't quite get a grasp on it. I mean, I have had sex with people before that I wasn't in a relationship with. I've just never done it with the intention, or rather, with no intention, of it going anywhere else."

He stays silent for several endless minutes. "So, you've been in love with—or at least falling in love with—everyone you've ever slept with? Is that what you're telling me?"

"I've never been in love."

Shit. I didn't mean to say that.

"Then we're really not all that different, are we?"

I have to think about that. But maybe what he's saying is true. Because I have slept with a number of men—and with Audrey—without being in love with them. Not real "in love," although I think I fancied myself sort of in love with Audrey. Maybe I still do. But I know what he means and it's not that.

"No. I suppose we're not."

"Okay. Okay. So, can you be here with me, just like this? Get to know each other. Sleep together. Enjoy each other?"

"Live in the moment, you mean."

"Something like that."

"Yes. I can do that," I say.

I'm not sure if it's true. But if the only other option is to stop, then this is what I'm choosing.

A poor choice, maybe. Because I could really feel something for Jack.

*Fuck.*

This is not the man to fall for.

But I know already it's too late. Too goddamn late.

# CHAPTER NINE

Dinnertime is a little weird. Audrey is still gone, with Charles, I suppose, and everyone pretends not to notice.

I have no idea how to act with Jack. He's off at one end of the kitchen with Leo, talking, laughing as they make an enormous salad. Every now and then he glances up and smiles at me for a brief moment, making me warm inside. But I have no idea what it means, what I'm supposed to do, how I'm supposed to respond.

I feel as though what's happened between us is private, it's *our* thing. And because I don't know what else may happen— or not happen—I don't want to make it public.

As I set the table I watch Jack through the doorway between the dining room and the kitchen, the easy manner he has with everyone, even Patrice. He seems compelled to hug her, to loop an arm around her shoulders, which she pretends annoys her, but which I can easily see she loves.

Who wouldn't love Jack?

*Not me.*

I am being ridiculous. Even more ridiculous over him than I was over Audrey. Because no matter what I say, aloud or to myself, I am having these entirely girlish fantasies about him. About permanence.

I have never done this before. Why now? Why him, Mr. Unobtainable? I really must be some sort of masochist.

Viviane comes through the door, a fistful of knives in her hand, Sid trotting at her heels.

"I forgot we'd need these—steak for dinner." She goes around the table, setting one at each place. "So, Tina, want to tell me what's up with you?"

"Hmm? Oh, nothing."

"Okay." She lets me get away with this for about ten seconds. "Now you want to tell me the truth?"

"Not really."

I sigh, straightening the silverware bit by minute bit, going from one place setting to another, until each one is perfectly lined up on the cloth napkins, relaxing into the small ritual. And after a few moments I look up and realize Viv is still there, watching me.

"I...I do this when I'm stressed," I explain, feeling a bit embarrassed.

She shrugs. "We all have our coping mechanisms," she says, making me feel a little less neurotic. "So, are you worried about the Jack and Audrey equation?"

I'm relieved that she knows, that she isn't beating around the bush. That she isn't judging.

"I'm confused. I just don't know what's going to happen next. With them. With Jack and me."

"With Audrey?"

"I feel like I'm pretty much out of the picture at this point, as far as she's concerned."

"Do you want to be?"

"I'm not one hundred percent certain, but...I'm really more

focused on Jack. I know that's not good. I mean, to be focused on him at all."

"Maybe not."

"Why do you say maybe, knowing what you know about him?"

"Because it's all growth, isn't it? Jack, Audrey, coming here."

"Yes, I guess so. Although I don't know that sleeping with half the group is exactly what my therapist meant by coming out of my shell on this trip."

"It's only one-third." Viviane grins at me.

I laugh. "And that's so much better."

"Could be worse. That's all I'm saying, doll."

"Thank you, Viv."

"For what?"

"For making me lighten up a bit."

"Lord knows you need it," she teases.

I groan. "I know!"

"So, all joking aside, what do you plan to do now?"

"Just take each day, see what happens. I feel like none of it is really up to me."

"Sure it is. You can decide if you want to be with him. Or not. You can turn him away if it's going to hurt you, Tina."

"Maybe." I fiddle with the silverware again. "Viv, the thing is, I'm not sure I can. If he wants me, I don't think I can say no."

She's quiet a moment. Then, "Tina, you do what you need to do. I can't say that's the best course of action where Jack is involved. But you can't help how you feel."

"I'm discovering that. I guess I've always thought I could. That I could just shut down. And I have, for a very long time. But since I've been here, really since things started with Audrey, I'm figuring out that I can't do that any longer. But maybe it's good for me. Maybe it's what I need. To feel *something,* even if it's not all good."

"Then maybe these experiences are worth something, no matter what happens."

"Yes. I think you're right. I think maybe this is what my therapist, Terry, wanted for me. Not to go through a terrible time, but just to experience…*something.* Because I think if we are really interacting with the world it can't all be good. But that's what life just *is.* And I need to learn how to deal with it."

Viv is smiling at me and nodding in agreement when Patrice comes in and sets the big wooden salad bowl on the table. "What's with all the gabbing? We have a hungry crew to feed. Steaks will be up in a few minutes."

Viviane gives her a grin. "Yes, ma'am."

"Viviane, I could use your help with the potatoes. You always give them a special touch."

"We can talk later," Viv silently mouths at me, and I smile and nod.

It felt good to talk with her, even if I didn't really get anywhere. I am no less excited to see Jack coming into the dining room laden with an armful of salad-dressing bottles. And when I sit, I am all too excited when he sits next to me. In fact, my body is blazing, my cheeks hot. I hope the others will just mark it off as sunburn.

Everyone finds their places at the big table, and we have our usual long, lazy meal, punctuated by conversation about the latest publishing industry gossip.

During dinner Jack's thigh rests against mine, and I have no idea if he's doing this on purpose. He is talking, animated, arguing with Leo over the psychology behind some horror comic book figure, sneaking bites of food to Sid, who has parked himself behind Jack's chair. And when I glance over at him, he smiles, but he smiles at everyone, doesn't he? It tells me nothing.

I can't eat much. My pulse is racing, my stomach in a small knot. My sex damp. Excruciating. But also lovely in some odd way. Exciting.

I can't remember the last time I had this sort of butterflies over anyone.

Dessert tonight is ice cream with a sauce made from fresh raspberries, but I can hardly touch mine.

"You're not eating your ice cream," Jack says.

"I can't," I tell him. "I'm too full."

"Mind if I have yours?"

"No, of course not."

I slide the bowl his way while he grins at me.

God, his teeth are beautiful. Perfect. And his eyes are dancing with the reflected light of the pillar candles Viviane always places in the center of the big table. And I'm on his left, so I can see the dimple in his cheek, the tattoo wrapping around the tight muscle of his upper arm. I want to run my fingers over the ink. I want to sigh in pure girlish admiration, but I don't.

Instead, I watch him eat the ice cream, spooning it between his lush lips, licking the raspberry sauce from the back of the spoon, his tongue darting out, pink and wet. I bite back a groan.

"We should do something special tonight," Viviane announces.

"What do you have in mind?" Kenneth asks. He's on his second bowl of ice cream, too.

"We should have our Exquisite Cadaver night."

"Oh, yes, let's!" Patrice chimes in, more enthusiastic than she usually is about anything.

Leo nods. "Sounds awesome. Let's do it."

"Everyone?" Viviane raises her brows in question, and Kenneth, Jack and I nod our agreement.

Even though all I can think of is getting back to my cottage, being alone with my vibrator. Or with Jack. But I know better than to expect anything.

As we stand up and start clearing the table, Jack brushes past me and whispers, "I'd rather take you back to bed and fuck you until you scream."

Lust is like a sunburst, lighting up my system, dazzling me momentarily. He's gone before I can answer.

We all help clean up, then sit back at the big dining table. Viviane has handed out pads of paper and pencils to each of us. Jack is beside me once more, distracting me with his presence, his whispered words echoing in my head.

*"…fuck you until you scream."*

*Oh, yes…*

"Okay, do you all know how this works?" Viviane asks, pouring more wine for everyone.

I seem to be the only one who hasn't played it before.

"I know it's the old parlor game played by the surrealists, but I could use more information."

"Yes, exactly," Patrice says. "It was started by André Breton and his group, sometime around 1925. Someone begins by writing a word on a piece of paper, then folding it before passing it on so the next person can't see what they've written, building a sentence. The surrealists believed you could create expressionistic poetry in this way. Nicolas Calas characterized this as 'the unconscious reality in the personality of the group' resulting from what Ernst called 'mental cognition.' The surrealists always said that poetry must be made 'by all and not by one.'"

Patrice is as passionate as I've ever seen her, her dark little bird eyes lighting up.

"Didn't they do it with art, too?" Leo asks, and I'm a bit surprised that he knows anything about the surrealists. Maybe I shouldn't be. Maybe everyone has more layers than anyone can easily see from the outside.

"Yes," Patrice answers, really warming to her subject now, I can tell by the flush in her sharp cheeks. "Some of them used drawings, rather than language, using the surrealist principle of metaphoric displacement. The results were fascinating."

"Tell us how you create the sentence again, Patrice," Kenneth says.

"The usual sequence is to write an adjective, a noun, an adverb, a verb, the word *the* and then an adjective and a noun. Thus the famous line *'The exquisite corpse drinks the new wine.'*"

"Thank you, Patrice," Viviane says, smiling to her and patting her hand. "That was very educational."

Patrice beams, her eyes glimmering.

"So, who wants to begin? Kenneth?" Viviane asks.

"Certainly."

He writes on a piece of paper, folds it, hands it to Leo, who does the same, then passes it to Jack. He pauses to consider, taking a long sip from his wineglass, scribbles something in pencil, then passes it to me. I add mine, pass it to Viviane, who hands it off to Patrice.

There is a sense of quiet anticipation around the table. A bunch of writers quietly geeking out over the written word. I love it.

"Okay," Viviane says, "here we have our first one." She reads, "'The fragrant gangster strokes the lovely earth.'"

Everyone laughs.

"Wow," Kenneth says. "That's almost beautiful. Except for the gangster, perhaps."

Leo blushes. "I'll try to be more poetic, keep up with the rest of you."

I'm laughing, too, but all I can think of is that Jack's contribution was the word *strokes*. Why does that make me all shivery inside?

We go again, this time ending up with "The slumberous monster kisses the angry lion." And one more time, the sentence reading "The timeless library releases the lambent fire."

These seem to become increasingly sensual to me, even sexual, particularly Jack's additions: *strokes, kisses, releases*. Or perhaps this is simply where my mind is going. But on the next round the result is "The imprisoned archer arouses the incredulous fire." And then "The imperious neophyte fucks the slumbering harvest."

"Jesus, Jack, are you sure you're not an erotica author?" Leo asks, laughing.

"Maybe I should be," he says, trying to look serious, but his dimple is flashing in his cheek.

*Or maybe he should just take me down to his cottage and fuck me senseless.*

I squirm in my chair. But I don't say this. Of course I don't.

I turn to Jack and smile, as in on the joke as anyone else at the table. Maybe more so. And he winks at me, a sly wink no one else can see, with his head turned in my direction.

I don't know what to think.

I am on fire.

Even worse when Jack strokes my thigh beneath the table. And it is no innocent touch. Oh, no. His fingertips trace a line over my knee, upward, then dipping down, up my inner thigh. I jump a little, turn to look at him, and he is still smiling at me, but he stops, moves his hand away. I turn away, my cheeks heating.

Unbearable, the ache between my thighs, in my breasts.

We play a little longer, switching places at the table, and therefore our parts in constructing the sentences. But Jack manages to use sensual language, the language of sex, every time. I can hardly stand it.

Is he sending some message to me? I'd like to think so, but probably this is just Jack being Jack. I have no idea now how serious he was when he whispered to me earlier, or if he was simply teasing me.

His brief touch was a tease. But again, I have no idea how much intent is behind it, if any.

Torture.

We play for nearly two hours before Kenneth begins to yawn.

"I've had too much wine. I need to get to bed," he says.

"Probably a good idea." Viviane stands up. "I want to hit the big farmer's market in Santa Barbara early tomorrow morning. Anyone coming with me besides Patrice?"

"I was planning to sleep in, but I might make it." Leo says, gathering our discarded bits of paper from the table.

"Wait, let's save these." Jack takes the folded scraps from Leo's hand, who shrugs and hands them over.

"Tina? You coming tomorrow?" Viviane asks.

"Yes. Sure."

"I'll come," Jack says, surprising me.

"I'll stay here with Sid, if you don't mind, Viviane," Kenneth says, yawning once more.

"Of course. All right, we leave by eight. I want to get there before everything is picked over. Everyone to bed. Get a good night's sleep."

Viv looks at me, gives a small nod of her head, a reassuring smile.

Everyone wishes each other a good-night, and I head out-side and down the path to my cottage, not wanting to know if Jack will follow me, invite me to be with him. But my heart is pounding.

The night air is cool, and I pause outside my door to look beyond the gnarled cypress trees. The moon is nearly full, shining down on the dark ocean, its silver orb reflected on the calm water. So beautiful it makes me ache inside. Or maybe it's not the beauty of the nighttime ocean. Maybe I'm just aching.

Sighing, I step up to the door, put my hand on the knob. And freeze when I hear footsteps behind me.

"Bettina."

I turn and find Jack standing there. The moonlight is cast-ing planes of light and shadow on his face, his beard stubble making his features appear darker, more mysterious. But he is a mystery to me, this man, despite his honesty.

"Hi, Jack. What are you doing here?"

He smiles, his teeth a flash of white in all those shadows. "I came to see you, of course."

I hate the hope shimmering in my system, fluttering in my belly. "What do you want, Jack?"

He steps forward. "I want to be with you. That's what I was trying to tell you earlier."

God, that's all I wanted to hear. All I needed.

I don't want to think about how badly I've needed to hear this all day.

He steps forward and I am unable to move as he descends upon me. And that's what it feels like, as though he is closing in. I feel his warmth, the sheer size of him, even before he touches me. My skin is cool from the evening air, but when he wraps his arms around me the heat of his body comes right through his shirt and mine.

He's nuzzling my hair, and I am melting, like some character in a romance novel. But I really cannot stop myself. I don't want to.

"Take me inside," he says. "I meant what I said earlier. I can't wait any longer."

He slides an arm around me and opens the door, pushes me inside. He's taking my clothes off as he walks me backward, until I fall, naked, onto the bed. He reaches to turn on the bedside lamp and I watch as he strips his clothes off, revealing tantalizing bits of smooth, lean muscle, golden skin, and finally, his cock. It's hard and beautiful and I sit up, lean forward, grab his hips and close my mouth over the swollen head.

"Ah, Bettina…" He sighs. "That's perfect, baby."

He tastes like he smells, that clean scent of fresh laundry, mixed with a bit of musk. I take him into my mouth, trying to swallow him, making my eyes water a little. But I don't care. I just want to suck him, to please him, to fill my body with his, somehow.

Using my hands, I pull him in closer, grasping his tight buttocks. I can hear his panting breath, his quiet moans. And I'm growing wetter and wetter, my pussy swelling with need.

Soon enough. Right now I am happy doing just this.

Jack's hands are in my hair, but gently. He's not one of those guys who force their cock down your throat, choking you. No, I'm doing that on my own, at my pace, even if it's making my jaw ache, making it hard to breathe.

"Christ, that's so good," Jack murmurs, his fingers tightening, his hips pumping slowly, his pace sensual. "I don't want to come like this, though. I want to fuck you, baby. I need to. To be inside your hot little cunt. I need it now."

He pushes me down on the bed, his cock slipping from my lips. I would feel almost deprived if he weren't already lowering his body over mine, holding my thighs apart. He has a condom in his hand, and he rolls it on quickly. Then he's pushing my knees up, until my sex is wide open to him.

"I love seeing you like this. Your innocent face, your wet pussy. God, what you do to me, girl."

My body surges, his guttural tone, his words, making me melt a little, my sex burning with liquid heat.

"Come on, Jack. Fuck me like you said you would."

"Oh, I will." He smiles, his face torn and loose with desire.

He is too beautiful like this, looking as if he's going to just come apart. I can't believe I do this to him. It feels glorious. Powerful.

He's holding me down with one hand on my shoulder, almost painfully. His other hand is holding one of my knees, bent nearly to my chest. But I love feeling so much under his command.

"Just do it, Jack," I beg.

He's watching me, his gaze on my face, as he slides the tip of his cock into me.

"Oh…yes, Jack."

Pleasure is like water, filling me up, making me swell with it.

He pushes his way in, slowly, until he's buried deep. He holds my face in his hand, his grip tight. His eyes are glittering, hungry.

"Bettina," he gasps, "I have to really fuck you now. Okay? I mean I have to just fuck you as hard as I can."

"Yes, please. Do it, Jack. I need it, too."

And I do. I need to feel taken over. I need to lose myself in him.

He begins a hard, frantic rhythm, his hips pistoning into me, and I am impaled by his cock, over and over. He's driving pleasure into me, forcing it into my body. And above me, his face is contorted with pleasure, but beautiful, still. More beautiful than ever.

I am at that keen edge, waiting, waiting, when he reaches down between us and pinches my clit. Immediately, I am coming, gasping, writhing, sensation driving deep. My sex clenches around his still-pounding cock, my climax hard and sharp and over quickly.

But he is still fucking me in long, magnificent strokes.

"I love it when you come, baby," he says between gritted teeth. "I want to make you come again."

"God, Jack. I don't…oh…I don't know if I can."

He pauses, his breath coming in ragged pants.

"Do you have a vibrator here?"

"Yes."

"Where?"

"In the nightstand."

He smiles. "Good girl."

Slipping his cock from me, he reaches over and finds my vibrator. He holds the plastic instrument in front of him, examining the length of it with his hand, running his fingertips over the bumps and ridges. "Very nice. Turn over."

I do as he asks. I'm not sure exactly what he has in mind. Not that it matters. My body is burning again simply thinking about it.

"Now spread those beautiful thighs for me. Yes, that's it. God, your ass is superb. Perfect."

He strokes a hand over the flesh there, and I shiver. When he slides his hand lower, brushing my pussy lips, I moan.

"You still want it, don't you? You need more."

"Yes, Jack."

I push back, trying to let him see how much I want him.

He snakes an arm around me, much as he did the first time he fucked me, pulling my body in closer, and his cock slips right in.

"Oh, God."

"What is it, baby?"

"It's just…you feel so good."

It's even better when he lowers the vibrator between my thighs, turns it on and presses it to my clit.

"Oh…"

He begins to fuck me again, his hips moving, pushing his cock deep into my sex. I love how deep he can go in this position, as though he's hitting the very center of my shivering body. Pleasure is like a wave, cresting, receding. His thrusting cock, the vibrator, are almost more than I can take. I am assaulted by sensation. But it is exactly what I need.

He leans in and bites the back of my neck, just hard enough that I wonder vaguely if it'll leave marks. But I love that idea, that he would mark me.

*Make me his.*

*Don't think. Not now.*

No, now I need to give myself over to pleasure. To him.

He moves faster, his breath panting in my ear, his cock driving into me, over and over. And the vibrator humming against my clit, as it grows harder moment by moment.

"Ah, baby, I'm going to come. Come with me."

He tenses and drives into me, harder, faster, pummeling me. And I can't take it; I come, shattering beneath him, *with* him. We moan together, gasp, shudder. My sex is clenching, his cock pulsing inside me, and I can feel the heat of his come through the condom.

Lovely, all of it.

Finally, it stops. We stay where we are for several moments.

I love the feeling of his big body pressed so close to mine, his heart beating against my back. I love the scent of him, especially after sex. I love the silky texture of his sweat on my skin.

I love…

*God, don't go there!*

My heart is hammering in my chest, as much from what I've nearly allowed myself to think as from the sex.

What is wrong with me? I've known this man for a little over a week in person, less than a year online, which hardly counts.

Maybe my head is just spinning with endorphins. Two mind-blowing orgasms in a row will do that, surely.

Yes, my mind is blown.

*God.*

I really have to get my head straightened out. I just need to calm down.

But later. Right now he is still with me, his body so close to mine, our skin stuck together, and it's too good. And when he slips from my body, rolling onto his back, he pulls me into his side, his arm under my shoulders, my head on his chest. Like any other couple after they make love.

I sigh.

"You okay?" he asks.

"Yes, fine. I'm great, actually."

"Mmm, me too."

He kisses the top of my head, and I have to force myself not to read too much into the sweet gesture, into every little thing he does. But my mind is spinning, both good and bad swirling through: bits of images, shadows, worries and those final shimmering waves of endorphins from coming.

I really am a mess.

"Bettina," he says, his voice sleepy.

"What?"

"I can feel you thinking."

It makes me laugh. "Okay, so I'm thinking."

"At least you waited until we were done. I think you did. It felt like it."

"Oh, my brain was turned off the whole time. Don't worry."

"But it turns on the second it's over?"

"Sometimes."

"And?"

"God, Jack."

"What?"

"You don't really want to know what's going through my head."

"Why not?"

I blow out a long breath. "Because you're a guy."

"Thanks for the stereotyping."

"Come on, Jack. You know what I mean."

He turns onto his side, facing me, and holds my chin in his hand, just as he did earlier, forcing me to look at him. "Bettina, I don't believe in sleeping with someone I'm not friends with. And friends talk to each other."

I nod a little. "So…is that why you don't want to be in a relationship? Because it's better just being friends, even with someone you're sexually involved with?"

"Believe me, no woman would want to be in a relationship with me. I'm the classic artist—selfish, totally in my head when I'm working. It's a helluva lot simpler to have sex with a friend. There aren't the same expectations. It keeps everything in perspective."

"I guess it does." I'm quiet a moment, trying to wrap my head around his reasoning. A part of me really wants to understand it, to believe it. "Is that why things work with you and Audrey?"

"That's part of it. It works because we both understand what it's about. And what it's not. There are no false expectations, no demands on each other outside of what happens in bed."

"And yet it bothers you sometimes."

It's his turn to be quiet, thoughtful. "Yeah. Sometimes. But I get over it quickly enough. How about you?"

"You mean the Audrey thing? It's complicated. The whole idea of being with a woman is new to me, so there are other issues involved. She's shown me new sides of myself, and I'm still processing what it all means. And to be with someone like Audrey, someone with such a powerful aura. Someone so…enchanting. She really made my head spin. But I'm not thinking of her so much anymore," I finish quietly.

Leaning in, he brushes a kiss across my lips, pulls back to look at me once more. He reaches out to tuck my hair behind my ear. "I'm not, either."

His tone is so low I can barely hear him. It's almost as though he doesn't want to say it. Or he doesn't want to believe it. But it feels true. Or maybe that's my wishful thinking.

God, I hope not.

My heart is hammering again, and I don't know if I'll be able to calm down this time. He's looking right at me, his eyes a liquid green, intense.

"Jack, please don't say that if you don't mean it."

"I never say anything I don't mean. I don't lie to my friends."

And there it is. That word. *Friends*. I've never cared before about being anything more to a man. But I do now.

*Fuck.*

This cannot be good.

"Bettina?"

"Yes?"

"I want to tell you something. I'm not sure why, but I do."

"Tell me, then."

"It's about Audrey."

"Okay."

I'm not sure I want to hear this. I'm pretty damn sure I don't. I hold my breath, waiting.

"She has come as close to hurting me as any woman has since...since my girl in college. And I haven't let her too close—that's not the problem. Maybe it's just that I want her, you know?"

This is not what I want to hear, but I can't ask him to stop.

"The thing is," he goes on, "nothing has ever made me feel better about her inevitable annual rejection than being with you."

My breath catches in my throat. I can't say anything. What could I say, anyway?

He pulls me in then, and I rest my cheek against his strong chest, trying not to let myself think that this only means I am still just second choice to him. That's not necessarily what he meant, is it? We're both quiet. Apparently he doesn't need me to respond. Which is good, because all I want to do is blurt out that I'm falling for him.

I will not do that.

My pulse is racing, hitching unevenly in my veins. But eventually, as Jack's breathing calms and his heartbeat beneath my cheek grows lazy, my body stills, and my mind follows.

I'm sleepy, spent. And it feels too good here, stretched out beside him. After a few minutes I'm struggling against the drowsiness that wants to overtake me. The darkness is like a blanket around us, just outside of the small circle of light cast by the dim bedside lamp. And I can hear the roar of the ocean through the closed window. It has become familiar to me, comforting. Almost as comforting as Jack's quiet, warm body next to mine. Eventually, I sleep.

# CHAPTER TEN

I wake in the dark. Jack must have turned off the light.

I know right away he's gone. But he's covered me with the throw blanket that normally sits on the back of the chair. Sweet, but not too sweet. He is, after all, gone. Slinking out in the middle of the night.

It's grown cold and I shiver. Pulling the small cotton throw around my bare shoulders, I get up and look out the window. It's dark, and I can't see anything but the faint amber glow from Jack's porch light.

I hate that I feel so damn empty. I know better. It's not as though I'm some dreamy teenager with her first crush. But I'm behaving as though I am. I hate that I can't seem to control how I feel. I couldn't with Audrey, and now I can't with Jack.

Is this supposed to be progress?

Anger simmers in my veins, suddenly.

I've been through all this fucking therapy, been told for months that I need to learn to open up again, to feel. But if this is where it leads me, this vacant sense of *aloneness,* maybe I was better off before, safely shut down.

But that can't be right, either.

*Fuck.*

I climb back into my empty bed, determined to sleep. I lay there for what feels like hours, my body tense, aching. I'm still awake as the sun begins to rise. But finally, my dry, stinging eyes close, and I fall into an exhausted, dreamless slumber.

"Bettina, wake up!"

It's Audrey. She's climbing onto the bed, looking fresh-faced and alert.

"What time is it?"

"Seven-thirty. You'd better get up if you're coming to the farmer's market."

"Maybe I'll stay here."

"Oh, come on. Come with us. It'll be fun."

My eyes feel glued together, but she's right, I should go. It'll be better than sitting here, brooding.

"Okay. I'm getting up."

I sit up, and the blanket drops away, and I am all too aware of my bare breasts. But it's not as though Audrey hasn't seen me naked before, and I feel too foolish to cover up. Foolish and a little turned on. I'm hoping she doesn't notice, or that she writes off my hard nipples as a reaction to the cool morning air.

But she hops up and heads toward the door. "We leave in half an hour. Hurry!"

I take a quick shower, assessing my sore muscles. My head aches, and my eyes have that scratchy feeling I always get when I've slept too little. Even after my shower, I'm still in a dream state as I pull on a pair of white capri-length cargo shorts and a tank top the same shade as the ocean in the afternoon. Looking into the bathroom mirror as I try to subdue my unruly hair into some sort of order, I can see that the color of the tank makes my gray eyes look more blue than usual. My eyes look enormous to me, the pupils large and round, and there are shadows underneath. I feel shadowed this morning.

*Yes, better to get out, just shake this off.*

I slip into a pair of flip-flops and make my way groggily to the main house, hoping for coffee. But when I get there everyone is already loading into Viviane's SUV, everyone being Viviane, Patrice, Leo and Audrey.

Leo, Audrey and I ride in the back, with Audrey in the middle, and I'm nervous, edgy. I haven't really spoken to her since she went off with Charles. I feel as if I should say something, but maybe later, when we have a moment alone. Not that I know what to say.

Scenery flashes by, a blur of brilliant colors in the morning sun, everything the cool tones of the sea: the green of the cypress and eucalyptus trees, the blazing blue sky. It's going to be hot today, but I can't wait to get to town and get my hands on a cup of coffee. Meanwhile, I'm sort of half-asleep, unable to think clearly, which is, perhaps, a good thing. I don't want to think too much right now. There's far too much to think about and I'd rather avoid it this morning.

We arrive in downtown Santa Barbara. I haven't seen much of it, and it's a pretty town. The buildings are all older architecture, a mix of old brick and early-twentieth stone and plaster, with iron benches on the sidewalks, and small, leafy trees. There are galleries and cafés everywhere, as there are in any California coastal tourist town, but this place has a calm, quiet feel to it. When I look down the long main street I can see the ocean, glinting pale and silvery in the morning sunlight.

We park two blocks away in a small open parking lot. As we all spill out of the car, Audrey leans over and whispers in my ear, "You smell like sex, Bettina."

She pulls away and flashes me a grin, and I blush, but don't say anything.

Has Jack already talked to her this morning? Or did he go from my bed to hers late last night? But no, she was next door with Charles, wasn't she?

I realize I have no idea.

I realize I have no right to question any of it.

I am in a lousy mood.

I lag behind the others a bit as we make our way down the street toward the section of Santa Barbara Avenue that's roped off for the farmer's market. White awnings cover the booths, but once we get right in there it's full of color. Produce, flowers, jars of homemade jam and honey, freshly baked bread. Finally, I see the coffee cart.

"I need to stop here," I call out.

"Me, too," Leo says, getting in line.

Viviane waves her hand absently; she and Patrice are bent over a table loaded with peaches, and Patrice is starting to bargain with the vendor already. I stand in line behind Leo, the scent of coffee nearly making me salivate. Luckily, he is quiet this morning. I don't think I can manage a normal conversation.

I wait, rubbing my eyes, only vaguely aware of my surroundings, obsessed with the idea of getting some caffeine into my system. I feel cranky and impatient. Too little sleep never agrees with me, but I feel worse than I should this morning. I don't want to think about why. I don't want to think at all.

A hand on my shoulder, and I turn to find Audrey has joined me. She slides her arm around my shoulders. "So," she says quietly, "are you going to tell me?"

"Tell you what?" I know exactly what she means, of course.

"About you and Jack."

"You already seem to know."

"Oh, we are tight-lipped this morning, aren't we?"

She's smiling, but I don't feel like making jokes. I just shrug.

"Okay, babe," she says. "You have every right not to share with me. But that doesn't mean I won't share with you." She grins at me, moves in closer and whispers, "Charles is amazing! The man can go forever. I can hardly walk. And he's the nicest guy. I think I really like him."

I imagine that's as committal as Audrey ever gets about anyone.

I really am cranky this morning.

"That's nice, Audrey," I tell her.

She looks at me, blinks, and there's hurt on her face.

"God, I'm sorry, Audrey. I'm just tired, I guess."

"It's okay." She's all softness again as she strokes my hair, asks, "Are you all right?"

"Yes. I guess so."

"Poor baby. Don't let him get to you. Don't let anyone get to you. Remember?"

"I remember."

I think back to our conversation, where she told me not to let anyone have that kind of power over me, and she's right. Jack said much the same thing to me. And I have to stop and wonder, since they are both telling me this, if that's what I do—let people have power over me—if it's so obvious.

She leans closer, her lips right next to my ear, and says, "Not anyone but me," and she kisses my cheek softly.

I shiver, desire like a tiny shard in my skin, prickling, tingling. Lighting me up.

But she's gone a moment later, moving toward one of the booths, stooping to examine a bunch of sunflowers. I pull in a breath, try not to stammer when Leo turns around and asks me if I'm just ordering coffee or some pastries, too.

"I'm not really hungry. The others might want something, though."

"Yeah, hold my place and I'll find out."

I close my eyes, commanding my heart to stop pounding, my stomach to stop fluttering.

Leo comes back and slips into line behind me, and I turn around to ask him what we should order for everyone. Only it's not Leo. It's Jack.

"Wh-what are you doing here?"

God, why must I talk like an idiot?

He smiles, that dazzling flash of strong, white teeth, and I am as smitten as I've ever been.

*Damn it.*

"I went for an early drive this morning and missed you guys leaving. Kenneth told me you'd come here."

"Ah."

"You look tired."

"I am."

"Sorry if I kept you up late."

He smiles again, but this time I'm not falling for it. At least, I'm pretending not to.

"Jack, not everything is about you."

"Okay…"

He shoves his hands into the pockets of his green cargo shorts and shrugs, looking down at the ground for a moment, then back up at me. And I can see that perhaps some of his cockiness is for show, something to protect him.

I feel like a total bitch, and I hate it.

"I'm sorry. I'm just…I was up a lot last night. I'm just tired, as you said. I'll be better once I've had some coffee."

"It's okay."

He rests a hand on my arm, and the heat of him burns right into my skin. How can I be so aroused and so irritated at the same time?

"I'm going to find that woman who sells the fresh-squeezed orange juice. Has anyone mentioned seeing her here again this year?" he asks.

"I don't think so. I don't know."

I just want him to go. I want some time to wake up, to try to get my head on straight. To get over seeing Jack and Audrey in the same place. It's been difficult ever since the three of us slept together. And things are getting more and more confusing for me all the time. Maybe I should just go home to Seattle, stop all this. Audrey. Jack.

But I know I have no intention of doing that.

"Okay. I'll wander around and see you later," Jack says.

"Okay. Sure. See you later."

He moves away, his hand slipping from my arm, stroking my skin, and I don't know if he meant it to be a sensual touch, but it is.

I watch him walk off, the way his broad shoulders move beneath the thin cotton of his T-shirt, his lazy gait, the breeze ruffling his dark hair. I let out a small, girlish sigh.

"Hey, you okay?" Leo asks, stepping back into line with me.

Why is everyone asking me that this morning?

"Yes, fine. I just wish this line would move faster."

"Looks like we're up next. No worries."

I ask for my large latte and Leo orders for the group: coffee and some lovely, fresh croissants. I add too much sugar to the steaming paper cup, blowing on it until I can sip the brew without scalding my tongue.

Audrey comes up beside me again, but this time I welcome her presence. We're walking in between the rows of stalls, a little behind Viviane and Patrice, who are clearly on a mission with the produce vendors.

"Better?" Audrey asks.

"Yes, thanks. The coffee is helping. More than I thought it would. The heat of it, even the scent, just makes me feel better."

"That's good." She bumps my hip with hers, smiling at me, and I smile back.

"I wonder sometimes how this one little thing, a good cup of coffee, can soothe me so much. It's not just that it wakes me up. Do you know what I mean?"

She nods, looping her hand through my free arm. "Growing up, my mom only drank coffee when we went out to dinner. I don't know why. But that was her ritual. Just like mine is always eating popcorn at the movies. No matter how stale or horrible it is, I have to have it."

I sip from my cup, thinking. "My parents drank coffee every morning, but it was usually on the run, on their way out to work. I remember, though, on Sundays, we'd sit around the kitchen table reading. It was one of the few times we all spent together on any regular basis, and it always smelled of coffee."

"Maybe that's why it comforts you," Audrey says. "It's familiar. It's attached to a ritual."

"Maybe."

"I think so much of how we respond to things, think about things, operate in our everyday lives, is about ritual. It happens a lot more than most people realize. Waking up, having breakfast, washing our hair. Most people do the same things in the same order each day."

"I know I do. I'm a little OCD, which I knew even before my therapist told me so. But I'm surprised to hear you do."

"Why?"

"Because you seem to be such a…free spirit. And I'm sorry to use such a clichéd term, but I can't think of anything else."

"Oh, I have my rituals. I'm fairly obsessive over them, actually. I have to have my toenails painted at all times. They've been painted every day of my life since I was sixteen. And I have to wash my hair every day. I can't stand not to."

"It's beautiful, your hair," I say, looking at it, the sun glinting in blue and gold on the nearly black strands of her long ponytail.

Audrey smiles at me, pulling me closer, her fingers stroking the back of my hand. My body is pressed into the plush side of her breast. And just like that our easy conversation has turned into something more. With her smoky-blue gaze on mine, she lifts my hand to her lips, brushes them over the skin, her tongue darting out, hot and wet.

Shocking, how good it feels, how pleasure runs from the back of my hand to my sex instantly. My breasts are aching, needing to be touched. I don't know what to do, how to react. Did anyone see that? Does it even matter?

I pull my hand away and sip my coffee, gulping too fast, and begin to cough.

She pats me on the back. "You all right?"

"Yes, I'm okay now. Thanks."

"Audrey," Viviane calls, "come look at these strawberries. I know how you love them."

Another quick smile, then she's gone, leaving me standing there with my pulse hammering in my veins.

I don't want her to be able to do this to me. Things are confusing enough with Jack. As much as I want to be with Jack, I still *want* Audrey. I don't understand it.

We stay for maybe another hour, wandering the stalls, Viviane and Patrice crowing over the gorgeous fruits and vegetables, the bargains. They've loaded Leo up with two heavy canvas bags as we walk back to the car. In the parking lot, Jack finds us. I'd almost forgotten he was there.

No, that's a lie. But I'd certainly tried to.

"Why don't you ride with me, Bettina," he asks, surprising me. "I'd rather not do the drive by myself. And I want to ask you some questions about a story idea I have. It's something I think you can help me brainstorm."

"Why me?" I ask.

"Oh, go with him," Audrey says. "It's too beautiful a day to drive up the coast alone. Go on, Bettina."

She gives me a gentle shove in his direction, just her small hand on my back, and I feel the heat of her in my bones. I turn to look at her, but her smile is entirely guileless.

Jack grabs my hand. "Come on," he says, then more quietly, "I promise not to bite."

I'm not so sure of that, but I go, anyway.

His dusty black truck is parked nearby, in the same lot. Jack silently holds the door for me. The truck is huge, and I have to hang on and pull myself up onto the seat. I set my small Indian-cotton purse down on the seat between us as Jack goes to the other side, climbs in and starts the engine.

We pull out of the lot and head to the 101, making our way back up the coast toward the small town of Bacara and Viviane's house. Jack has turned the stereo on, and the cab of the truck is filled with the low murmur of a Puccini opera. Not quite what I expected, but there are a lot of things about Jack that surprise me. It's one of the things I find most interesting about him. But it also makes me nervous. Except when I'm in bed with him. Then everything just flows and I am as unselfconscious as I've ever been in my life. Wanton.

I slip my sunglasses on and from the corner of my eye I look surreptitiously at his profile, which is outlined against the noontime sun shining over the ocean to our left. The sky is a brilliant, incredible blue, the ocean that lovely mixture of green and gray, going darker as my eye follows it out toward the horizon. In the far distance is the tiny silhouette of a ship. But my eye is drawn back to Jack when he turns his head, catching me watching him.

"Hey, Bettina," he says, not really saying anything at all, but his voice is low, husky, and it sends shivers through me.

"Hey," I answer.

"I saw you and Audrey hanging out today."

"Did you? I didn't see you after you left this morning."

"I was around. I didn't want to bother you."

"You wouldn't have bothered me."

"No?" he asks, raising one brow at me before turning back to the road. "You didn't give me that impression before you had your coffee."

"Yes, well, I hadn't had my coffee yet."

"Yeah, so you said." He's quiet a moment, just driving. "Was that it, Bettina?"

"Was what…what?"

He lets out a long sigh. "Okay. We can talk about something else. But you sure are stubborn."

I smile at him. "I can be. I like to think of it as one of my more charming qualities."

He laughs, and just like that, the tension is gone. I feel my shoulders dropping, my neck relaxing, even my jaw.

"So, no bags from the farmer's market?" he asks me.

"Nope. Viviane and Patrice are kind of territorial over the produce."

"Yeah, they are."

"I don't mind. I just like going, looking at everything, watching the people."

"I like to people watch, too. It's a favorite pastime of writers, I think."

"It is. How else are we going to create our characters if we don't have an enormous well of personalities to draw from? I love to watch people in places like that and make up stories about them. I like to try to figure out what goes on in everyone's head."

"We're a weird lot, aren't we?" He's grinning, and I find myself wishing I were on his other side, so I could see the dimple flashing in his cheek.

"Yes. We do seem to be. Most of the writers I know have these strange childhood stories. Or at least, the way we respond to things that happened in our childhoods is maybe a little different from the average person's."

"You think we're more sensitive?" he asks.

"I've always thought so. Maybe all creative personalities are. Painters, musicians. Maybe that's why we're able to do what we do, because we attach more emotion to things than others do. I don't know, maybe I'm being presumptuous."

"No, I think you're onto something. But I think it's good stuff as well as the bad that we feel more of."

"What good stuff have you responded strongly to in your life, Jack?" I ask him.

"Ah, that's easy. My sisters."

"I didn't know you had sisters."

"Eliza and Katie. They're twins, four years younger than I am."

"I always wanted to have a sister."

"Oh, don't get me wrong. They're a pain in the ass."

I can hear the pride, the affection, in his voice.

"So, you're close?"

He nods. "They're too far away. I don't like that. I can't keep an eye on them from a distance, which I remind them of regularly. It drives them crazy, especially since I'm not actually willing to move to be closer, so they think I'm being hypocritical. Maybe I am. And I know I go overboard in wanting to protect them. If we lived in the same city they'd really learn to hate me. Katie came to Portland for a few months, but she fell for a guy in L.A. and moved away. She's been with him ever since. They got married last year, so I guess it's a good thing. She's a teacher, like my mother was. Eliza still lives in the small town in Oregon where we were raised. She writes, too. Children's books."

"I didn't know you were raised in Oregon. I got the impression you've only been in Portland a few years."

"About eight years. But I was raised in Coos Bay, right on the Pacific. It's beautiful country, but too quiet for me. I spent too many years traveling to go back there. But I've always loved the ocean. That's one reason I love to come here every summer."

"Where have you been, Jack?" I ask him, wanting to know. Wanting to know everything, suddenly.

I can't get enough of him, in any way, on any level. And it's so cozy in the cab of his truck, with the music playing softly, the brilliant day outside warming me. And Jack opening up to me, telling me about his life.

"All over Europe. Spain, Germany, Italy, Czech Republic. I did that right before college, did the hostel-and-backpack thing, then went back a few years ago once I started to make money off my writing. I saw France and Italy again. It was like a whole new experience, staying in hotels. I'm still not sure which trip I liked better. I've also spent some time in Costa Rica, Argentina, Brazil. And I've been to Japan. Really loved Kyoto."

"You set one of your books there. The one that came out two years ago."

"Yeah." He turns his head, giving me a strange look, as though he thinks it's odd I would know.

"What's your favorite place?" I ask him.

"There's something I like about every place I've been, but you know, I love New Orleans. That city is just magic. But it's too hot to live there. I like Portland. I like the fog, the grayness of it. I like the loneliness of it. The sadness. Maybe that makes me macabre."

"Well, I don't think that's what makes you macabre." I laugh and he turns to flash one of his dazzling grins at me. "But that's one of the things I love about Seattle, too. I love feeling insulated by the fog and the gray and the rain. I think it's the only sort of place I could live."

"So, what about you, Bettina? Where have you been?"

"Not far. I'm just now getting to a point in my life where I'm feeling brave enough to see something of the world. This trip is sort of where I'm starting."

"You mean you've never been out of Seattle?"

"Not much. I've gone up to Victoria a few times. I've been to San Francisco. I loved it there. It has my fog." I laugh again, and he laughs with me, and I feel too much that we are on the same page, somehow.

*Don't get used to it.*

"You have to travel, Bettina. You absolutely have to do it."

"I know. I hope to." I shift in my seat, my hand finding the cool glass of the window, my fingertips resting there.

"No, you can't hope to. You have to *make* it happen." His voice is certain, passionate. He glances over at me, his eyes a blaze of green, before focusing on the road once more. "We should go somewhere. We should take off from here at the end of the summer and just go. Where would you like to see?"

I'm certain he's not serious, so I play along.

"I'd like to see New Orleans, actually. I hear the food there is fantastic."

"It is. And the architecture is incredible. There's an aura about that city that's unlike any other place in the world. It's sad and tragic and romantic."

Why does my heart pound hearing him say that last word?

I am being totally ridiculous. Just because a man like Jack can say the word romantic doesn't mean he is. Except that he is.

*Damn it.*

The passion with which he speaks about his travels, his fierce love for his sisters, both of these things tell me he isn't unable to love. So why is it he can't love a woman, other than in the sort of distracted way he loves Audrey?

Horrible twist in my stomach at that thought. But I have to know more.

"How long have you and Audrey been coming to these retreats?" I ask, then wish I'd kept my mouth shut.

"I've been coming for about six years, Audrey for three." He's quiet a moment. Then, "But what you really want to know is how long Audrey and I have been sleeping together. Isn't that it, Bettina?"

The knot in my stomach pulls tighter. I don't want to admit this to him. I don't want to admit it to myself. But it's too late, isn't it?

"Yes, I suppose so. I know it's none of my business."

"You're right, it's not," he says, though not unkindly. "But I don't mind telling you. We've been together off and on ever since we met. It's gotten to be habit, almost. I'm beginning to wonder if it's more that than anything else at this point."

He looks thoughtful, his dark brows drawn together. I have to force myself not to read too much into this.

I am just so surprised at how he's opening up to me, how he seems to really *talk* to me. I'm not used to men doing this. But I have to stop and ask myself if maybe I haven't been open to it myself, if I haven't allowed that in my life because I've been too busy protecting myself. Until now.

What's changed for me? Is it about who Jack is? Is it about having been in therapy this long, having done some of the inside work?

I think it's all that. But I also think some of it is about Audrey. About her opening me up in a new way, the power of her charm—if you want to call it that, and I don't know what else to call it—sort of forcing me to open up. And not just sexually, but some inner part of myself. Something about her has taught me to take a few risks.

I'm still pretty sure falling for Jack is a poor risk to take. One guaranteed to leave me in the dust. And I'm still struggling with this. I can't figure out if I should stop myself or not. Or if I even can.

"You're quiet," Jack says.

"I'm thinking."

"About?"

I laugh. "Do you always do that? Insist on knowing what goes on in everyone's head?"

He turns to me, smiling. He is so damn beautiful, his eyes that deep mossy green in the afternoon light. "Yeah. I always do. You might as well get used to it."

He says this as though he'll be around. As though we really will travel together, go to New Orleans at the end of the summer. As though he wants to spend more time with me. But on what terms?

How would I feel if Audrey was invited along, too? It's entirely possible.

I don't even want to consider that.

The future is all too uncertain, and I hate it. I like every-thing to be nice and tidy and predictable, everything in its place. But nothing about Jack—or Audrey—or my feelings or experiences with either of them, is at all tidy. Which is probably why it's been so powerful for me.

Or maybe I'm simply overthinking the hell out of everything.

The sun is blazing when we pull into Viviane's driveway. Her SUV is already parked, and it looks as if everything has been unloaded. I start to get out, but Jack puts a hand on my arm. I shiver with the heat of his fingertips on my bare skin, my sex going damp at this simple touch.

"Want to go for a swim?" he asks me. "It's too hot to stay inside, or to sit on the beach and write."

He's smiling at me, his palm still warm on my skin, so I can hardly say no. I nod my head.

"Yes. I'd love to swim."

I'd love to do anything that involves him, frankly.

We get out and pass by the kitchen windows. Everyone is inside, talking, preparing lunch, probably. I'm a little hungry, but I'd rather be alone with Jack.

We walk around the side of the house, coming out on the edge of the back patio, and take the path to the guest cottages, where Jack leaves me with a wave to get changed.

Inside my cottage, I strip quickly, and find my panties damp. I want him again. Need to have him pretty damn soon or I may lose my goddamn mind.

I slip into my favorite bikini, which is a silvery gray with some dark blue embroidery on it, slather sunblock onto my skin. I'm more tanned than I've ever been in my life, but still fairly pale compared to Jack. Or Audrey. I try not to think of her as I grab the big, colorful beach towel I bought before I left Seattle and head outside.

Jack hasn't reached the beach yet, so I find a soft spot in the sand and lay my towel down, sit and look out at the water.

This place is beautiful, serene. But every nerve in my body, my brain, is lit up with that keen edge of awareness as I wait for Jack to arrive.

When he does I go sort of tense all over, but in some lovely way. There is something entirely sensual about being alone on the beach with him, both of us half-naked in our swimsuits. He sits next to me, close enough that I can smell his skin, which smells a bit of soap from his morning shower still, and very faintly of sweat. But I like it.

I like him.

I more than like him.

I sound like a fourteen-year-old in my head.

"I brought a bottle of water for you," Jack says, handing it to me.

"Thanks." I rub my thumb over the cool moisture clinging to the clear plastic.

"You're thoughtful today," he says.

"Yes."

I turn to him, and he's facing the water. Behind his dark sunglasses his eyes are narrowed. I can't tell what he's thinking.

"Jack, I'm sorry I'm being so moody."

He shrugs, a magnificent ripple of shoulders. The skin there is tanned a little more than elsewhere on his body, with a few freckles. I want to touch them, put my fingertips on those small spots, trace lines from one to another. I shiver, clench my hands around my water bottle.

"Everyone's allowed an off day. Maybe you just need some exercise. Come on. Let's get in the water."

He grabs my hand and pulls me up. I go without protest, quiet until he drags me into the ocean, which is a little too cool against my skin, and I yelp.

Jack laughs. "Come on. It's not so bad."

"I know. I'm just a big baby about it."

"Here, I'll help."

He pulls my body close to his as he takes us deeper, reminding me of that day in the water with Audrey, but soon enough I forget all about her as the waves rush around us, pushing at the small of my back. Through his sunglasses I can see that his gaze is on my face. His holds a small smile. And I am entranced by him, as though he's put some spell on me.

He is every bit as magical as Audrey, in his way. My body melts all over as he pulls me closer, holding me tighter. I can smell sun and salt on him, that lovely whiff of his sweat. And when he leans in and kisses me, it is as though the impact of his lips on mine wipes out everything else.

His kiss is hot, powerful, his tongue delving into my mouth. I taste him, swallow him up, and he does the same to me. We are on exactly that same sensual page, and this time I know I am not imagining it.

Overwhelming. Beautiful.

The ocean flows and recedes around us and I no longer feel the cold. The sun overhead is not nearly as brilliant as the heat blooming between us. And the entire earth just falls away, leaving nothing but the two of us. No sand, no sea. Just our bodies pressed together, our lips, our hands.

I am lost once more.

# CHAPTER ELEVEN

A wave crashes into us, knocking us over, the salty water in my eyes, my mouth, and I am immediately back in my body. Jack hangs on to me, pulling my head up from beneath the water.

"I've got you," he says. "You okay?"

"Yes."

And I am. I want to laugh at the absurdity of it, that magical moment, just killed.

Or maybe not.

Jack pulls me back into him, and I can feel his erection hard against my belly.

"Good," he says. "Because I have plans for you, girl."

He presses his hips into me, leans down and kisses my neck, and pulls me a little deeper, until we are in the water up to our necks, my body floating in his embrace, my feet unable to touch the bottom. His hands reach beneath the sea and wrap my legs around his waist, and I feel open to him, even with my bikini on, keeping my not-quite-naked sex from touching him.

"Bettina," he whispers into my ear, but if he says anything else it is lost in the ocean's thunder. In my blossoming need.

I'm quiet as he reaches down between us and slips his fingers inside me. Just a small gasp from between my lips as he begins to pump, his fingers curled to hit my G-spot, his thumb pressing hard on my clit.

I would be soaking wet if I weren't already, the sea washing away my juices, other than what hides inside of me, making his hand slippery, deep in my pussy.

His other hand is pushing my bathing suit top to one side, then cupping my breast, his fingers pulling on my nipple. Pleasure is like the water, heavy in my body, and I float on it, on the waves washing through me.

He pumps faster, and I arch my hips into his hand.

"Harder, Jack."

"I need to make you come, baby."

I feel helpless, weightless, his body and the salt of the water holding me up. My sex is beginning to clench already, but I don't want this to be over so soon. I bear down on his fingers, bury my face in his shoulder, taste the salt water on his skin. And still he pumps harder, faster, his finger squeezing my nipple. It hurts. And it feels amazing, pleasure shafting from my breast to my sex. Everything feels swollen with need: my nipples, my pussy. My clit is rock hard. I'm going to come.

When I do it's with a hard jerk, and my body spasms all over. I cry out, but it's lost in the sound of the gulls crying overhead, in the pounding of the surf. Pleasure flows through me, wave upon wave, hot and wet. The taste of his skin is in my mouth, some elemental sense of his fingers inside my body, as though I am hyperaware even as I'm coming, my climax fierce, unraveling me.

"Ah, that was good, baby," Jack tells me as the last shudders roll through me.

He shifts me, moving my legs down a little lower, closer to his body, until I feel his rigid cock poking at me through his swim trunks and my bikini. I want him to fuck me, but I don't know how it's possible, out here in the ocean.

"Jack, I want you to come, too," I tell him when I can speak again.

"Here, Bettina." His voice is rough as he guides my hand inside his shorts, and his cock fills my palm. So hard and full, and I want him inside me so badly it hurts, my sex pulsing, filling with need once more.

"That's so good," he growls in my ear. "Let me come into your hand."

"Yes," I gasp, wrapping my fingers around him, and stroking.

"Hey, Jack! Bettina!"

*Fuck.*

Audrey is waving to us from the shore. Charles is with her. I let go, but Jack murmurs to me, "No, don't stop," and guides my hand back to his cock.

I keep stroking him, and he smiles at me before turning his head and yelling back to Audrey, "Hi!"

"God, Jack," I whisper.

"Just keep going."

He pushes my body from his and turns, until I am behind him, my arm wrapped around his waist, my hand fisted around his cock. His hips pump into my palm, between my grasping fingers.

"What's up?" he yells to Audrey and Charles.

"We just wanted to say hello," Charles yells. "How's the water?"

"Great! Isn't it, Bettina?"

He slips a hand behind him, dipping beneath my suit, and

immediately finds my hungry sex once more, pressing his fingers into me in one hard thrust.

I nod, trying not to gasp. I can't speak. He's really pushing into my hand now, his cock growing harder by the second. And I love it, his silky, hard flesh, his fingers moving inside me, the knowledge that I am doing this to him, that he is doing this to me. That a few yards away people are watching us, without knowing. Or maybe they do. I don't care. I pump him harder, hear his quiet groan above the crashing waves, and smile.

"Maybe we should join you," Charles yells to us. But Audrey slips an arm through his, whispers something in his ear, making him smile. "Perhaps another time," he says.

"We'll see you guys later!" Audrey calls, and she and Charles wave again and turn to go.

As we watch their retreating backs, Jack groans, his hips jerking hard, and he comes. Heat fills my hand for a moment before the sea takes it away. His fingers slide from my pussy, and he turns me again in the water until he's facing me once more.

He holds me tight as we float, both of us panting a little.

"I need to really fuck you," he tells me, his green gaze on my face, his brows drawing together. There is something there, maybe just the aftermath of his orgasm. It's too hard to tell, with my heart still pounding so fiercely I can barely breathe. "I need to rest first," he says, "but then I need to be inside you. Come with me, Bettina. I want you naked on my bed, laid out on the sheets so I can see you."

"Yes…"

"Let's go."

We make our way out of the water, the waves dragging at us, as though they want to reclaim us, make us part of the sea. And I'm not so sure I'd mind, to be lost on the ocean with Jack.

I feel weak as I stagger onto the sand. Jack grabs my towel and his, our water bottles, and somehow manages to juggle it all so he can hold on to my hand as we walk to his cottage.

Once in the shade of the bent cypress trees, I'm cold, shivering, even in the afternoon heat. We go into his cottage, and he drops everything and brings a towel from the bathroom, strips my suit off and dries me.

He is tender with me, gentle, as he kneels in front of me to rub my legs with the towel. The rough texture of it is wonderful on my skin, the sight of his damp, dark curls, his strong back. He pauses to kiss my belly, and I am wet again, needing him.

Standing, he runs the towel over my shoulders, then my breasts, and my nipples go hard.

"I love your breasts," he says, palming them, and I surge into him, my eyes fluttering closed.

I can't get enough of him. I really can't.

He lets me go and quickly dries himself, and I can see that his cock is half-hard again already.

I want him. So badly my mouth is watering, my sex clenching, my thighs tense.

He comes up close to me and begins to dry my hair with the damp towel. But I just want him to finish. I want to be laid out on his bed, as he said. I want him to fuck me there.

Finally, he drops the towel.

"Lie down with me, girl."

He takes my hand and pulls me with him onto the bed, onto my back, the cotton quilt cool and soft on my naked flesh. I think he's going to spread my thighs, to settle between them. But he lies on his back, one hand in mine.

"Christ, I'm tired," he says, closing his eyes.

I am filled with disappointment. Which doesn't really make sense. At least he wanted me here with him.

But my body is aching, tight with need.

I take a deep breath, try to calm down.

"Do you want to nap?" I ask him.

"A nap would be perfect. I need to sleep for a while."

"Should I go?"

"What? No, of course not."

His hand grips mine tighter. My chest knots up and suddenly I want to cry.

What the hell is wrong with me?

I bite my lip, try to breathe, deep calming breaths: in through my nose, out through my mouth, as I learned from the antianxiety tapes my therapist gave me.

"Bettina, tell me a story," Jack murmurs, his voice heavy with sleep.

"A story? What do you mean?"

"Yeah. About you. A true story. Something important."

Am I imagining how intimate a situation this is? Because that's what it feels like. And it's good and terrifying at the same time.

*Calm down.*

"Okay. Let me think a minute."

What bit of truth do I want to tell him about? I find I want to tell him everything. Partly as a sort of experiment, to see if he'll still want me. And partly simply because I want him to *know*.

"Okay. Here's a true story about me, Jack. I've been in therapy for almost two years."

"Mmm…why?"

"Because my writerly neurosis goes beyond the point where it's healthy. Because for much of my adult life I've barely been able to force myself to leave the house most days. Because I have difficulty with intimacy. Because while I've done my share of sleeping around, I do it for the wrong reasons. And I don't allow myself to really care for anyone but a handful of old and loyal friends."

"What else?"

I laugh, a small, harsh sound. "Isn't that enough?"

"I don't know. I've never been to therapy."

"Yes, it's enough."

"I guess it's enough if the therapy helps."

"Yes."

"So, does it help?"

"Yes, it has. Quite a lot. I doubt I'd be here now if it didn't."

"Then I'm glad. I'm glad it makes you feel better. I'm glad you're here."

He pulls my hand to his lips, kisses the back of it, drops it to his chest. And I lie there with my heart hammering.

Will he think I'm crazy? Will he judge me? But it doesn't seem as if he's judging me. Or maybe he's already half-asleep and hasn't really heard me.

Maybe I need to give him more credit.

His breathing shifts, becomes shallower, and I know he's drifting into sleep. I doubt I'll be able to sleep, with Jack lying next to me, both of us naked, the afternoon sun shafting through the window, making the dust motes dance, lighting up his beautiful skin in a warm golden glow.

His lashes are so dark against his cheeks. So long, for a man. I want to touch them, to run my fingers over the tips. But I don't do it. Instead I lie still beside him and watch him breathe, the gentle rise and fall of his chest, understanding how alive he is. He is more alive than anyone I've ever known. Stronger. Even more so than Audrey.

It always comes back to her, somehow. I don't know how

to make it stop. Maybe it won't stop until I'm away from this place. But that'll mean I'll be away from Jack, too.

*Too soon to think about that.*

No, right now I'm here with him. He is right here next to me, and anything is possible. I'd like to believe that, anyway. Maybe I will, if even for a while. Maybe I need to try to stop all my usual dissection and enjoy what's happening here.

I think about some of the teachings of the Tao I've read about in my search for serenity. About letting go the inevitable, not struggling against it, because doing so serves no purpose other than to exhaust me. Maybe now would be a good time to put that principle into practice.

Because the truth is, I am absolutely powerless over what Jack does or thinks, or how he feels about me. I hate it, but that's the reality of the situation.

Somehow, this idea comforts me, rather than making me feel more frustrated, and I bask in that comfort as I let myself drift off.

Plenty of time to dwell on my control issues tomorrow.

When I wake up, the sun is setting in a blaze of orange and pink. The colors are flooding in through the window. I realize immediately that I am alone on the bed. I sit up.

"Hey."

Jack is standing there, smiling at me, and I am awash in relief.

He's dressed in a pair of army-green board shorts and nothing else. Lovely.

"I went up to the house and grabbed a picnic. I didn't want you to get dressed. I didn't want you to leave my bed."

I sit up, and he frowns at me, although he doesn't look too serious about it.

"Just stay there," he says.

"What? Why?"

"Don't move. Hang on."

He goes to the small dresser on one side of the room, rummages around a little, comes back with a camera in his hand. It's not one of those small digitals everyone uses, it's the real thing, an old Olympus, I can see from the name engraved on the front, with a long, heavy lens.

"Oh, no," I tell him, grabbing a pillow and pulling it over the front of my body.

"Why not? You're too damn beautiful, Bettina. And this light is flawless. Come on. Just a few shots."

"I'm not beautiful," I say, hugging the pillow tighter.

His brows draw together. "You really don't know how beautiful you are, do you?"

He's coming closer, moving slowly across the floor, his bare feet scuffing on the wood.

I shake my head. "I'm not."

"But you are." His voice has gone soft as he sits down on the bed and runs a hand down my spine. His palm is warm and dry. "You're beautiful, girl. Your skin. Your hair. You know I love your breasts." His hand finds one beneath the pillow, his fingers stroking gently, and I arch into his touch; I can't help myself. "But it's your eyes that really get to me. They're like quartz, but shadowed. I can see all the way down into you through your eyes. I can see your pain. I can see your strength."

"I'm not strong."

I feel so damn vulnerable, with him saying these things to me. But he seems so certain, so sincere, I no longer really know how *not* to believe him.

"You don't perceive yourself in the same way others do. Most of us don't. It's okay. But let me show you what I see, okay? If you don't like the pictures, you can tear them up.

Burn the film. Whatever you want. But let me show you the incredible girl I see."

I am aware that he's talking to me as if I'm a spooked horse, soothing me. But I find myself responding to it, wanting to open up. He does that to me.

I let the pillow fall away, and ask, "What do you want me to do?"

He smiles. "Lie on your stomach, yes, just like that, and tip your head a little so the light catches in your hair. Ah, that's perfect."

He holds the camera to his eye, pauses to make some sort of adjustment and snaps a few shots, the camera making a tiny whirring, clicking sound.

"Good. Now roll onto your side, lay your head on the pillow. And just relax."

I try, following his directions as he takes me through a series of poses. He's clicking away, and I'm beginning to feel panicky. Too naked. Too open to him, as though the camera can see even more deeply than he can. And some part of me wants him to see everything. But that's just too damn frightening to contemplate.

I curl up, covering myself. "You said just a few shots."

"I did, didn't I?" He comes to the bed, leans over me and kisses me on the lips, softly. "Okay, we can be done. Thank you."

"For what?"

"For trusting me."

His eyes are that deep, gleaming green that I love. Mysterious. Thoughtful. Do I trust him? I'm still not sure. Maybe I don't really trust anyone.

The sun is really going down now, but the room is still lit up in amber, the light gentle, a chiaroscuro mix of shadow and color, everything a little soft around the edges. He kisses me again, and I melt, as I always do.

"Do you want to eat? Are you hungry?" Jack asks.

"Starving."

I realize as I say it that it's true. I haven't had anything all day other than my coffee at the farmer's market that morning, which feels like a thousand years ago.

Jack kisses me one last time, then gets up and starts piling things on the bed: a bowl of red grapes, their ruby skin glistening with tiny droplets of water, a hunk of crusty Italian bread, a plate of cheese and thinly shaved slices of prosciutto, a bowl of dark green olives. There's also a bottle of red wine and two short, round glasses.

"I should get dressed if we're going to eat," I say, but everything looks too good, and all I have here is my bathing suit, which is lying on the floor, crumpled and damp.

"Don't," he says, unbuttoning his shorts and stepping out of them.

He is gorgeously naked underneath. He climbs up onto the bed, sitting across from me, the picnic between us. He slices the cheese with a small knife, pulls the bread apart and hands a piece to me, along with some of the cheese. I bite into it; it's a nice mild Fontina, a little smoky, and it melts on my tongue.

"Here, you have to try it with these garlic-stuffed olives," Jack tells me. "Viviane gets them from a guy in town. They're amazing. That little bit of salt is the perfect accent."

He pops an olive into my mouth and I chew, the flavor acrid and earthy and wonderful.

"You're right. It's perfect."

This day is perfect. Too perfect, and I have a horrible feeling it's all going to be taken away from me somehow. But I try to ignore it, to distract myself with the flavors of the food, the mild bite of the wine in my glass and Jack's naked body so close to mine.

"Jack?"

"Mmm, what?"

"It's your turn to tell me a true story."

"Okay." He smiles, then sits quietly a moment. "Okay. A true story. When I was a kid, my dad was my hero. I mean, I totally worshipped him. I followed him around like a puppy. Everything he did was gold. I realized later that some of it was because he wasn't around much. I didn't know then what he was doing, why he was gone so often. I just wanted to make him notice me. I wanted him to be proud of me.

"I did some pretty stupid stuff. Once I tried to mow the lawn while he was away, but I was only eight and the mower was too powerful for me, so the lawn ended up in patches and I took out half my mom's flowers."

I smile at him. "That's sweet."

"Yeah, maybe." He stops, sips his wine in a sort of aggressive manner, as though he's tossing back a shot of whiskey. "But then I tried to teach myself to drive a few years later. I was twelve. Could barely reach the pedals of my mom's car. I wanted to show him that I was a man, you know? So I backed it out of the driveway. I didn't know that he was coming home, pulling into the driveway just as I was backing out. I ran right into him, smashed the front of his car. He sprained his hand, had a whiplash injury. He was furious with me."

"I'm sorry, Jack." I don't know what else to say. His face has frozen up a little, as though he doesn't want the hurt to be seen on the surface. But I see it. I do. And it makes my chest ache.

He takes a long swallow of his wine, slowly this time, and then another. "Yeah, kids do stupid things."

"Yes, they do."

"Sometimes adults do, too."

He goes quiet, and I sit with him, silent for a bit, just sipping my wine, watching him. Shadows cross his face in a series, one after another.

Finally I ask him, "Are you thinking about Sheri, Jack?"

He shrugs. "Not in that way. Not like she's some lost love. She wasn't ever that to me, which was the problem, for her, anyway. But thinking about being an idiot, yeah."

"You never loved her?"

"If I had, would I have cheated on her?"

"I don't know. People do."

"Yeah. Maybe. I don't think that's what love is."

"What do you think it is?"

"I don't know." He runs a hand through his hair. "I guess I don't have an answer for that." He lets out a short, sharp laugh. "Pretty ridiculous that I'm thirty-five years old and I don't even know what love is. All I know is what it isn't."

This conversation is making me uncomfortable, and I'm not sure why. I usually adore this sort of philosophical challenge. Maybe it's the wrong topic for us.

"We don't have to talk about this, Jack. I'm sorry."

"Ah, don't be sorry. I was the one getting morbid."

He throws back another swallow of wine, emptying his glass. Standing, he refills it and tops off mine, even though I haven't asked him to, then he starts to pick up plates and bowls and sets them on the small table.

"Let me help you," I offer.

"No, that's okay. I've got it."

The sun is down now, and outside I hear the last calls of the gulls as night closes in. I can feel the evening fog, a faint layer of damp on my skin, and I shiver. Jack turns around, comes to sit on the bed with me, looping an arm over my bare shoulder. His skin is hot, lovely. I breathe him in, his skin and the scent of sex, which I am really coming to love.

"Take a walk with me, Bettina."

"Now?"

"Yeah."

"I'll have to go next door and get some clothes."

"I have this big tunic shirt. It'll be like a dress on you. Wait one sec."

He gets up, rummages around in the dresser, pulls out a long-sleeved white shirt in some light, gauzy fabric. He brings it to me, helps me slip it over my head, then pulls his shorts back on, along with a black T-shirt.

"Come on."

We go down to the beach, my hand in his, the dark sort of enveloping us. It would be lonely by myself, but with Jack I don't feel at all alone. Not as long as he's here with me. Tomorrow may be a different story. But for now, everything just feels good.

"It's beautiful here at night," I tell him as we make our way down the dunes toward the shoreline. The moon shines down on the water, a flat half disc hanging in the velvet sky. The light on the water is silvery and mysterious, like some sort of elemental magic, something about the earth and the water and the air. "I've never hung out on a beach after dark before I came here. I like it. I like the sound of the ocean when I can't see it. I mean, it's out there, I can almost see it. But I can *feel* it more, if that makes sense."

"It does."

Jack's hand tightens on mine and he turns to me. In the dim moonlight I can see that he's watching me closely. And I feel that it means something, but I don't know what. And just as quickly I am doubting myself. I am being overly romantic. Girlish.

I am never overly romantic and girlish.

But when he leans in and brushes a kiss across my lips before turning to lead me down the beach once more, I sigh softly. I'm glad he can't hear me, that the heavy white noise of the ocean covers up my sentimental moment.

We walk a bit longer, toward the light shining down onto the sand from the next house over. Charles's house. It strikes me that maybe we should stop, and I don't know why neither of us does, but we both move on, closer and closer. As we approach it I can hear music playing, some sort of jazz piece. Jack and I both stop, finally, and stare up at the place. There's an enormous picture window overlooking the beach, taking advantage of the incredible view, and against the light coming through it we can see the dark silhouettes of Audrey and Charles sitting on the narrow front deck. They are seated at opposite sides of a table, a bottle of wine and some glasses between them, but they are leaning in toward each other. And over the music I catch the faint sound of Audrey's laughter.

My stomach knots up. I don't know why. Is it because I can see the magic of Audrey's attention focused on someone other than me? Or because I can feel Jack tensing beside me?

"Let's go back," Jack says, gripping my hand for a moment.

"Does it bother you?" I ask him quietly. I can't help myself.

"I…" He stops for a moment. "Maybe it's an automatic reaction. Because I'm here with you. And I want to be, Bettina."

I nod my head. "Okay. Okay." I pause, thinking, trying to figure this all out. "It's okay that you still want her, Jack. So do I. I can't help it. You can't, either. That's just Audrey."

"Yeah. It's not the same anymore for me, though. I don't buy into it as much as I used to. Into her charm."

"But it's still there. And it's undeniable."

"Yeah. But maybe you and I just need to accept this about each other, about her. Because sometimes I feel like she's always here with us, even when she's not."

I've felt that, too, as though Audrey is a sort of obstacle between us, even though she's what drew us together.

When did I start to worry about there being obstacles between us? It's not like this is going anywhere. This is a summer fling, just as Audrey was for me, just as she always is for Jack, and now for Charles. When this retreat is over, I won't see him until the next one, if even then. And meanwhile, he and Audrey may see each other, be together.

Why does that make my stomach hurt?

But it is suddenly crystal clear to me that while I still have desire for Audrey, it's not the same at all as my feelings for Jack. It's Jack I am absolutely aching over.

*Fuck.*

"Bettina?" His hand is on my face, cupping my cheek, and I don't want to read any more into this gesture than might be there. "Can we just let it be?"

He's asking to keep things simple. Okay. I get that.

"Yes. Sure."

He draws me in closer, his arms around me. "Let's go back to my cottage. Get into bed together again."

I nod my head. I don't want him to hear the emotion that's clogging my throat, so I don't say anything. But I don't need to. He takes my hand and we move back the way we've come. The surf is pounding in my ears, or maybe it's my blood, which is heating again, despite the emotions. Or maybe more so because of what I'm feeling.

He pushes his red door open and I follow him inside. He hasn't let go of my hand for a moment.

"Jack? Are you going to close the door?"

He shakes his head. His eyes are glittering, dark and un-readable in the faint light from the bedside lamp. "I'm going to take you outside, Bettina. I want to smell the beach and the night. Okay?"

I smile. I can't help myself. "Yes. Please."

He grins at me then, and even through that almost boyish expression I can see the lust in the softness of his face, his mouth loose and lush, and a shiver runs up my spine.

He lets me go long enough to grab a condom from the drawer in his nightstand and takes my hand once more, and we go out into the night, passing by the stand of trees at the edge of the property. And that's when we hear it: Audrey's high, tinkling laugh, like fairy dust floating on the sea breeze, soft and sultry. We both know that laugh. And it stops us in our tracks. His grip tightens around my hand, and he pulls me closer to the trees, to a space where we can peer through, where we can see Charles's house.

The light is on in the living room, still, and they are on the front deck. It's dark, but with the light coming through the window I can see he has her bent over the railing, and she is completely naked. I can just make out the outline of her plush breasts, her slim torso, the curve of her back. Behind her, Charles is all fine, smooth muscle. And my sex heats, desire making my legs weak.

"Jack, we shouldn't…"

"Yeah, but you want to as much as I do. I can hear it in your voice," he whispers. He comes up behind me, his arms slipping around my waist, and before I can think about it, his hand slips beneath the hem of the long shirt I'm wearing, his fingers finding my cleft immediately. "Ah, you're wet. I knew you would be."

"We can't just watch them." I know my argument is weak,

but I feel that I should state the obvious. "We shouldn't be doing this."

"Which is exactly what's going to make it so good," he growls in my ear.

A small whoosh of air escapes me as his fingers find my clit.

I will do whatever he wants at this moment, and he knows it. He knows he's got me. But I don't care. All I want is him, any way he wants me. I just don't care.

"Do it, Jack," I whisper as he moves my hair aside and draws his tongue up the back of my neck. "Just do whatever you want to me."

I thought I was lost in him before. But now I know this is only the beginning. I have no idea where it will end.

# CHAPTER TWELVE

"God, Jack…"

"Baby, this is going to be so good," he whispers into my hair.

I lean into him, loving the solid strength of his body behind me. And even more, his hand between my thighs, his clever fingers playing with my clit, tugging on my pussy lips, teasing me. And his mouth hot and wet on my neck.

I am soaking, shivering with need.

He reaches around with his other hand and draws mine behind me, wrapping my fingers around his cock, which is hard as glass, but with that velvet-soft skin all over the solid shaft.

"Look at them," he says to me. "She's so into him. She's as wet as you are right now. We both know how wet she gets."

"Yes…"

His fingers slide into my opening, into that wet heat, and I clench in pleasure.

"You'd love to fuck her, wouldn't you?"

"Oh, yes."

"And I'd love to fuck you, baby. And I will."

He pushes my shirt up with his free hand. I am naked underneath, open to the cool air, which feels lovely on my skin, the breeze caressing me like another lover.

I watch as Charles pulls off his pants, moving in close behind Audrey. I can see the shape of his hard cock behind her. Then he presses against her body, and I hear her laughter again as he smacks her ass.

Jack pinches mine and I jump. But he shoves his fingers deep into my pussy at the same time, and all I can do is gasp and arch into him.

"Good, baby?"

"Yes, it's good. Do it again."

A low chuckle from him, then he pinches my clit and my ass at the same time, his fingers really twisting the flesh on my ass, and pleasure and pain flow through me in equal measures. And Charles smacks Audrey again, then again, the sound growing louder. She's groaning now, backing into him. And it is so damn hot: Jack's hands on me, watching Audrey with Charles, the pain and pleasure, which I have never before experimented with. But with Jack, anything would be good.

"I need to fuck you, Bettina."

I am breathless, wanting, my legs shaky. "Yes, I need you to. Do it, Jack."

"Move in closer to the tree, hold yourself up. Yes, that's it."

The bark is a bit rough beneath my palms, the rich scent of the cypress filling my head. My shirt—Jack's shirt—is hiked up over my hips, and I am naked and outdoors and vulnerable. And I love it.

I hear Jack unzip his shorts as he moves in behind me, then his hand is on my lower back, pressing me down a bit.

"Spread for me, girl, yeah, and bend over."

I do as he asks, hanging on to the tree for support, my gaze still on Audrey and Charles. He is grabbing her around the waist, and I can see his erect cock moving closer, then her cries as he slides into her. And at that moment, Jack uses his hand to spread the lips of my sex wide, and plunges in.

"Jack!"

"Shh, they'll hear us."

He clamps a hand over my mouth, and for some reason that just makes me melt. My body goes soft all over, filled with pleasure, with his hard cock inside me. His hand slips from my mouth.

"Fuck me, Jack," I whisper between his fingers. "Come on."

He moves deeper, his cock sliding in my juices, and his fingers are working furiously on my hard little clit, which is swollen with need. Pleasure is an arrow piercing into my body, over and over. He is fucking me in rhythm with Charles fucking Audrey, and I know he's watching them, as I am. When Charles picks up the pace, slamming into Audrey, Jack does the same to me. And I swear I feel it as though it is both Jack and Charles, as though I am both Audrey and myself. Pleasure doubled, intensified. Lovely.

My climax is bearing down on me, hot, furious, even these first glimmering surges. As Jack plunges into me, I gasp, "Jack…I have to tell you…"

"What is it, baby?" He is breathless, his voice rough.

"I have to tell you…oh…" I inhale, my gaze focused on Audrey and Charles, my body focused on Jack's cock driving in and out of me. "I listened to you. With Audrey. I listened and…oh, God…"

"Tell me," he demands, his hips slowing down, his fingers stilling.

Torture.

"I listened to you two together. And it was so…hot."

He moans, asks me, "What else, Bettina?"

"I got off, listening to you fucking her."

"Christ, Bettina."

He slams into me then, his cock hard and driving, pleasure burrowing deep into my body.

"Come for me now, baby." His voice is a low growl, full of need to match my own. "Come for me like you did listening to us fuck, Audrey and me."

He pinches my clit again between his fingers, rolls it, the motion hard, demanding. And I come apart, my climax knifing into me, my body arching. My palms bite into the bark of the tree, and it hurts, but that small pain, his hurting fingers, his pummeling cock, are all a part of it. I come so hard I want to scream, but I swallow it down hard, and nothing comes out but a series of sharp gasps.

"Ah, baby. You feel so damn good. Fuck, Bettina."

Jack tenses, his hips slamming harder and harder, his mouth on my neck again, biting this time. And he grunts into my skin, pushing, pushing, his cock going deep, his free hand going around my waist, holding me so tightly I can barely breathe. But it's all good. Wonderful.

I'm shivering, the air cooling my skin now. All is quiet at the house next door. I have forgotten all about Audrey and Charles. They must have finished, gone inside. I don't know. I don't care. All I care about are the shimmering waves of post-orgasm flowing up my spine, through my belly. And Jack's hands going gentle on my body. He is smoothing my hair, as if to make up for pulling so hard, even though he had to know I loved it. Loved feeling so *possessed* by him.

And then he does the most amazing thing. He picks me up, and holding me in his arms, he carries me into his cottage without saying a word. Once inside, he lays me down on the bed, covers me with his body. He's holding himself up on his elbows, just looking into my face. His brows are drawn together. I don't know what to think; I can barely think at all, still half-numb from my orgasm, as if all the blood has drained from my head.

But Jack keeps staring at me, so intensely, and soon I come out of my stupor enough to wonder what he's thinking.

"Jack?"

"Shh."

He strokes my hair from my face, and my heart thuds heavily, then begins to hammer. What does this mean? For him? For me?

"I want to make you come again," he says finally.

"Oh, I don't need to. Not yet."

"Do it because I want you to," he demands quietly, his gaze still glittering with something I find impossible to read.

I nod, melting for him already, and he slides down between my legs, his mouth going right to my sex. His fingers pry open my swollen lips, and I am wet, needy once more for him even before his tongue touches me.

He licks me, long, slow strokes of his tongue, and in moments I am squirming. Then he pushes his tongue inside me, like some small, silken cock, wet and gorgeously soft.

"God, Jack…"

My hands go into his hair, and it is nearly as soft as his tongue. But his tongue…so hot as it slips from my body, goes back to licking at my hard little clit. And I am boneless, helpless against the pleasure washing over me. Helpless against the arching of my hips against his face. And when his fingers plunge into me, I gasp, moan, his fingers pushing the pleasure ever deeper into my body.

He moves faster, fucking me with his fingers, licking my clit, then sucking it into his mouth, his tongue swirling over the tip. And I am shivering all over with a fast-moving pleasure. It's fast yet soft, sultry, like honey moving through my system.

"Jack, please..."

I arch harder, and he fucks me harder, his fingers burrowing deep into my aching and somehow hungry pussy, no matter how much he has fed it already. He sucks my clit into his mouth, sucking, sucking, and I come. Into his hot, lovely mouth, my climax spiraling through me, making me dizzy.

"Jack! God, oh, God..."

He is licking my juices from me as my body calms, licking me clean, causing little frissons of pleasure to echo through me.

"Jack..." I sigh.

He moves up until he is lying next to me. As he kisses my cheek, my closed eyelids, I can smell my own ocean scent on his face. And when he kisses my lips, opening them with his tongue, I taste myself, my desire, my come. But there is something more here, something more than that hot magic that is my orgasm, and his.

He burrows into my neck, kissing the tender flesh there. And something is happening inside me. Something I have been dying for, even though I didn't know it before. It is a sort of opening up. And it's lovely and terrifying.

I can't think about it now.

His body is warm next to mine, and I allow myself that comfort. I let myself drift on those sleepy currents, nearly irresistible.

*Don't think, don't think.*

I close my eyes, breathe him in, and just let myself *be.*

When I open my eyes the light is still on, a small beacon casting warmth and shadow across the wood floor. Jack is asleep next to me, the pattern of his breathing long and shallow. Outside, the sky is swallowed up in darkness, no moon or stars penetrating the layers of fog, and it is like a bowl of night covering everything: the beach, this cottage, the two of us in bed. I can feel it all in some universal way, that sense of darkness, of it protecting me somehow, protecting us. The magic of it.

Am I foolish to think these things? Or maybe a little crazy?

I turn to him, his head pillowed next to mine. His face is less rugged in slumber. Still beautiful. And I remember that look on his face earlier, that intensity. My heart begins to flutter once more.

What I saw there was emotion. I may not know what it means, but it was...important.

I am filled with an uncertainty that seems at odds with the satisfaction in my body. I am filled with fear.

Jack's arm is heavy across my stomach, and suddenly I feel as if I can't breathe, as if my skin is too small for my body, tight all over. I bite my lip, draw in a deep breath, but it doesn't help.

I can't stay here with him. I cannot stay here and let my mind wander into these dark waters, where it seems possible to believe in some liquid and constantly shifting way that he will want me.

Carefully, holding what little breath I have in my lungs, I slip out from beneath his arm, praying he won't wake up. He doesn't. And I am free, pulling my discarded bathing suit on, then moving silently to the door and carefully closing it behind me. I am as quiet as the mouse I have always been.

It's so dark out, and now it just makes me feel alone as I creep back to my cottage. Once inside, I flick on the lights. Everything is perfectly neat, in order, as I always leave it. As everything in my life must be.

I move into the bathroom, where my thick-toothed comb, my hair serum, my body lotions and skin creams are all lined up like little soldiers across the counter. I lay my toothbrush and tube of toothpaste next to everything else, then touch each object, one at a time, silently counting, something I haven't done for a long while. But I am as compelled now as I have ever been, my breath coming in short, shallow gasps as I seek comfort from the old ritual I thought I was done with.

*Fuck.*

Pulling my hand back, I stare at myself in the mirror above the sink, meeting my own fevered gaze there. My hair is a mess of tangled curls, my cheeks flushed. My lips are swollen from kissing Jack.

Why do I want to cry?

*Fuck!*

With one sharp sweep of my hand I scatter my row of soldiers on the floor. The small clattering sound is satisfying somehow.

I do not want to feel this. I don't want to feel this shit I thought I'd dealt with. Isn't that what therapy was for? And it seemed to be working. It got me here, got me out of the safety of Seattle, of my apartment, my small circle of old friends, my daily rituals that had seemed so damn crucial to my existence. I was out in the world, wasn't I? Meeting new people. Audrey. Jack.

*Jack.*

Why was he bringing it all back, this old fear of...everything?

I do not want to feel like this! Can I simply decide not to?

I lean into the counter, holding myself up with my palms against the edge, letting it bite into my flesh. I force myself to slow my breathing. To stop counting each breath.

After a while, I pull my still-damp suit off and get into the shower. The hot water soothes me, quiets me. When I get out I clean up the little mess I made, putting everything back on the counter and resisting the urge to straighten each object.

The bed looks too neat to me now, and I yank on the covers, messing it up a little before climbing beneath the cool sheet. My body is buzzing, but it's only the aftermath of sex, not the hard-edged anxiety I felt leaving Jack's cottage. Still, I lay in the dark, listening to the ocean pounding inexorably on the sand, the soft murmur of crickets chirping in the cypress trees, and it's a long time before I sleep.

Breakfast at the house is the same as it's been most mornings, which I, of course, take comfort in. Patrice and Viviane cooking, with some help from Leo, who is whistling to himself. Kenneth is feeding Sid bits of bacon, and the entire kitchen is fragrant with the rich, salty scent. Everyone greets me in their own way: Patrice with a nod, Viviane with a kiss on the cheek as I pass her. Leo and Kenneth just say good-morning, both smiling at me.

Jack and Audrey are absent. I refuse to think about that. About them.

I pour myself a cup of coffee from the endless pot Viviane keeps on the counter, and help Kenneth carry into the dining room steaming platters of scrambled eggs, baskets of toast folded into colorful cotton napkins, saucers with small pats of butter, bowls of jam.

We've just sat down and everyone is pouring orange juice and filling their plates when Jack comes in. He is unshaven, as he often is this early. I've always found it sexy. But this morning it only seems to add to the cloud hovering over him, his eyes stormy. He glances once at me, a frown on his face, and I look away. I can't bear it, that he seems to be annoyed with me. And I think to myself that I don't know what I've done, but the truth is, I do. I left again. I'm sure I'll hear about it from him later, when we're alone.

*Alone. With Jack.*

I shiver, then cover it up by taking a bite of toast, the strawberry jam sweet enough on my tongue to slide over the bitter taste in my mouth, left there by my own foolishness.

Jack is quiet while he eats. Mostly he sips coffee and broods, pushing his eggs and bacon around on his plate. I'm doing pretty much the same. I can't help but wonder if it's really me he's mad at, or if the problem is that Audrey hasn't come back. I remember what he said to me, about how it still bothers him sometimes, and it makes my stomach pull into a tight little knot. Maybe he's jealous of her time with Charles. Maybe last night meant more to me than it did to him, and what I thought I saw on his face, in his eyes, was nothing more than post-sex endorphins.

I don't want him to want her. But hell, *I* still want her, in some small way. How can I possibly blame him?

My head is spinning again.

He excuses himself and gets up from the table before the rest of us are finished.

"What bit him in the ass?" Leo asks before stuffing an entire piece of toast into his mouth.

"Oh, shush, Leo," Viviane admonishes, ever the mother to us all. "Maybe he's hungover."

"Yeah, I don't think so," he says, glancing at me.

I wonder if he knows. If he saw us together last night. But it shouldn't matter, should it? We're both adults, Jack and I. We're not doing anything wrong. That's just my old habit kicking in, feeling as if everyone is judging me. Leo probably could care less who sleeps with whom, other than in the most passing, gossip-happy way. I'm being paranoid.

I can't eat any more, but I wait until everyone is done to get up. I don't want to follow Jack so quickly.

But of course that's exactly what I want. I want to run after him and explain why I left. Beg him to forgive me. To take me back to his cottage and fuck me until I'm senseless. Until I can't think anymore. That seems to be the only time I am completely at peace.

I force myself to help to clear the table, load the dishwasher, wiping the counters after Patrice and Kenneth have gone out to sit on the terrace and Leo has gone upstairs to shower. As I'm drying my hands on a cotton dish towel, Viviane comes up next to me and asks quietly, "Are you okay, Tina?"

"What? Yes. Fine. I'm fine."

She takes my chin in her hand. "Are you?"

I am horrified to find my eyes filling with tears. But I shake my head, shake them away.

"Oh, honey," she says. Her big brown eyes are soft with worry.

"No. I'm fine. I promise. I don't know what's gotten into me."

She stares into my eyes for a long time as I blink them dry. Then, "You can talk to me anytime, you know."

"I know. I think…I just need to get my head straight. Figure out what I want. What I don't want, too."

"Good girl. I'm glad to see you standing up for yourself, taking care of yourself." Viviane smiles at me and I smile back.

"Yeah, I guess I am. Although it feels a lot more like I'm floundering around with no direction."

"You just need to pick one and follow it, babe."

"I'm trying."

"You'll do it. I have confidence in you."

I laugh, the tears wanting to surface again, but I swallow

them back. "That's one of the nicest things anyone has ever said to me."

"I mean it, Tina." She smiles again, rubs my back for a moment. "Want to come down to the beach and write? Or do you want some time alone today? I can make excuses to the group, if you like."

"Maybe…maybe I will take some time for myself."

"Okay. You know where to find us."

I nod. Viviane goes upstairs, leaving me alone in the kitchen. It's still full of cooking smells and golden morning light. I pour some more coffee and drink it while leaning on the counter, gazing out the window.

Outside, the long leaves of the eucalyptus trees are moving in the breeze, just a delicate fluttering, making them look like clusters of green and white and brown butterflies. My stomach is filled with that same fluttering.

I cannot stop thinking about him. I want to and don't want to in equal measures. I want the relief of being able to let my mind wander, to stop worrying over what this all means: his behavior, mine. At the same time, I want to indulge in those girlish fantasy scenarios: Jack kissing me, telling me…what? That he loves me?

I scoff to myself, take another sip of coffee. The hot liquid scalds my tongue and I spill some onto the counter.

My heart is hammering.

"Fuck," I say quietly.

"It's just spilled coffee," Jack says from behind me.

"Fuck," I say again, whirling to face him. "You startled me."

"Sorry."

He doesn't look sorry. He looks furious. Furious and darkly sexy, as always, but maybe more so now. Furious suits him.

"You're angry," I say to him.

"Damn right I'm angry."

I hate that he's so beautiful right now, his eyes a blaze of dark green, his lush mouth set beneath the haze of beard stubble, making his jaw look sharper, more defined. And some part of me just wants to kiss him, because he wouldn't be angry if he didn't care that I left. The ache in my stomach slides open and the flutter is back.

God, I'm fucked up.

"Tell me why, Jack."

"You want me to tell you why I'm mad, Bettina? All right, I'll tell you."

He advances on me, until he is right next to me. Until I can smell sex on him, the scent of the two of us the night before: sweat and skin and come.

I can only look up at him, waiting. That scent has me dumbstruck with wanting.

He jams a hand into his dark hair and I see him pull in a long breath.

"I'm mad because this is bullshit. Bullshit. I can get this shit from Audrey. It's like her all over again. This fucking, then sneaking away in the middle of the night."

"I didn't sneak," I say.

"Didn't you?"

"I—"

"Stop it, Bettina."

Anger surges in me suddenly, an unfamiliar but potent wave of it. "You stop it, Jack. What do you expect of me? I'm not Audrey. I'm not you. I'm not used to this casual-sex thing. I don't get the protocol. Am I supposed to pretend like everything is perfect and lovely because we're having sex? That never knowing if you'll still want me the next day is just fine with me? If that's how you want to play it, Jack—and you've made it abundantly clear that that's how you do things—then you can't begrudge me my defense mechanisms. So pardon me if the only way I can fuck you is not to allow myself to linger after. I may be a writer, but I can't imagine my way into pretending everything is normal. There is nothing normal about this. This thing where you can't forget about Audrey even when you're with me. Hell, I can't handle that *I* can't forget about her! This is all just too…weird and confusing. I'm not that sophisticated, Jack."

"It's not about being sophisticated, Bettina. Fuck."

"What is it then? Why don't you explain it to me?"

He shakes his head, his face shutting down, his eyes going even darker. "I can't."

My eyes are burning with tears, damn it. "Well, that's incredibly helpful, Jack. And a bit cowardly."

He looks as if I've slapped him. Maybe I have. But I can't take this anymore. I've let him know how I feel. If he wasn't still hung up on Audrey, he would tell me now. If he wanted to be with me, I've given him the opportunity to say so. But he remains silent, his hand in his hair again.

I shake my head. "I'm going."

I try to push past him, but he grabs my arm. I turn to look at him, waiting, my pulse hot and racing.

"Don't do this, Bettina."

"Why not? Can you give me one good reason, Jack?"

But he just shakes his head mutely. I pull my arm from his hand so hard it hurts. But it's nothing compared to the ache in my chest.

He can't give me a reason to stay because he doesn't have one.

Fuck.

I turn and walk out the door, and he doesn't try to stop me.

# CHAPTER THIRTEEN

I yank open the blue door to my cottage, every bit as furious now as Jack was. Maybe more so. I stomp inside, my flip-flop–covered feet making a sort of ridiculous slapping noise on the wood floor, which stops me and makes me think for a moment.

He cares. There's no reason for him to be upset if he didn't.

But he doesn't care enough.

I flop down on the bed, toe my sandals off, letting them drop onto the floor, where they fall with a small *thunk* that satisfies me somehow. I think I understand suddenly why some people punch walls when they're mad. And just as quickly, I realize this is one of the first times in my life I've truly been angry with anyone, that I've felt this, *allowed* myself to feel this.

How absurd is it that this is progress for me? But it is.

I cover my eyes with my hands, pressing, trying not to think; it's making my brain hurt. And I jump when the door slams open, crashing into the wall.

Jack is standing there, his face grim.

"Jack, you scared the hell out of me!"

Oh, yes, I'm still mad. And it feels good.

He is silent, watching me for a moment. Then he crosses the room so damn fast I don't have time to realize what's happening until he's on me, his hands pressing my shoulders down into the pillows. His mouth comes down on mine, hard and bruising. I don't want to return his kiss, but I do, my lips opening, my tongue twining with his.

I'm still mad. But his mouth is so sweet, some mixture of coffee and that Jack taste I could never describe, writer or not. And his cock is hardening against my thigh, that and his hot, thrusting tongue, the weight of his body on mine making me melt beneath him.

He pulls his mouth away long enough to mutter, "Goddamn it, Bettina," as he tears his shirt over his head, then mine.

I help him wordlessly, our clothes coming off quickly. And just as quickly he is rolling a condom down over his rigid cock and spreading my thighs with his, just sort of pushing my legs out of the way so he can get inside me.

One sharp thrust and he's in, and I'm so damn wet it doesn't hurt; he just slides home. Our hips angle and pump, bones clashing together, and I think from some vague distance that I'll have bruises when this is over. Doesn't matter, though. What matters is Jack's mouth on the rise of my breast, biting into my flesh, my hands on his shoulders, nails digging into his smooth skin. Jack fucking me, fucking me, until I can barely breathe. Then his hand going down between us and pinching at my clit.

Pleasure rises, crests, and my anger, that bit I can still feel, joins with his, driving us both on. We are panting, groaning, Jack muttering a few curses as he slams into me. And I am taking it, loving it, needing it.

Soon his fingers and his cock are really working their

magic, and I come, a hard, shattering torrent of sensation, rocking me.

"Jack…fuck! Jack…"

"I'm coming," he tells me from between clenched teeth.

His body jerks, thrusting harder, and I hold on to him, as though I will drown. Maybe I will, without him.

Scary thought. I shove it away, focus on the hard push of his chest against mine as he gasps for breath, the scent of his sweat, the wetness sticking our bodies together.

"Bettina," he says finally.

"What?"

"Don't fucking do that again. Okay?"

"Okay."

He's quiet for a minute. Then, "Do we need to talk about this?"

"No."

And I don't. For once, I really want to not think, not talk.

"Okay," he says, leaning in to brush his lips along my jaw, then over my lips. "Okay."

Then he's kissing me, and I'm kissing him back, and it's not like those pre-sex kisses that are all about heat and need and spiraling desire. No, this is just about kissing each other, our lips meeting, parting, meeting again, the soft touch of our tongues. And his mouth is so soft on mine, my head is spinning.

*Don't think.*

I shut my brain off, just let it go blank, and lose myself in Jack. I shut out the fear and the questions and the doubt with which I am constantly torturing myself. And it feels good.

I've been here for just over a month. Time has gone by in a blur of sunny days spent writing on the beach, meals with the group, swimming in the ocean. My writing is going well. Viviane has been teaching me to cook in a wok. Jack has been teaching me how to come almost instantly and in more ways than I ever imagined.

He's also taught me something about staying in the moment. He still hasn't promised me anything, but I'm learning to be with him without that. I'm still uncertain what it is I want from him, ultimately, what it is I truly need. Meanwhile, he gives me everything I desire.

The others know, even though no one says anything, other than an occasional veiled remark. But none of it is cruel. Audrey, on those rare days when she comes back to the group from Charles's house, is quiet. She'll sit across from us on the sand, glancing up from her notepad, and sometimes I'll catch her doing it, catch the expression in her smoke-blue eyes. Sometimes she looks merely curious, as though she wants to ask me about it, what's going on between Jack and me. Sometimes I swear she looks almost hurt.

Jack thinks she's just upset that neither of us has gone to her, confided in her. But what's happening with Jack and me now feels private. I want it to be. We've already shared plenty with Audrey. This is *ours*.

Anyway, I don't understand what she has to be upset about. She's with Charles every night and often during the day. She has her life. We have ours.

I miss her. Maybe Jack does, too. I'm not sure I want to know. I miss her magic, the dynamic light that is Audrey. I miss the sex a little, too, as impossible as that seems. Jack has satisfied my body in every way. Well, almost every way. Being with Audrey was different. Softer. Safer. I miss that feeling, and I just miss *her*. It makes me sad. And that's how Jack finds me this morning when he wakes up. We're in his bed, and the fog is heavy beyond the sheer curtains. The rumble of the ocean seems muffled by it, a white blanket of quiet outside.

"What's up, baby?"

Oh, I love it when he calls me that; it makes me shiver all over. But not so much today.

"I don't know."

"Come here."

He pulls me into his arms, and I lay my head against his chest, breathing him in, as I've done so often these past weeks. But today it doesn't comfort me as it has.

"Jack?"

"Hmm?"

"Do you think it's possible that some of us…that I…can't be made happy?"

"Why would you say that?"

"Because I should be happy now."

"Aren't you?"

He shifts so that he can look at me, his dark brows drawn together. God, he's beautiful.

I really should be happy.

"I…I don't know what I am. Sometimes I am. But sometimes I let myself think too much."

"Then don't think."

He laughs and pulls me in tighter, kissing my head, but I struggle, pulling away to sit up.

"Jack, please don't do that."

He sits up, too. "Don't do what?"

"Don't condescend. I'm not some little thimblehead."

"I know that." He's looking hard at me now, his green eyes gone dark. "Don't you think I know that?"

Why am I doing this? Making him angry? But I can't seem to help myself.

"I just think…I can't stop thinking about Audrey. And about you. I mean, what exactly are we doing here, Jack?"

He sighs softly, as though he knows he shouldn't let me hear him, the classic male sound that means some woman wants to talk about emotions and they don't want to deal with it. I have never been that woman before. I sigh, too.

Finally he says, "We're just being together. Enjoying each other."

"And then what?"

He looks at me, his brows drawing together over his mossy-green eyes. They are so damn beautiful. He is so damn beautiful.

My chest feels heavy, as though anticipating something I don't want to hear. But I don't even know what I do want to hear. I'm a mess. As usual.

"I don't know."

I sigh once more, turn away.

"I don't know what you want me to say," he tells me. "I want what we have right now. I don't know how to think beyond this. But tell me, Bettina, do you? Because from what you've said, we are in exactly the same place when it comes to this stuff. Relationships."

"I…" I shake my head. "No. You're right. I don't even understand why I'm doing this."

But as he pulls me back into his arms I know I'm lying. I know exactly why I'm doing this.

I'm in love with Jack.

I have a new secret now. But I'm good at keeping secrets. My whole fucking existence has been a secret, unnoticed until now.

And so I fall into his embrace as I always do, smiling,

letting his kisses, his touch, soothe me, so I can pretend it's not true.

But it is. I'm in love with Jack.

We're on the beach, having just finished a picnic lunch. Jack and Leo have gone back up to the house to help Kenneth with some car problem, and Viviane and Patrice are lounging beneath the umbrella, heads together, brainstorming some plot issue of Viv's.

Which leaves Audrey and me.

She's been writing furiously on her notepad today, but after the men have gone she puts her pen down on the colorful woven blanket and watches me. I keep trying to write for a few minutes, scribbling on my pad of paper, but she's distracting me. Finally I lay my pen down, too.

"What is it, Audrey?" My voice is a little sharper than I intended.

"Want to walk with me?"

I do. And I don't. I'm a little afraid of being alone with her. Afraid of what we'll talk about. What we won't.

"Sure. Yes." I turn to Viviane and Patrice. "Will you two be here for a bit?"

"For a while," Viviane answers. "You can leave your things here, if you want. If you're not back when we go, we'll take everything with us."

I nod and Audrey and I stand up. She turns to head north, in the opposite direction from Charles's place, and I follow.

The day is hot, the sun beating down on the water, making it sparkle so brilliantly I can't really look at it, even with my sunglasses on. Even the damp, foam-strewn sand at the water's edge is warm beneath my bare toes.

We're quiet until we've walked a ways up the beach, leaving Viviane and Patrice behind us.

"So," I say.

Audrey turns to me.

"So."

She smiles at me, brilliantly, the old Audrey once more, and the sense of awkwardness disappears, leaving me wondering why it was there to begin with.

"I've missed you," I tell her, the words pouring out before I can stop them.

"I've missed you, too. And Jack."

My heart stutters for a moment, but then she says, "You two seem happy together. I'm glad."

"I...thanks." I look down, digging my big toe into the sand, sweeping it in an arc as I shove my hands into the pockets of my shorts.

"Just remember what I said, Bettina. About not letting them get to you." Her gaze is a little intense now, but that's Audrey, isn't it?

"I remember."

And I do. Even though I've let myself go a little, with Jack, a part of me is still intent on protecting myself. From hurt. From love, maybe.

I don't like to think of what I'm doing that way, but there it is. It's the truth.

We walk a little farther, Audrey wandering closer to the waves washing up on the beach, pausing, the cool water swirling around her ankles. I stand next to her and let the waves move the sand in and out in thick, wet surges beneath my feet. And I have once more that sensation of the world filling me up and falling away that I so loved as a child. Only now it feels like some sort of symbol for my life.

I hate it when I get philosophical.

"He and Viv used to be together, you know," Audrey says

so quietly I can barely hear her over the hammer of waves on the shore.

"What?"

"They used to have a thing. It wasn't serious. Well, not for Jack, of course. But Viv..."

"Viviane what...?"

Audrey turns to me. Her smoke-blue eyes are enormous, the whites as white as her beautiful teeth. The contrast against her summer-tanned skin is dazzling.

She says simply, "Viviane's heart was broken."

"I...oh."

I don't know what to say. I hate to hear this. I love Viviane.

I love Jack.

"Audrey, why are you telling me this? It's none of my business."

"Isn't it? You're with Jack now, Bettina, and I'd hate to see the same thing happen to you. I care about you, you know." There's an edge to her voice now that makes me uncomfortable. Why is she really telling me this?

I nod.

"And," she goes on, "I think you're a bit...fragile sometimes."

It sounds like an accusation. Or am I imagining things? My insecurities getting out of hand again. "You think I'm fragile?"

"Don't be so insulted, Bettina," she says a little too carelessly. "I just meant that you've been hurt before."

"Haven't we all, Audrey? Aren't we all a bit fragile somewhere along the line? Aren't you?"

As I say it I understand that it's true. She's being a little harsh with me, a little mean, but I feel for her. All of Audrey's magic and brilliance is real, but some of it, at least, is to cover up.

It's to protect that part of her that, just like me, is still a little girl who's afraid of the world. It makes me angry and makes me love her all at the same time.

Which still doesn't explain why I'm crying.

I shake my head and wipe at my cheeks with the back of my hand. "I just realized that I'm not the only one who's scared sometimes."

"Maybe," she says grudgingly. She isn't looking at me anymore, and I can feel the walls going up around her.

She's angry with me. Half pretending not to be. She pretends a lot. I wonder if that brilliant smile she gave me earlier was even real, or some sort of setup, then hate myself a little for even thinking this.

"What are you afraid of, Audrey?"

She shrugs. "Everything."

Her answer hits me like a punch to the stomach. It's as though I was the one who said that word. It's as though the last few minutes have been a slowly blossoming epiphany, despite her passive-aggressive behavior. And I'm a little less scared, because she shares that with me.

Still, in the back of my mind is the image of Jack with Viviane. And Audrey. I don't like it.

Is he scared, too? Is his habit of sleeping with everyone merely an escape for him the way books and staying locked in my house have been for me?

But I don't have time to think about it; Audrey takes my hand in hers, and the old heat is there, instantly. She's looking at me, those eyes, that fairy magic, focused on me in such a way, the rest of the world has ceased to exist for her. I understand now that this is part of her power. But I find myself mostly immune to it. Mostly.

She leans in, pulling me closer, and I am surrounded by her

lovely scent, like flowers and citrus and the beach itself. She brushes her lips over mine, whispers, "Come on, Bettina."

Her lips are soft, sweet. But I pull back. This is not what I want, even though my physical desire for her is still there, sharp and beating like a pulse between my legs. But my head, my heart, knows this isn't right for me.

I smile, and because I don't want to hurt her, reach up and run my hand over her hair. But she pulls away, a sharp, jerking motion. Her dark, elegant brows are drawn together, her lovely red mouth in a small pout.

"What is it with you, Bettina? Don't tell me you don't want me, that the sex isn't good enough, because we both know damn well it is."

Her eyes are a blue blaze of fury. She's really angry now, full-blown mad, and it makes me want to apologize, which is what I usually do. But I know there's nothing to apologize for. I don't owe her this.

"Audrey, I've wanted you from the moment I met you, I can't deny that. But…my heart is with Jack. And no matter what happens with him, that's where I'm at right now. That's where I want to be."

"Okay, fine." Audrey nods her head, takes a step back, frowning. "Whatever. I understand."

"Do you?"

She smiles, then, all brilliance again, but it's fake, I can tell. Other than the smile, her face is pure stone. "Yes. Absolutely. And I'm happy for you. For both of you. Just watch out for Jack. He's a user, you know. Always has been. He's just like me, Bettina. And I'm not sure you're the kind of girl who can handle it."

Her words are cruel. I don't believe her. I know she's hurt, feeling rejected. But I know there's no point in arguing with her. I don't want to do that. I swallow my hurt, look out to sea.

"Just take care of yourself, okay?" she says, her voice a little softer. "Promise me you'll do that."

"I will. I'm learning how, whether you believe that or not. Being with each of you has taught me something about that."

I turn to look at her and she just stares at me, her smoky-blue eyes clouded, shuttered. I can't quite fathom what she's thinking at this point. I don't want her to be angry with me. But I'm not going to lie to her, either.

Finally, she shrugs. "I'm going back."

We move down the beach, a little distance between us as we walk, and it makes me feel sad. She stops to pick up a shell, puts it into my hand, folding my fingers over it. She doesn't say anything, but I feel it as a gift from her. Her not fighting me for Jack is a gift, because I would surely lose.

After lunch with the group I go to my cottage, and find Jack waiting for me there. He pulls me into his arms with a growl.

"What took you so long?"

"I was helping clean up. Which you could be better about, Jack."

"I was much more interested in getting you alone and naked," he says, nuzzling into my neck.

"I admit that sounds better than washing pots and pans."

He's dragged me over to the bed, laying me down on my back, his long body next to mine, propped up on one elbow.

"So what else did you do today?" he asks me, and I love this; that he wants to know about my day. It feels so normal.

"I wrote a bit. This book is going okay right now. I'm at that point where it all seems to be falling into place."

"That's great."

"Yes. I did a good ten pages, by hand, anyway, on my notepad. I'll type it all up later. And then Audrey and I took a walk on the beach."

"Oh?"

"Yes. We talked. It was…good, I think."

"Good."

He leans in and kisses my neck, his lips soft against my skin.

"Jack?"

"Hmm?"

"Have you talked to her lately?"

"Not much. She's always with Charles."

"But you have talked."

"Sure." He keeps kissing me, but I feel a little cold, suddenly.

"Have you talked to her about…us?"

"Not really."

"Why not?"

Why is a knot growing in my stomach?

"Because it's private." He props himself up to look at me, his eyes dark and mossy. "This is just us, you and me, right?"

"Right."

"But you're worried about me being with her again? Sleeping with her?" he asks.

"She's just so…beautiful. And special."

"So are you, Bettina."

I shake my head. "I don't have what she has, Jack. I'm realistic about that. But then, few people do. Audrey draws people to her like a magnet."

"Yeah, she does. We've both been drawn in, haven't we?

But everything is temporary with her. We've already talked about that. One moment you're the center of her universe and the next you cease to exist. And I've already told you I'm pretty tired of that shit."

"Still, it's hard to hold myself up next to that, you know?"

"You don't have to."

"But I do. I know what I am, Jack—an ordinarily pretty girl who's too shy and lacks faith in herself. I have a good mind, I believe that. But…that's it."

"Christ, Bettina, why do you do that? Are you trying to make me believe that? Or yourself?"

"It's just what's true. I don't have the Audrey magic."

"I don't want that from you! It's not even real. She's not quite real."

I'm quiet a moment, thinking about what he's saying. Wondering how the conversation got here, with Jack angry and me feeling so defensive.

"What do you want, Jack?"

"Christ."

He runs a hand over his dark hair, his mouth settling into a thin line.

"Jack, you've admitted you still think about her. That's hard for me. And you've also told me from the start that you're as much a free spirit sexually as she is. This thing with you two has gone on for a long time. What's to stop it? And I know about you and Viviane, too."

I regret those words instantly, but it's too late. I don't even know what point I was trying to make in saying it.

His eyes are darker than ever. Stormy, cold. "Then you know I hurt her."

I nod. "Yes."

"That kind of thing is exactly why I know better than to

make you any promises. I don't want to do that to anyone. Not to her, not to you. I'm no good at long-term relationships. The few I've had have always ended badly."

"Do you mean Sheri?"

"That was the worst of it, but yeah. That taught me to be honest about who I am."

"Who are you, Jack? What are you trying to tell me?"

He pulls in a breath, blows it out. "I'm selfish, in the worst way a writer can be. I need to lock myself up for weeks at a time and work with no distractions. I'm demanding, the worst kind of creative personality. The classic artistic temperament, right?" He lets out a small, bitter laugh.

"Jesus, Jack, I can say the same for myself."

He sits up, pushing his back against the pillows at the head of the bed, his gaze somewhere on the wall over my shoulder. I sit up, too, but don't move closer to him. My stomach is churning.

"The difference is that no one in your life nearly died because of it, Bettina."

*Shit.*

"I know that," I say quietly.

"And I am my father's son. That's the example I grew up with."

"You aren't him, Jack. That's such a cop-out. You can choose differently."

"Maybe."

"But you're choosing not to."

"Fuck, Bettina." His hand is in his hair again in the way he has when he's angry or confused. Defensive. "I don't fucking know what I'm doing."

Neither do I. All I know is that I want him. That I want what I apparently can't have.

After a while I say quietly, not looking at him because I can't, "Maybe you need to figure that out, Jack."

"Yeah. Yeah."

A long pause before he gets up and goes to the door while my blood beats in my veins, a hot and unsteady pulse.

"We can…we can talk more later, Bettina. Okay?"

I nod. "Okay."

What else can I say?

Then he's gone. And I feel as empty as I ever have in my life.

# CHAPTER FOURTEEN

I've spent the rest of the day in bed, pretending to nap in the soft, midday heat. Jack and I have lain together on days like these in this bed, in his, touching and fucking and kissing. Talking. It's too quiet now.

I pick up a book and read the same page over and over as the sun begins to set outside, and soon it's too dark to read, so I put the book down.

They'll be serving dinner up at the main house, but I feel too awful to face anyone. They'll know something is wrong, especially Viviane, and I don't want to talk to anyone about it. Except Jack. But what is there to say?

I feel adrift. Powerless.

Audrey's words come back to me, what she says about not letting anyone have that much power over you. I know she's right. I just don't feel strong enough to fight it. To fight for him. And why should I, if he's not willing?

Maybe because the truth is that I'm stronger than he is? Is that possible?

I roll over and lean off the edge of the bed to open the window. It's cooling off outside. The sun is a burning orange

ball in the distant sky, sinking to meet the darkening crest of
the waves. I breathe in the ocean air, letting the salt fill my
lungs.

Why the hell should I let him go without a fight? Maybe it's
time I fought for something, became braver than that image
I've always had of myself, that frightened little girl. Maybe,
for once, there's someone who's more afraid than I am.

I get out of bed, slip on a pair of jeans, a light cotton sweater,
slide my feet into a pair of sandals. I glance back at the bed,
but resist the urge to straighten the rumpled covers, the dented
pillows. I don't want to be that person anymore. That's what
this whole summer has been about. Now more than ever.

Pulling open the door, I step out into the night, following
the path of pebbles that runs between Jack's cottage and mine.
It's not quite dark yet, but his porch light is on, burning faintly
amber, cutting through the fog that rolls in off the water every
evening.

I step closer and see that the front door is partway open,
light spilling out, illuminating the edges of the doorway. I
move closer still, and blink against that soft light, my eyes,
my brain, taking several moments to adjust.

Jack is inside. And in his arms is Audrey. Her dark hair
hangs like a curtain of silk down her back, which is to me. Jack
is too involved in kissing her to notice me in the doorway. I
can see from where I stand, my heart stuttering in my chest,
that his brows are drawn together. His hands are on her bare
shoulders. And I realize she is topless, wearing nothing but a
pair of denim shorts that barely cover the smooth cheeks of
her ass. And I think for one stupid moment how sexy she is
like this: half-dressed, with her hair loose.

I am an idiot. For too many reasons.

I shake my head, manage to gasp through my constricted
throat, "Fuck, Jack."

His head jerks up, and he pushes Audrey from him to stare at me.

"Bettina…"

I turn and run, down to the beach, toward the crashing, churning waves. Oh, I'm not thinking of jumping in. No, I simply need to get the hell out of there, to breathe. Need the power of the ocean to wash away the hard pit of grief in my stomach.

I reach the sand and sort of fall down. There is too much emotion in my body for me to stand.

*Stupid, stupid…*

But I shake my head. It's not me who's stupid, goddamn it! It's him.

*Fuck.*

The tears come then, and I hate them. But I also know they aren't my usual tears of self-pity. It's just grief, just a terrible, weighty sadness. And I know for the first time what it feels like to have my heart broken. But only because, finally, I've given it to someone.

*Jack.*

A part of my mind is waiting for him to come after me, but I am far too much a realist to think he actually will do that. He'll stay in there with Audrey, continue to sabotage whatever we could have had, because that's how he's set up. He's been honest enough with me about it. I can't expect any more of him; that wouldn't be fair. That wouldn't be realistic.

Sometimes being a realist sucks.

I sit for a long while, watching the moon, the water, the fog sifting through the dark sky. I want to contain my sadness, but I can't do that anymore. And the tears are gentle enough that they feel cathartic. They are gentle because even though this is fucking awful, I understand how much I've learned, from Jack, from Audrey. I can't hate either of them.

I can't hate myself anymore.

Wiping my tears on my sleeve, I breathe in, out, trying to calm myself, and I even manage to do it after a while. Finally, the tears stop.

The sky is dark now, inky all over, except for the nearly full moon. And where it touches the water, reflecting, it gives just enough silvery light to see by. I lie back in the sand, which is still warm from the day, allowing my brain to empty, hoping for peace, and finding a little of it in that bottomless arc overhead.

The ocean's throaty roar fills my ears, and it's comforting, as though the sound itself is a blanket, holding me on the earth. It helps to make the inside of my head quiet. I am soothed by earth and water, and this is exactly what this place has been for me since I arrived, despite what I'm feeling now, the confusion I've been through. And I'm grateful.

But I'm still angry.

I realize it is possible to be all these things at once.

"Bettina?"

His voice is like a fine, smoke-deep whiskey, just as it was the first time I heard it.

I take in a long breath before I sit up, and he kneels down on the sand next to me. I can see the glittering dark of his eyes as he looks at me. He reaches to brush sand from my back, and I want to just sink into him and enjoy his touch. But I can't do it.

"Fuck you, Jack," I say quietly.

He exhales, a slow breath. "You have every right to be angry."

"Yes, I do."

"I need to explain."

"No, you don't. I understand, Jack. You've been perfectly

honest with me. I don't have to like it. I don't have to like *you* right now. But you don't need to explain anything to me."

"Damn it, Bettina. I do." He grabs my arm, holds on tightly enough to hurt. His eyes are a pair of blazing beacons in the dark, the moonlight catching them as it does the waves.

I sit up straighter. "What could you possibly have to say to me, Jack?"

"That what you saw was a fucking mistake."

"Yes, it was."

My stomach is roiling, my pulse hammering. The anger is making me stronger, and I let it flow through me like a burning tide.

"No. That's not what I mean. I mean it wasn't what it looked like. Not exactly."

"Not exactly? Are you kidding me?"

"Will you just listen to me, Bettina? Just listen? Because there's more to tell you."

I exhale on a sigh. "Okay. Okay."

He lets his hand drop away, moving to grasp the back of his neck in his palm.

"Audrey came to me tonight. And we were talking about… about you. About us. She reminded me how alike we are, Audrey and me. That neither of us is about to change and that I have to accept that the way she has about herself."

"That's bullshit."

Oh, I'm really fuming now.

"Yeah. Maybe. But an hour ago I wasn't seeing it that way. All I could see was the truth in what she said. The truth I've believed most of my life. She talked about how maybe we belonged together, she and I, that we deserve each other in some perverse way, and that made sense to me."

"That's bullshit, too."

He's massaging the back of his neck, his head down.

"Yeah." He raises his gaze to mine, then, looking right at me, right through me. I can feel it, even in the dark. "You make me realize that, Bettina. How much of my self-perception is bullshit. A cop-out, as you said before."

"But when you're with Audrey you believe whatever she tells you?"

"No. No. Well, maybe for a few minutes. Because her message is my own, and that's powerful. It's carved into my brain. That I don't have enough to offer you, or anyone."

"You know what I think, Jack? I think you use your history as an excuse not to admit to your feelings, not to grow as a person. And believe me, I know, because that's exactly what I've done for most of my life. But not anymore. Not for me. And if that's where you're at, then maybe Audrey is right. You should be with her. Maybe you do deserve each other. Because I deserve better."

I wait for him to argue the point, but he's dropped his gaze once more, his hand still at the back of his neck.

"Fuck, Jack. That's what I thought."

I get up and head for my cottage, my heart a terrible, keen ache in my chest. I don't bother to look back to see if he's following me.

My cottage is too damn lonely; I feel that the moment I step inside. I turn around and go up to the main house, almost too numb to cry. Wanting only to be more numb still.

It's quiet in the kitchen as I let myself in through the back door. There's a small light on above the stove. I find a half-empty bottle of Cabernet on the counter, open it and look for a glass.

"Want some company, Bettina?"

Viviane.

I start shaking then. Something about her gentle voice loosens me up inside. I grasp the glass and turn to her silently.

"Oh, honey."

She comes to me and takes me in her arms. She's soft and safe, and I need this so much, just to feel loved. And I do.

"Viviane…he…God, I don't know where to begin."

"You don't have to, babe. I understand."

"It fucking hurts."

"Yes, it does."

She's rocking me as we stand there, and I realize suddenly what this must be like for her, having been hurt by him herself.

I pull back a little, wipe my streaming eyes.

"I'm sorry, Viviane. I forgot that you and Jack…Audrey told me…"

"It's okay. It was a long time ago. He helped me to get over losing Malcolm. It's really fine now, I promise. Come on, let's sit down."

She takes my hand, the bottle of wine, and I'm still gripping my glass. We sit in front of the empty fireplace in the great room at one end of the big, cozy kitchen. Viviane pours the wine for me, puts the glass back into my hand.

"You know…" Viviane pauses, waits for me to swallow my wine. "I've never seen Jack look at anyone the way he looks at you. Not even Audrey. He's different with you. Different than he was with me. With me, I always knew it wasn't permanent."

"I'm sorry, Viviane."

"Don't be. We had a lovely summer. But Jack is special, isn't he? No one can resist him. You've seen how Leo follows him around like a puppy. He was hard to give up, but I got over it. Well, mostly. There's some tiny bit that lingers, that comes alive when I see him for the first time each year. It's like a small splinter permanently buried under my skin. But it goes away more quickly each time. And now it's really nothing more than an uncomfortable moment. So, please, don't feel that you have to apologize to me, Bettina. I never really loved Jack. Not the way you do."

"Is it that obvious?"

She smiles, nods. "No more obvious than that he loves you back."

"No, I don't think so."

"He hides it well. He's good at that. But I've known him a while. And I can see it, even if he can't."

"That's the problem, Viviane. I need to hear it from him. And if he can't see it, if he's not willing to, then what chance do we have? I'm not going to beg him to love me. I shouldn't have to."

"No, you're right. I'm sorry, babe. I'm sorry he's hurt you. But, Tina, you are so much stronger than you were when you came here. And I'm glad to see it."

There are still tears in my eyes, but I smile through them. "So am I."

We sit quietly together while I finish my wine. After a while I grow sleepy, from the wine, perhaps, but also from the emotional toll of the day. Viviane hugs me, gives me a good-night kiss on the cheek, and I wander back outside, following the path to my cottage. I swing the door open.

Jack.

He looks completely disheveled, his dark hair spiky from running his hands through it. And even now I can't help but appreciate the way his low-slung cargo shorts hang on his narrow hips, the tight span of his white, V-neck T-shirt across his chest, his broad shoulders. Angry or not, he is still beautiful to me.

"I was looking for you," he says.

"It took you a while, Jack. I've been up at the house for over an hour. And I was on the beach for probably an hour, too, before you came after me. Is this all you've got, Jack? Am I some sort of afterthought?"

"No. Of course not. Christ, Bettina, this is hard for me."

"Forgive me if I'm not too sympathetic."

My eyes are damp again, and it's pissing me off, all of this crying.

"Okay. I deserved that."

"Yes."

He steps closer and I have to steel myself not to draw back. My body wants this closeness too much, and it's terrifying.

"Bettina," he starts again, "I'm sorry."

"Okay. That's a start."

"I understand that I betrayed you. Even though we've had no agreement about exclusivity I...I betrayed my own feelings for you. You're right. I've been a fucking coward. I've hidden behind excuses that have sounded perfectly sane to me all these years. Until now."

He takes another step, until he's close enough that I can feel the heat of his body. I realize I'm still holding the brass doorknob in my hand, the metal cool and hard in my palm. I can't speak. I don't know what to say yet.

"I am so goddamn sorry." His voice is heavy with emotion, and he takes a moment, swallows hard. "And you should know that I sent her away. That Audrey came to me and I followed her lead for a minute or two, but when you came in and I saw the look on your face, the hurt, I knew I'd gone too far in a direction I really didn't want to take. And I'm sorry, I'm fucking sorry, Bettina, that I didn't run after you. But I had to think. There is so much going through my brain and I don't know how to handle it. This is all new territory for me."

"What is, Jack?" I ask, my voice a whisper.

He watches me for several moments, in that way he has.

He is looking inside me, and seeing me, all of me, and not turning away. "Loving you."

"Jesus, Jack."

My head is spinning, my heart racing. I can't help the tears pooling in my eyes. But this time I don't care.

"Tell me again, Jack."

He shakes his head and for one agonizing moment I'm afraid he's changing his mind. But then he says, "Not like this. Come here."

He pulls me into his arms, and I melt into him, his arms strong and warm around me, his chest pressed against mine.

"I love you, Bettina. Do you love me?"

I lean my head against his wide chest, and hear his heart beating. "Yes. I love you."

"Fuck," he breathes.

"That's not the usual reply."

"Yeah. There's nothing usual about us."

"Yes." I stand there, breathing him in. But I know this is not the whole answer. "So, what now?"

"I don't know. We live in different cities."

"Seattle and Portland aren't that far from each other."

"You're right. They're not. We'll figure that part out. And we still need to see New Orleans together."

"Yes." I smile, then it fades away as another thought invades my mind. "And Audrey? Will she come into play?"

His body tenses a bit; I can feel his arms and his stomach tightening. "I could ask you the same question."

"Yes. That's fair." I pull back enough to look at him. He is so beautiful, his face soft with emotion, a bit tormented still. "She's like some ethereal creature to me, almost too beautiful to be real, even now. I understand what you meant about that, about her not being real. I feel…sad for her insubstantial existence. Do you know what I mean? And I don't mean that in any condescending way. But having this, knowing love, finally, it hurts to know she doesn't."

I feel a bit self-conscious saying this to him. I'm not used to discussing love this way. But he's nodding his head.

"She came to me tonight because she wants what we have. She knew it even before I was able to admit it. But she's not ready for it, that much is obvious. I believe she cares about us both."

"Yes, I think so, too, despite her horrible behavior, trying to seduce each of us just today."

"You didn't tell me that." He raises an eyebrow but doesn't press me further.

"No."

"It's okay."

"Nothing happened, Jack. I turned her away."

"I wish I had. I wish to God I hadn't given in, even for a moment."

I'm quiet for a few breaths, waiting for him to say more, but he remains silent.

"Jack. Neither of us has said how we feel about Audrey. About whether or not she's still in the picture."

"I care about her. I feel sorry for her. And she still holds that attraction. That pull. For both of us, I think." His gaze is searching mine.

"Yes." My heart is a hammer in my chest.

"But I want to be with you. I don't want to fuck this up. And Audrey will fuck this up. She's good at that."

"Yes."

"But you're not telling me not to see her, talk to her?"

"No. You need to make your own choices, Jack. And I just have to hope you choose not to hurt me. I have to believe you can do that."

"I can. I want to." He strokes my hair, his fingers brushing my cheek. "You've changed so much this summer. You're different."

"I have changed. And as painful as this whole thing has been for me, I've learned from both of you, you and Audrey. I feel stronger because I'm able to let the anger go and love her, still." He's watching me very closely, his lips parted a bit, his eyes gleaming and tender in a way I've never seen them. "I don't think I'd be where I am right now if things hadn't happened exactly the way they did. So, while I can't regret that, I have no desire to be with her again. I simply want to keep inside that bit of her magic that's rubbed off on me."

"You have your own magic, you know. You always have."

He squeezes me tighter, our bodies so close I swear I can feel the hard beating of his heart against mine. "Bettina…I don't know how good at this I'll be. I don't want to let you down. But I don't know what the hell I'm doing."

"Neither do I. But I know one thing, Jack. The past does not have to make us who we are. We have to choose."

"I get that. You've made me get that. And I want to be different. Because of you. But I'm not going to be any good at this. At believing I deserve this, maybe. Not at first. But if you can just hang in there with me…"

He smiles at me, wraps me in his arms and kisses me, hard. His mouth is all sweet, wet heat, and I love the feel of it, his lips pressed against mine, the sweep of his tongue. And his body pressed so close to mine, his cock a rigid shaft against my belly. I want him. I need him. I love him.

He lowers me onto the bed, somehow tearing our clothes off as we go, so that by the time my body hits the blue-and-white quilt, I am wearing nothing but my panties. They come off quickly, too, and I am aching and glad when he slips a condom over his gorgeous cock and pushes between my thighs.

It's too good, the weight of his body on mine, his cock slipping inside me, the frissons of pleasure racing over my skin. And as he pumps into me, those mossy eyes looking into mine, looking inside me, as he always does, I am nothing but pleasure and fire and his scent in my head, filling me up.

My climax bears down on me, pleasure rising like some inexorable tide. And all the time his gaze on mine, shining with tenderness. When I come it is like another sort of epiphany, coming with love and into love and into Jack, as much as it is him coming into me when he tenses and calls my name.

After, we stay perfectly still, breathing each other in. He kisses me, over and over. I can taste the salt of his sweat on his lips, and my own, mingling. Sweeter than anything has ever been before.

"What now, Jack?" I ask him once more.

But whatever it will be, it's enough for now. I still have so much to learn. So does he. But we'll be together when we can. And in between I will learn to live my life. To be happy. No matter what happens. But at least, finally, I have someplace to start.

A Hell's Eight erotic adventure from national bestselling author

# SARAH McCARTY

Before his trade became his name, "Tracker" Ochoa was a scrawny Mestizo runaway. Now as fearsome as he once was frightened, he's joined the notorious Hell's Eight… and they have a job for him.

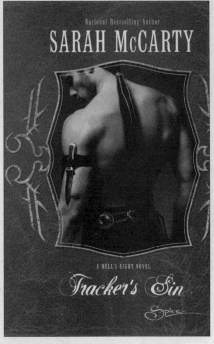

He must rescue kidnapped heiress Ari Blake and deliver her safely to the Hell's Eight compound—by any means necessary. Turns out that includes marrying her if he means to escort her and her infant daughter across the Texas Territory. Tracker hadn't bargained on a wife— especially such a fair, blue-eyed beauty. But the pleasures of the marriage bed more than make up for the surprise.

Tracker's well-muscled bronze skin and dark, dangerous eyes are far more exciting than any of Ari's former debutante dreams. In the light of day, though, his deep scars and brooding intensity terrify her. But he's her husband and she's at his mercy. With the frontier against them and mercenary bandits at their heels, Ari fears she'll never feel safe again.

Tracker, too, remembers what fear feels like. Though he burns to protect Ari, to keep her for himself always, he knows that money, history—and especially the truth—can tear them apart.

"If you like your historicals packed with emotion, excitement and heat, you can never go wrong with a book by Sarah McCarty."—*Romance Junkies*

www.Spice-Books.com

SSMC60548TR

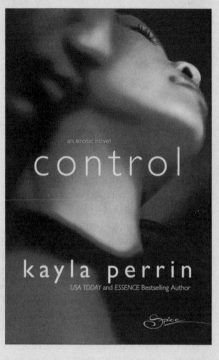

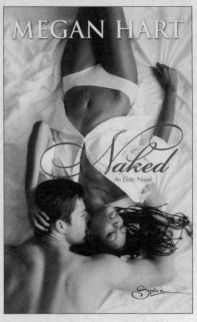

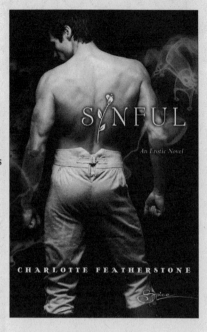

# ALISON's WONDERLAND

## ALISON TYLER

Over the past fifteen years, Alison Tyler has curated some of the genre's most sizzling collections of erotic fiction, proving herself to be the ultimate naughty librarian. With *Alison's Wonderland,* she has compiled a treasury of naughty tales based on fable and fairy tale, myth and legend: some ubiquitous, some obscure—all of them delightfully dirty.

From a perverse prince to a vampire-esque Sleeping Beauty, the stars of these reimagined tales are—like the original protagonists—chafing at unfulfilled desire. From Cinderella to Sisyphus, mermaids to werewolves, this realm of fantasy is limitless and so *very* satisfying.

Penned by such erotica luminaries as Shanna Germain, Rachel Kramer Bussel, N.T. Morley, Elspeth Potter, T.C. Calligari, D.L. King, Portia Da Costa and Tsaurah Litzsky, these bawdy bedtime stories are sure to bring you (and a friend) to your own happily-ever-after.

> "Alison Tyler has introduced readers to some of the hottest contemporary erotica around."—*Clean Sheets*

www.Spice-Books.com

SAT60545TR